ORSON SCOTT CARD
THE CHANGED MAN

A TOM DOHERTY ASSOCIATES BOOK
NEW YORK

THE CHANGED MAN

Previously published as book one of *Maps In Mirror* by Orson Scott Card (Tor, 1990)

A Tor Book
Published by Tom Doherty Associates, Inc.
175 Fifth Avenue
New York, N.Y. 10010

TOR® is a registered trademark of Tom Doherty Associates, Inc.

Cover art by Paul Scanlan

ISBN: 0-812-53365-8

First edition: April 1992

Printed in the United States of America

0 9 8 7 6 5 4 3 2 1

To Charlie Ben,
who can fly

CONTENTS

INTRODUCTION

I CAN'T WATCH HORROR or suspense movies in the theatre. I've tried—but the tension becomes too much for me. The screen is too large, the figures are too real. I always end up having to get up, walk out, go home. It's more than I can bear.

You know where I end up watching those movies? At home. On cable TV. That little screen is so much *safer*. The familiar scenes of my home surround it. And when it gets too tense, I can flip away, watch reruns of *Dick Van Dyke* or *Green Acres* or some utterly lame depression-era movie until I calm down enough to flip back and see how things turned out.

That's how I watched *Aliens* and *The Terminator*— I never have watched them beginning-to-end. I realize that by doing this I'm subverting the filmmaker's art, which is linear. But then, my TV's remote control has turned viewing into a participatory art. I can now per- form my own recutting on films that are too upsetting for my taste. For me, *Lethal Weapon* is much more pleasurable when intercut with fragments of *Wild and Beautiful on Ibiza* and *Life on Earth*.

Which brings us to the most potent tool of storytellers. Fear. And not just fear, but dread. *Dread* is the first and the strongest of the three kinds of fear. It is that tension, that waiting that comes when you know there is something to fear but you have not yet identified what it is. The fear that comes when you first realize that your spouse should have been home an hour ago; when you hear a strange sound in the baby's bedroom; when you realize that a window you are sure you closed is now open, the curtains billowing, and you're alone in the house.

Terror only comes when you see the thing you're afraid of. The intruder is coming at you with a knife. The headlights coming toward you are clearly in your lane. The Klansmen have emerged from the bushes and one of them is holding a rope. This is when all the muscles of your body, except perhaps the sphincters, tauten and you stand rigid; or you scream; or you run. There is a frenzy to this moment, a climactic power—but it is the power of release, not the power of tension. And bad as it is, it is better than dread in this respect: Now, at least, you know the face of the thing you fear. You know its borders, its dimensions. You know what to expect.

Horror is the weakest of all. After the fearful thing has happened, you see its remainder, its relics. The grisly, hacked-up corpse. Your emotions range from nausea to pity for the victim. And even your pity is tinged with revulsion and disgust; ultimately you reject the scene and deny its humanity; with repetition, horror loses its ability to move you and, to some degree, dehumanizes the victim and therefore dehumanizes you. As the sonderkommandos in the death camps learned, after you move enough naked murdered corpses, it stops making you want to weep or puke. You just do it. They've stopped being people to you.

This is why I am depressed by the fact that contemporary storytellers of fear have moved almost exclusively toward horror and away from dread. The slasher movies almost don't bother anymore with creating the sympathy for character that is required to fill an audience with dread. The moments of terror are no longer terrifying because we empathize with the victim, but are rather fascinating because we want to see what creative new method of mayhem the writer and art director have come up with. Ah—murder by shish-ka-bob! Oh, cool—the monster poked the guy's eye out from *inside* his head!

Obsessed with the desire to film the unfilmable, the makers of horror flicks now routinely show the unspeakable, in the process dehumanizing their audience by turning human suffering into pornographically escalating "entertainment." This is bad enough, but to my regret, too many writers of the fiction of fear are doing the same thing. They failed to learn the real lesson of Stephen King's success. It isn't the icky stuff that makes King's stories work. It's how much he makes you care about his characters before the icky stuff ever happens. And his best books are the ones like *The Dead Zone* and *The Stand* in which not that much horror ever happens at all. Rather the stories are suffused with dread leading up to cathartic moments of terror and pain. Most important, the suffering that characters go through *means something*.

That is the artistry of fear. To make the audience so empathize with a character that we fear what he fears, for his reasons. We don't stand outside, looking at a gory slime cover him or staring at his gaping wounds. We stand inside him, anticipating the terrible things

EUMENIDES IN THE FOURTH FLOOR LAVATORY

L IVING IN A fourth-floor walkup was part of his revenge, as if to say to Alice, "Throw me out of the house, will you? Then I'll live in squalor in a Bronx tenement, where the toilet is shared by four apartments! My shirts will go unironed, my tie will be perpetually awry. *See what you've done to me!*"

But when he told Alice about the apartment, she only laughed bitterly and said, "Not anymore, Howard. I won't play those games with you. You win every damn time."

She pretended not to care about him anymore, but Howard knew better. He knew people, knew what they wanted, and Alice wanted *him*. It was his strongest card in their relationship—that she wanted him more than he wanted her. He thought of this often: at work in the offices of Humboldt and Breinhardt, Designers; at lunch in a cheap lunchroom (part of the punishment); on the subway home to his tenement (Alice had kept the Lincoln Continental). He thought and thought about how much she wanted him. But he kept remembering what she had said the day she threw him out: If you ever come near Rhiannon again I'll kill you.

He could not remember why she had said that. Could not remember and did not try to remember because that line of thinking made him uncomfortable and one thing Howard insisted on being was comfortable with himself. Other people could spend hours and days of their lives chasing after some accommodation with themselves, but Howard was accommodated. Well adjusted. At ease. I'm OK, I'm OK, I'm OK. Hell with you. "If you let them make you feel uncomfortable," Howard would often say, "you give them a handle on you and they can run your life." Howard could find other people's handles, but they could never find Howard's.

It was not yet winter but cold as hell at three A.M. when Howard got home from Stu's party. A must attend party, if you wished to get ahead at Humboldt and Breinhardt. Stu's ugly wife tried to be tempting, but Howard had played innocent and made her feel so uncomfortable that she dropped the matter. Howard paid careful attention to office gossip and knew that several earlier departures from the company had got caught with, so to speak, their pants down. Not that Howard's pants were an impenetrable barrier. He got Dolores from the front office into the bedroom and accused her of making life miserable for him. "In little ways," he insisted. "I know you don't mean to, but you've got to stop."

"What ways?" Dolores asked, incredulous yet (because she honestly tried to make other people happy) uncomfortable.

"Surely you knew how attracted I am to you."

"No. That hasn't—that hasn't even crossed my mind."

Howard looked tongue-tied, embarrassed. He actually was neither. "Then—well, then, I was—I was wrong, I'm sorry, I thought you were doing it deliberately—"

"Doing what?"

"Snub—snubbing me—never mind, it sounds adolescent, just little things, hell, Dolores, I had a stupid schoolboy crush—"

"Howard, I didn't even know I was hurting you."

"God, how insensitive," Howard said, sounding even more hurt.

"Oh, Howard, do I mean that much to you?"

Howard made a little whimpering noise that meant everything she wanted it to mean. She looked uncomfortable. She'd do anything to get back to feeling right with herself again. She was so uncomfortable that they spent a rather nice half hour making each other feel comfortable again. No one else in the office had been able to get to Dolores. But Howard could get to anybody.

He walked up the stairs to his apartment feeling very, very satisfied. Don't need you, Alice, he said to himself. Don't need nobody, and nobody's who I've got. He was still mumbling the little ditty to himself as he went into the communal bathroom and turned on the light.

He heard a gurgling sound from the toilet stall, a hissing sound. Had someone been in there with the light off? Howard went into the toilet stall and saw nobody. Then looked closer and saw a baby, probably about two months old, lying in the toilet bowl. Its nose and eyes were barely above the water; it looked terrified, its legs and hips and stomach were down the drain. Someone had obviously hoped to kill it by drowning—

it was inconceivable to Howard that anyone could be so moronic as to think it would fit down the drain.

For a moment he thought of leaving it there, with the big-city temptation to mind one's own business even when to do so would be an atrocity. Saving this baby would mean inconvenience: calling the police, taking care of the child in his apartment, perhaps even headlines, certainly a night of filling out reports. Howard was tired. Howard wanted to go to bed.

But he remembered Alice saying, "You aren't even human, Howard. You're a goddam selfish monster." I am not a monster, he answered silently, and reached down into the toilet bowl to pull the child out.

The baby was firmly jammed in—whoever had tried to kill it had meant to catch it tight. Howard felt a brief surge of genuine indignation that anyone could think to solve his problems by killing an innocent child. But thinking of crimes committed on children was something Howard was determined not to do, and besides, at that moment he suddenly acquired other things to think about.

As the child clutched at Howard's arm, he noticed the baby's fingers were fused together into flipperlike flaps of bone and skin at the end of the arm. Yet the flippers gripped his arms with an unusual strength as, with two hands deep in the toilet bowl, Howard tried to pull the baby free.

At last, with a gush, the child came up and the water finished its flushing action. The legs, too, were fused into a single limb that was hideously twisted at the end. The child was male; the genitals, larger than normal, were skewed off to one side. And Howard noticed that where the feet should be were two more flippers, and near the tips were red spots that looked like putrefying sores. The child cried, a savage mewling that reminded Howard of a dog he had seen in its death throes.

(Howard refused to be reminded that it had been he who killed the dog by throwing it out in the street in front of a passing car, just to watch the driver swerve; the driver hadn't swerved.)

Even the hideously deformed have a right to live, Howard thought, but now, holding the child in his arms, he felt a revulsion that translated into sympathy for whoever, probably the parents, had tried to kill the creature. The child shifted its grip on him, and where the flippers had been Howard felt a sharp, stinging pain that quickly turned to agony as it was exposed to the air. Several huge, gaping sores on his arm were already running with blood and pus.

It took a moment for Howard to connect the sores with the child, and by then the leg flippers were already pressed against his stomach, and the arm flippers already gripped his chest. The sores on the child's flippers were not sores; they were powerful suction devices that gripped Howard's skin so tightly that it ripped away when the contact was broken. He tried to pry the child off, but no sooner was one flipper free than it found a new place to hold even as Howard struggled to break the grip of another.

What had begun as an act of charity had now become an intense struggle. This was not a child, Howard realized. Children could not hang on so tightly, and the creature had teeth that snapped at his hands and arms whenever they came near enough. A human face, certainly, but not a human being. Howard threw himself against the wall, hoping to stun the creature so it would drop away. It only clung tighter, and the sores where it hung on him hurt more. But at last Howard pried and scraped it off by levering it against the edge of the toilet stall. It dropped to the ground, and Howard backed quickly away, on fire with the pain of a dozen or more stinging wounds.

It had to be a nightmare. In the middle of the night, in a bathroom lighted by a single bulb, with a travesty of humanity writhing on the floor, Howard could not believe that it had any reality.

Could it be a mutation that had somehow lived? Yet the thing had far more purpose, far more control of its body than any human infant. The baby slithered across the floor as Howard, in pain from the wounds on his body, watched in a panic of indecision. The baby reached the wall and cast a flipper onto it. The suction held and the baby began to inch its way straight up the wall. As it climbed, it defecated, a thin drool of green tracing down the wall behind it. Howard looked at the slime following the infant up the wall, looked at the pus-covered sores on his arms.

What if the animal, whatever it was, did not die soon of its terrible deformity? What if it lived? What if it were found, taken to a hospital, cared for? What if it became an adult?

It reached the ceiling and made the turn, clinging tightly to the plaster, not falling off as it hung upside down and inched across toward the light bulb.

The thing was trying to get directly over Howard, and the defecation was still dripping. Loathing overcame fear, and Howard reached up, took hold of the baby from the back, and, using his full weight, was finally able to pry it off the ceiling. It writhed and twisted in his hands, trying to get the suction cups on him, but Howard resisted with all his strength and was able to get the baby, this time headfirst, into the toilet bowl. He held it there until the bubbles stopped and it was blue. Then he went back to his apartment for a knife. Whatever the creature was, it had to disappear from the face of the earth. It had to die, and there had to be no sign left that could hint that Howard had killed it.

He found the knife quickly, but paused for a few moments to put something on his wounds. They stung bitterly, but in a while they felt better. Howard took off his shirt; thought a moment and took off all his clothes, then put on his bathrobe and took a towel with him as he returned to the bathroom. He didn't want to get any blood on his clothes.

But when he got to the bathroom, the child was not in the toilet. Howard was alarmed. Had someone found it drowning? Had they, perhaps, seen him leaving the bathroom—or worse, returning with his knife? He looked around the bathroom. There was nothing. He stepped back into the hall. No one. He stood a moment in the doorway, wondering what could have happened.

Then a weight dropped onto his head and shoulders from above, and he felt the suction flippers tugging at his face, at his head. He almost screamed. But he didn't want to arouse anyone. Somehow the child had not drowned after all, had crawled out of the toilet, and had waited over the door for Howard to return.

Once again the struggle resumed, and once again Howard pried the flippers away with the help of the toilet stall, though this time he was hampered by the fact that the child was behind and above him. It was exhausting work. He had to set down the knife so he could use both hands, and another dozen wounds stung bitterly by the time he had the child on the floor. As long as the child lay on its stomach, Howard could seize it from behind. He took it by the neck with one hand and picked up the knife with the other. He carried both to the toilet.

He had to flush twice to handle the flow of blood and pus. Howard wondered if the child was infected with some disease—the white fluid was thick and at least as great in volume as the blood. Then he flushed seven more times to take the pieces of the creature down the drain. Even after death, the suction pads clung tightly to the porcelain; Howard pried them off with the knife.

Eventually, the child was completely gone. Howard was panting with the exertion, nauseated at the stench and horror of what he had done. He remembered the smell of his dog's guts after the car hit it, and he threw up everything he had eaten at the party. Got the party out of his system, felt cleaner; took a shower, felt cleaner still. When he was through, he made sure the bathroom showed no sign of his ordeal.

Then he went to bed.

It wasn't easy to sleep. He was too keyed up. He couldn't take out of his mind the thought that he had committed murder (not murder, not murder, simply the elimination of something too foul to be alive). He tried thinking of a dozen, a hundred other things. Projects at work—but the designs kept showing flippers. His children—but their faces turned to the intense face of the struggling monster he had killed. Alice—ah, but Alice was harder to think of than the creature.

At last he slept, and dreamed, and in his dream remembered his father, who had died when he was ten. Howard did not remember any of his standard reminiscences. No long walks with his father, no basketball in the driveway, no fishing trips. Those things had happened, but tonight, because of the struggle with the monster, Howard remembered darker things that he had long been able to keep hidden from himself.

"We can't afford to get you a ten-speed bike, Howie. Not until the strike is over."

"I know, Dad. You can't help it." Swallow bravely. "And I don't mind. When all the guys go riding around after school, I'll just stay home and get ahead on my homework."

"Lots of boys don't have ten-speed bikes, Howie."

Howie shrugged, and turned away to hide the tears in his eyes. "Sure, lot of them. Hey, Dad, don't you worry about me. Howie can take care of himself."

Such courage. Such strength. He had got a ten-speed within a week. In his dream, Howard finally made a connection he had never been able to admit to himself before. His father had a rather elaborate ham radio setup in the garage. But about that time he had become tired of it, he said, and he sold it off and did a lot more work in the yard and looked bored as hell until the strike was over and he went back to work and got killed in an accident in the rolling mill.

Howard's dream ended madly, with him riding piggyback on his father's shoulders as the monster had ridden on *him*, tonight—and in his hand was a knife, and he was stabbing his father again and again in the throat.

He awoke in early morning light, before his alarm rang, sobbing weakly and whimpering, "I killed him, I killed him, I killed him."

And then he drifted upward out of sleep and saw the time. Six-thirty. "A dream," he said. And the dream had woken him early, too early, with a headache and sore eyes from crying. The pillow was soaked. "A hell of a lousy way to start the day," he mumbled. And, as was his habit, he got up and went to the window and opened the curtain.

On the glass, suction cups clinging tightly, was the child.

It was pressed close, as if by sucking very tightly it would be able to slither through the glass without breaking it. Far below were the honks of early morning traffic, the roar of passing trucks: but the child seemed oblivious to its height far above the street, with no ledge to break its fall. Indeed, there seemed little chance it would fall. The eyes looked closely, piercingly at Howard.

Howard had been prepared to pretend that the night before had been another terribly realistic nightmare.

He stepped back from the glass, watched the child in fascination. It lifted a flipper, planted it higher, pulled itself up to a new position where it could stare at Howard eye to eye. And then, slowly and methodically, it began beating on the glass with its head.

The landlord was not generous with upkeep on the building. The glass with thin, and Howard knew that the child would not give up until it had broken through the glass so it could get to Howard.

He began to shake. His throat tightened. He was terribly afraid. Last night had been no dream. The fact that the child was here today was proof of that. Yet he had cut the child into small pieces. It could not possibly be alive. The glass shook and rattled with every blow the child's head struck.

The glass slivered in a starburst from where the child had hit it. The creature was coming in. And Howard picked up the room's one chair and threw it at the child, threw it at the window. Glass shattered and the sun dazzled on the fragments as they exploded outward like a glistening halo around the child and the chair.

Howard ran to the window, looked out, looked down and watched as the child landed brutally on the top of a large truck. The body seemed to smear as it hit, and fragments of the chair and shreds of glass danced around the child and bounced down into the street and the sidewalk.

The truck didn't stop moving; it carried the broken body and the shards of glass and the pool of blood on up the street, and Howard ran to the bed, knelt beside it, buried his face in the blanket, and tried to regain control of himself. He had been seen. The people in the street had looked up and seen him in the window. Last night he had gone to great lengths to avoid discovery, but today discovery was impossible to avoid. He was ruined. And yet he could not, could never have let the child come into the room.

Footsteps on the stairs. Stamping up the corridor. Pounding on the door. "Open up! Hey in there!"

If I'm quiet long enough, they'll go away, he said to himself, knowing it was a lie. He must get up, must answer the door. But he could not bring himself to admit that he ever had to leave the safety of his bed.

"Hey, you son-of-a-bitch—" The imprecations went on but Howard could not move until, suddenly, it occurred to him that the child could be under the bed, and as he thought of it he could feel the tip of the flipper touching his thigh, stroking and ready to fasten itself—

Howard leaped to his feet and rushed for the door. He flung it wide, for even if it was the police come to arrest him, they could protect him from the monster that was haunting him.

It was not a policeman at the door. It was the man on the first floor who collected rent. "You son-of-a-bitch irresponsible pig-kisser!" the man shouted, his toupee only approximately in place. "That chair could have hit somebody! That window's expensive! Out! Get out of here, right now, I want you out of this place, I don't care how the hell drunk you are—"

"There was—there was this thing on the window, this creature—"

The man looked at him coldly, but his eyes danced with anger. No, not anger. Fear. Howard realized the man was afraid of him.

"This is a decent place," the man said softly. "You can take your creatures and your booze and your pink stinking elephants and that's a hundred bucks for the window, a hundred bucks right now, and you can get out of here in an hour, an hour, you hear? Or I'm calling the police, you hear?"

"I hear." He heard. The man left when Howard counted out five twenties. The man seemed careful to avoid touching Howard's hands, as if Howard had become, somehow, repulsive. Well, he had. To himself, if to no one else. He closed the door as soon as the man was gone. He packed the few belongings he had brought to the apartment in two suitcases and went downstairs and called a cab and rode to work. The cabby looked at him sourly, and wouldn't talk. It was fine with Howard, if only the driver hadn't kept looking at him through the mirror—nervously, as if he was afraid of what Howard might do or try. I won't try anything, Howard said to himself, I'm a decent man. Howard tipped the cabby well and then gave him twenty to take his bags to his house in Queens, where Alice could damn well keep them for a while. Howard was through with the tenement—that one or any other.

Obviously it had been a nightmare, last night and this morning. The monster was only visible to him, Howard decided. Only the chair and the glass had fallen from the fourth floor, or the manager would have noticed.

Except that the baby had landed on the truck, and might have been real, and might be discovered in New Jersey or Pennsylvania later today.

Couldn't be real. He had killed it last night and it was whole again this morning. A nightmare. I didn't really kill anybody, he insisted. (Except the dog. Except Father, said a new, ugly voice in the back of his mind.)

Work. Draw lines on paper, answer phone calls, dictate letters, keep your mind off your nightmares, off your family, off the mess your life is turning into. "Hell of a good party last night." Yeah, it was, wasn't it? "How are you today, Howard?" Feel fine, Dolores, fine—thanks to you. "Got the roughs on the IBM thing?" Nearly, nearly. Give me another twenty minutes. "Howard, you don't look well." Had a rough night. The party, you know.

He kept drawing on the blotter on his desk instead of going to the drawing table and producing real work. He doodled out faces. Alice's face, looking stern and terrible. The face of Stu's ugly wife. Dolores's face, looking sweet and yielding and stupid. And Rhiannon's face.

But with his daughter Rhiannon, he couldn't stop with the face.

His hand started to tremble when he saw what he had drawn. He ripped the sheet off the blotter, crumpled it, and reached under the desk to drop it in the wastebasket. The basket lurched, and flippers snaked out to seize his hand in an iron grip.

Howard screamed, tried to pull his hand away. The child came with it, the leg flippers grabbing Howard's right leg. The suction pad stung, bringing back the memory of all the pain last night. He scraped the child off against a filing cabinet, then ran for the door, which was already opening as several of his co-workers tumbled into his office demanding, "What is it! What's wrong! Why did you scream like that!"

Howard led them gingerly over to where the child should be. Nothing. Just an overturned wastebasket, Howard's chair capsized on the floor. But Howard's window was open, and he could not remember opening it. "Howard, what is it? Are you tired, Howard? What's wrong?"

I don't feel well. I don't feel well at all.

Dolores put her arm around him, led him out of the room. "Howard, I'm worried about you."

I'm worried, too.

"Can I take you home? I have my car in the garage downstairs. Can I take you home?"

Where's home? Don't have a home, Dolores.

"My home, then. I have an apartment, you need to lie down and rest. Let me take you home."

Dolores's apartment was decorated in early Holly Hobby, and when she put records on the stereo it was old Carpenters and recent Captain and Tennille. Dolores led him to the bed, gently undressed him, and then, because he reached out to her, undressed herself and made love to him before she went back to work. She was naively eager. She whispered in his ear that he was only the second man she had ever loved, the first in five years. Her inept lovemaking was so sincere it made him want to cry.

When she was gone he did cry, because she thought she meant something to him and she did not.

Why am I crying? he asked himself. Why should I care? It's not my fault she let me get a handle on her . . .

Sitting on the dresser in a curiously adult posture was the child, carelessly playing with itself as it watched Howard intently. "No," Howard said, pulling himself up to the head of the bed. "You don't exist," he said. "No one's ever seen you but me." The child gave no sign of understanding. It just rolled over and began to slither down the front of the dresser.

Howard reached for his clothes, took them out of the bedroom. He put them on in the living room as he watched the door. Sure enough, the child crept along the carpet to the living room; but Howard was dressed by then, and he left.

He walked the streets for three hours. He was coldly rational at first. Logical. The creature does not exist. There is no reason to believe in it.

But bit by bit his rationality was worn away by constant flickers of the creature at the edges of his vision. On a bench, peering over the back at him; in a shop window; staring from the cab of a milk truck. Howard walked faster and faster, not caring where he went, trying to keep some intelligent process going on in his mind, and failing utterly as he saw the child, saw it clearly, dangling from a traffic signal.

What made it even worse was that occasionally a passerby, violating the unwritten law that New Yorkers are forbidden to look at each other, would gaze at him, shudder, and look away. A short European-looking woman crossed herself. A group of teenagers looking for trouble weren't looking for him—they grew silent, let him pass in silence, and in silence watched him out of sight.

They may not be able to see the child, Howard realized, but they see something.

And as he grew less and less coherent in the ramblings of his mind, memories began flashing on and off, his life passing before his eyes like a drowning man is supposed to see, only, he realized, if a drowning man saw this he would gulp at the water, breathe it deeply just to end the visions. They were memories he had been unable to find for years; memories he would never have wanted to find.

His poor, confused mother, who was so eager to be a good parent that she read everything, tried everything. Her precocious son Howard read it, too, and understood it better. Nothing she tried ever worked. And he accused her several times of being too demanding, of not demanding enough; of not giving him enough love, of drowning him in phony affection; of trying to take over with his friends, of not liking his friends enough. Until he had badgered and tortured the woman until she was timid every time she spoke to him, careful and long-winded and she phrased everything in such a way that it wouldn't offend, and while now and then he made her feel wonderful by giving her a hug and saying, "Have I got a wonderful Mom," there were far more times when he put a patient look on his face and said, "That again, Mom? I thought we went over that years ago." A failure as a parent, that's what you are, he reminded her again and again, though not in so many words, and she nodded and believed and died inside with every contact they had. He got everything he wanted from her.

And Vaughn Robles, who was just a little bit smarter than Howard and Howard wanted very badly to be valedictorian and so Vaughn and Howard became best friends and Vaughn would do anything for Howard and whenever Vaughn got a better grade than Howard he could not help but notice that Howard was hurt, that Howard wondered if he was really worth anything at all. "Am I really worth anything at all, Vaughn? No matter how well I do, there's always someone ahead of me, and I guess it's just that before my father died he told me and told me, Howie, be better than your Dad. Be the top. And I promised him I'd be the top but hell, Vaughn, I'm just not cut out for it—" and once he even cried. Vaughn was proud of himself as he sat there and listened to Howard give the valedictory address at high school graduation. What were a few grades, compared to a true friendship? Howard got a scholarship and went away to college and he and Vaughn almost never saw each other again.

And the teacher he provoked into hitting him and losing his job; and the football player who snubbed him and Howard quietly spread the rumor that the fellow was gay and he was ostracized from the team and finally quit; and the beautiful girls he stole from their boyfriends just to prove that he could do it and the friendships he destroyed just because he didn't like being excluded and the marriages he wrecked and the coworkers he undercut and he walked along the street with tears streaming down his face, wondering where all these memories had come from and why, after such a long time in hiding, they had come out now. Yet he knew the answer. The answer was slipping behind doorways, climbing lightpoles as he passed, waving obscene flippers at him from the sidewalk almost under his feet.

And slowly, inexorably, the memories wound their way from the distant past through a hundred tawdry exploitations because he could find people's weak spots without even trying until finally memory came to the one place where he knew it could not, could not ever go.

He remembered Rhiannon.

Born fourteen years ago. Smiled early, walked early, almost never cried. A loving child from the start, and therefore easy prey for Howard. Oh, Alice was a bitch in her own right—Howard wasn't the only bad parent in the family. But it was Howard who manipulated Rhiannon most. "Daddy's feelings are hurt, Sweetheart," and Rhiannon's eyes would grow wide, and she'd be sorry, and whatever Daddy wanted, Rhiannon would do. But this was normal, this was part of the pattern, this would have fit easily into all his life before, except for last month.

And even now, after a day of grief at his own life, Howard could not face it. Could not but did. He unwillingly remembered walking by Rhiannon's almost-closed door, seeing just a flash of cloth moving quickly. He opened the door on impulse, just on impulse, as Rhiannon took off her brassiere and looked at herself in the mirror. Howard had never thought of his daughter with desire, not until that moment, but once the desire formed Howard had no strategy, no pattern in his mind to stop him from trying to get what he wanted. He was *uncomfortable*, and so he stepped into the room and closed the door behind him and Rhiannon knew no way to say no to her father. When Alice opened the door Rhiannon was crying softly, and Alice looked and after a moment Alice screamed and screamed and Howard got up from the bed and tried to smooth it all over but Rhiannon was still crying and Alice was still screaming, kicking at his crotch, beating him, raking at his face, spitting at him, telling him he was a monster, a monster, until at last he was able to flee the room and the house and, until now, the memory.

He screamed now as he had not screamed then, and threw himself against a plate-glass window, weeping loudly as the blood gushed from a dozen glass cuts on his right arm, which had gone through the window. One large piece of glass stayed embedded in his forearm. He deliberately scraped his arm against the wall to drive the glass deeper. But the pain in his arm was no match for the pain in his mind, and he felt nothing.

They rushed him to the hospital, thinking to save his life, but the doctor was surprised to discover that for all the blood there were only superficial wounds, not dangerous at all. "I don't know why you didn't reach a vein or an artery," the doctor said. "I think the glass went everywhere it could possibly go without causing any important damage."

After the medical doctor, of course, there was the psychiatrist, but there were many suicidals at the hospital and Howard was not the dangerous kind. "I was insane for a moment, Doctor, that's all. I don't want to die, I didn't want to die then, I'm all right now. You can send me home." And the psychiatrist let him go home. They bandaged his arm. They did not know that his real relief was that nowhere in the hospital did he see the small, naked, child-shaped creature. He had purged himself. He was free.

Howard was taken home in an ambulance, and they wheeled him into the house and lifted him from the

stretcher to the bed. Through it all Alice hardly said a
word except to direct them to the bedroom. Howard
lay still on the bed as she stood over him, the two of
them alone for the first time since he left the house a
month ago.

"It was kind of you," Howard said softly, "to let me
come back."

"They said there wasn't room enough to keep you,
but you needed to be watched and taken care of for a
few weeks. So lucky me, I get to watch you." Her voice
was a low monotone, but the acid dripped from every
word. It stung.

"You were right, Alice," Howard said.

"Right about what? That marrying you was the worst
mistake of my life? No, Howard. *Meeting* you was my
worst mistake."

Howard began to cry. Real tears that welled up from
places in him that had once been deep but that now
rested painfully close to the surface. "I've been a monster, Alice. I haven't had any control over myself. What
I did to Rhiannon—Alice, I wanted to die, I wanted to
die!"

Alice's face was twisted and bitter. "And I wanted
you to, Howard. I have never been so disappointed as
when the doctor called and said you'd be all right. You'll
never be all right, Howard, you'll always be—"

"Let him be, Mother."

Rhiannon stood in the doorway.

"Don't come in, Rhiannon," Alice said.

Rhiannon came in. "Daddy, it's all right."

"What she means," Alice said, "is that we've checked
her and she isn't pregnant. No little monster is going
to be born."

Rhiannon didn't look at her mother, just gazed with
wide eyes at her father. "You didn't need to—hurt your-

self, Daddy. I forgive you. People lose control sometimes. And it was as much my fault as yours, it really was, you don't need to feel bad, Father."

It was too much for Howard. He cried out, shouted his confession, how he had manipulated her all his life, how he was an utterly selfish and rotten parent, and when it was over Rhiannon came to her father and laid her head on his chest and said, softly, "Father, it's all right. We are who we are. We've done what we've done. But it's all right now. I forgive you."

When Rhiannon left, Alice said, "You don't deserve her."

I know.

"I was going to sleep on the couch, but that would be stupid. Wouldn't it, Howard?"

I deserve to be left alone, like a leper.

"You misunderstand, Howard. I need to stay here to make sure you don't do anything else. To yourself or to anyone."

Yes. Yes, please. I can't be trusted.

"Don't wallow in it, Howard. Don't enjoy it. Don't make yourself even more disgusting than you were before."

All right.

They were drifting off to sleep when Alice said, "Oh, when the doctor called he wondered if I knew what had caused those sores all over your arms and chest."

But Howard was asleep, and didn't hear her. Asleep with no dreams at all, the sleep of peace, the sleep of having been forgiven, of being clean. It hadn't taken that much, after all. Now that it was over, it was easy. He felt as if a great weight had been taken from him.

He felt as if something heavy was lying on his legs. He awoke, sweating even though the room was not hot. He heard breathing. And it was not Alice's low-pitched, slow breath, it was quick and high and hard, as if the breather had been exerting himself.

Itself.

Themselves.

One of them lay across his legs, the flippers plucking at the blanket. The other two lay on either side, their eyes wide and intent, creeping slowly toward where his face emerged from the sheets.

Howard was puzzled. "I thought you'd be gone," he said to the children. "You're supposed to be gone now."

Alice stirred at the sound of his voice, mumbled in her sleep.

He saw more of them stirring in the gloomy corners of the room, another writhing slowly along the top of the dresser, another inching up the wall toward the ceiling.

"I don't need you anymore," he said, his voice oddly high-pitched.

Alice started breathing irregularly, mumbling, "What? What?"

And Howard said nothing more, just lay there in the sheets, watching the creatures carefully but not daring to make a sound for fear Alice would wake up. He was terribly afraid she would wake up and not see the creatures, which would prove, once and for all, that he had lost his mind.

He was even more afraid, however, that when she awoke she *would* see them. That was the one unbearable thought, yet he thought it continuously as they relentlessly approached with nothing at all in their eyes, not even hate, not even anger, not even contempt. We are with you, they seemed to be saying, we will be with you from now on. We will be with you, Howard, forever.

And Alice rolled over and opened her eyes.

QUIETUS

I T CAME TO him suddenly, a moment of blackness as he sat working late at his desk. It was as quick as an eye-blink, but before the darkness the papers on his desk had seemed terribly important, and afterward he stared at them blankly, wondering what they were and then realizing that he didn't really give a damn what they were and he ought to be going home now.

Ought definitely to be going home now. And C. Mark Tapworth of CMT Enterprises, Inc., arose from his desk without finishing all the work that was on it, the first time he had done such a thing in the twelve years it had taken him to bring the company from nothing to a multi-million-dollar-a-year business. Vaguely it occurred to him that he was not acting normally, but he didn't really care, it didn't really matter to him a bit whether any more people bought—bought—

And for a few seconds C. Mark Tapworth could not remember what it was that his company made.

It frightened him. It reminded him that his father and his uncles had all died of strokes. It reminded him of his mother's senility at the fairly young age of sixty-eight. It reminded him of something he had always known and never quite believed, that he was mortal and that all the works of all his days would trivialize gradually until his death, at which time his life would be his only act, the forgotten stone whose fall had set off ripples in the lake that would in time reach the shore having made, after all, no difference.

I'm tired, he decided. MaryJo is right. I need a rest.

But he was not the resting kind, not until that moment standing by his desk when again the blackness came, this time a jog in his mind and he remembered nothing, saw nothing, heard nothing, was falling interminably through nothingness.

Then, mercifully, the world returned to him and he stood trembling, regretting now the many, many nights he had stayed far too late, the many hours he had not spent with MaryJo, had left her alone in their large but childless house; and he imagined her waiting for him forever, a lonely woman dwarfed by the huge living room, waiting patiently for a husband who would, who must, who always had come home.

Is it my heart? Or a stroke? he wondered. Whatever it was, it was enough that he saw the end of the world lurking in the darkness that had visited him, and like the prophet returning from the mount things that once had mattered overmuch mattered not at all, and things he had long postponed now silently importuned him. He felt a terrible urgency that there was something he must do before—

Before what? He would not let himself answer. He just walked out through the large room full of ambitious younger men and women trying to impress him by working later than he; noticed but did not care that they were visibly relieved at their reprieve from another endless night. He walked out into the night and got in his car and drove home through a thin mist of rain that made the world retreat a comfortable distance from the windows of his car.

The children must be upstairs, he realized. No one ran to greet him at the door. The children, a boy and a girl half his height and twice his energy, were admirable creatures who ran down stairs as if they were skiing, who could no more hold completely still than a hummingbird in midair. He could hear their footsteps upstairs, running lightly across the floor. They hadn't come to greet him at the door because their lives, after all, had more important things in them than mere fathers. He smiled, set down his attaché case, and went to the kitchen.

MaryJo looked harried, upset. He recognized the signals instantly—she had cried earlier today.

"What's wrong?"

"Nothing," she said, because she always said Nothing. He knew that in a moment she would tell him. She always told him everything, which had sometimes made him impatient. Now as she moved silently back and forth from counter to counter, from cupboard to stove, making another perfect dinner, he realized that she was not going to tell him. It made him uncomfortable. He began to try to guess.

"You work too hard," he said. "I've offered to get a maid or a cook. We can certainly afford them."

MaryJo only smiled thinly. "I don't want anyone else mucking around in the kitchen," she said. "I thought we dropped that subject years ago. Did you—did you have a hard day at the office?"

Mark almost told her about his strange lapses of memory, but caught himself. This would have to be led up to gradually. MaryJo would not be able to cope with it, not in the state she was already in. "Not too hard. Finished up early."

"I know," she said. "I'm glad."

She didn't sound glad. It irritated him a little. Hurt his feelings. But instead of going off to nurse his wounds, he merely noticed his emotions as if he were a dispassionate observer. He saw himself; important self-made man, yet at home a little boy who can be hurt, not even by a word, but by a short pause of indecision. Sensitive, sensitive, and he was amused at himself: for a moment he almost saw himself standing a few inches away, could observe even the bemused expression on his own face.

"Excuse me," MaryJo said, and she opened a cupboard door as he stepped out of the way. She pulled out a pressure cooker. "We're out of potato flakes," she said. "Have to do it the primitive way." She dropped the peeled potatoes into the pan.

"The children are awfully quiet today," he said. "Do you know what they're doing?"

MaryJo looked at him with a bewildered expression.

"They didn't come meet me at the door. Not that I mind. They're busy with their own concerns, I know."

"Mark," MaryJo said.

"All right, you see right through me so easily. But I was only a little hurt. I want to look through today's mail." He wandered out of the kitchen. He was vaguely aware that behind him MaryJo had started to cry again. He did not let it worry him much. She cried easily and often.

He wandered into the living room, and the furniture surprised him. He had expected to see the green sofa and chair that he had bought from Deseret Industries, and the size of the living room and the tasteful antiques looked utterly wrong. Then his mind did a quick turn and he remembered that the old green sofa and chair were fifteen years ago, when he and MaryJo had first married. Why did I expect to see them? he wondered, and he worried again; worried also because he had come into the living room expecting to find the mail, even though for years MaryJo had put it on his desk every day.

He went into his study and picked up the mail and started sorting through it until he noticed out of the corner of his eye that something large and dark and massive was blocking the lower half of one of the windows. He looked. It was a coffin, a rather plain one, sitting on a rolling table from a mortuary.

"MaryJo," he called. "MaryJo."

She came into the study, looking afraid. "Yes?"

"Why is there a coffin in my study?" he asked.

"Coffin?" she asked.

"By the window, MaryJo. How did it get here?"

She looked disturbed. "Please don't touch it," she said.

"Why not?"

"I can't stand seeing you touch it. I told them they could leave it here for a few hours. But now it looks like it has to stay all night." The idea of the coffin staying in the house any longer was obviously repugnant to her.

"*Who* left it here? And why us? It's not as if we're in the market. Or do they sell these at parties now, like Tupperware?"

"The bishop called and asked me—asked me to let the mortuary people leave it here for the funeral tomorrow. He said nobody could get away to unlock the church and so could we take it here for a few hours—"

It occurred to him that the mortuary would not have parted with a funeral-bound coffin unless it were full.

"MaryJo, is there a body in this?"

She nodded, and a tear slipped over her lower eyelid. He was aghast. He let himself show it. "They left a corpse in a coffin here in the house with you all day? With the kids?"

She buried her face in her hands and ran from the room, ran upstairs.

Mark did not follow her. He stood there and regarded the coffin with distaste. At least they had the good sense to close it. But a coffin! He went to the telephone at his desk, dialed the bishop's number.

"He isn't here." The bishop's wife sounded irritated at his call.

"He has to get this body out of my office and out of my house tonight. This is a terrible imposition."

"I don't know where to reach him. He's a doctor, you know, Brother Tapworth. He's at the hospital. Operating. There's no way I can contact him for something like this."

"So what am I supposed to do?"

She got surprisingly emotional about it. "Do what you want! Push the coffin out in the street if you want! It'll just be one more hurt to the poor man!"

"Which brings me to another question. Who is he, and why isn't his family—"

"He doesn't have a family, Brother Tapworth. And he doesn't have any money. I'm sure he regrets dying in our ward, but we just thought that even though he had no friends in the world someone might offer him a little kindness on his way out of it."

Her intensity was irresistible, and Mark recognized the hopelessness of getting rid of the box that night. "As long as it's gone tomorrow," he said. A few amenities, and the conversation ended. Mark sat in his chair staring angrily at the coffin. He had come home worried about his health. And found a coffin to greet him when he came. Well, at least it explained why poor MaryJo

had been so upset. He heard the children quarreling
upstairs. Well, let MaryJo handle it. Their problems
would take her mind off this box, anyway.

And so he sat and stared at the coffin for two hours,
and had no dinner, and did not particularly notice when
MaryJo came downstairs and took the burnt potatoes
out of the pressure cooker and threw the entire dinner
away and lay down on the sofa in the living room and
wept. He watched the patterns of the grain of the coffin,
as subtle as flames, winding along the wood. He remembered having taken naps at the age of five in a
makeshift bedroom behind a plywood partition in his
parents' small home. The wood grain there had been
his way of passing the empty sleepless hours. In those
days he had been able to see shapes: clouds and faces
and battles and monsters. But on the coffin, the wood
grain looked more complex and yet far more simple. A
road map leading upward to the lid. An engineering
drawing describing the decomposition of the body. A
graph at the foot of the patient's bed, saying nothing to
the patient but speaking death into the trained physi-
cian's mind. Mark wondered, briefly, about the bishop,
who was even now operating on someone who might
very well end up in just such a box as this.

And finally his eyes hurt and he looked at the clock
and felt guilty about having spent so long closed off in
his study on one of his few nights home early from the
office. He meant to get up and find MaryJo and take her
up to bed. But instead he got up and went to the coffin
and ran his hands along the wood. It felt like glass,
because the varnish was so thick and smooth. It was as
if the living wood had to be kept away, protected from
the touch of a hand. But the wood was not alive, was
it? It was being put into the ground also to decompose.
The varnish might keep it alive longer. He thought
whimsically of what it would be like to varnish a

corpse, to preserve it. The Egyptians would have nothing on us then, he thought.

"Don't," said a husky voice from the door. It was MaryJo, her eyes red-rimmed, her face looking slept in.

"Don't what?" Mark asked her. She didn't answer, just glanced down at his hands. To his surprise, Mark noticed that his thumbs were under the lip of the coffin lid, as if to lift it.

"I wasn't going to open it," he said.

"Come upstairs," MaryJo said.

"Are the children asleep?"

He had asked the question innocently, but her face was immediately twisted with pain and grief and anger.

"Children?" she asked. "What is this? And why tonight?"

He leaned against the coffin in suprise. The wheeled table moved slightly.

"We don't have any children," she said.

And Mark remembered with horror that she was right. On the second miscarriage, the doctor had tied her tubes because any further pregnancies would risk her life. There were no children, none at all, and it had devastated her for years; it was only through Mark's great patience and utter dependability that she had been able to stay out of the hospital. Yet when he came home tonight—he tried to remember what he had heard when he came home. Surely he had heard the children running back and forth upstairs. Surely—

"I haven't been well," he said.

"If it was a joke, it was sick."

"It wasn't a joke—it was—" But again he couldn't, at least didn't tell her about the strange memory lapses at the office, even though this was even more proof that something was wrong. He had never had any children in his home, their brothers and sisters had all been discreetly warned not to bring children around poor

MaryJo, who was quite distraught to be—the Old Testament word?—barren.

And he had talked about having children all evening.

"Honey, I'm sorry," he said, trying to put his whole heart into the apology.

"So am I," she answered, and went upstairs.

Surely she isn't angry at me, Mark thought. Surely she realizes something is wrong. Surely she'll forgive me.

But as he climbed the stairs after her, taking off his shirt as he did, he again heard the voice of a child.

"I want a drink, Mommy." The voice was plaintive, with the sort of whine only possible to a child who is comfortable and sure of love. Mark turned at the landing in time to see MaryJo passing the top of the stairs on the way to the children's bedroom, a glass of water in her hand. He thought nothing of it. The children always wanted extra attention at bedtime.

The children. The children, of course there were children. This was the urgency he had felt in the office, the reason he had to get home. They had always wanted children and so there *were* children. C. Mark Tapworth always got what he set his heart on.

"Asleep at last," MaryJo said wearily when she came into the room.

Despite her weariness, however, she kissed him good night in the way that told him she wanted to make love. He had never worried much about sex. Let the readers of *Reader's Digest* worry about how to make their sex lives fuller and richer, he always said. As for him, sex was good, but not the best thing in his life; just one of the ways that he and MaryJo responded to each other. Yet tonight he was disturbed, worried. Not because he could not perform, for he had never been troubled by even temporary impotence except when he had a fever and didn't feel like sex anyway. What bothered him was that he didn't exactly care.

He didn't *not* care, either. He was just going through the motions as he had a thousand times before, and this time, suddenly, it all seemed so silly, so redolent of petting in the backseat of a car. He felt embarrassed that he should get so excited over a little stroking. So he was almost relieved when one of the children cried out. Usually he would say to ignore the cry, would insist on continuing the lovemaking. But this time he pulled away, put on a robe, went into the other room to quiet the child down.

There was no other room.

Not in this house. He had, in his mind, been heading for their hopeful room filled with crib, changing table, dresser, mobiles, cheerful wallpaper—but that room had been years ago, in the small house in Sandy, not here in the home in Federal Heights with its magnificent view of Salt Lake City, its beautiful shape and decoration that spoke of taste and shouted of wealth and whispered faintly of loneliness and grief. He leaned against a wall. There were no children. There were no children. He could still hear the child's cry ringing in his mind.

MaryJo stood in the doorway to their bedroom, naked but holding her nightgown in front of her. "Mark," she said. "I'm afraid."

"So am I," he answered.

But she asked him no questions, and he put on his pajamas and they went to bed and as he lay there in darkness listening to his wife's faintly rasping breath he realized that it didn't really matter as much as it ought. He was losing his mind, but he didn't much care. He thought of praying about it, but he had given up praying years ago, though of course it wouldn't do to let anyone else know about his loss of faith, not in a city where it's good business to be an active Mormon. There'd be no help from God on this one, he knew. And not much help from MaryJo, either, for instead of being strong as she usually was in an emergency, this time she would be, as she said, afraid.

"Well, so am I," Mark said to himself. He reached over and stroked his wife's shadowy cheek, realized that there were some creases near the eye, understood that what made her afraid was not his specific ailment, odd as it was, but the fact that it was a hint of aging, of senility, of imminent separation. He remembered the box downstairs, like death appointed to watch for him until at last he consented to go. He briefly resented them for bringing death to his home, for so indecently imposing on them; and then he ceased to care at all. Not about the box, not about his strange lapses of memory, not about anything.

I am at peace, he realized as he drifted off to sleep. I am at peace, and it's not all that pleasant.

"Mark," said MaryJo, shaking him awake. "Mark, you overslept."

Mark opened his eyes, mumbled something so the shaking would stop, then rolled over to go back to sleep.

"Mark," MaryJo insisted.

"I'm tired," he said in protest.

"I know you are," she said. "So I didn't wake you any sooner. But they just called. There's something of an emergency or something—"

"They can't flush the toilet without someone holding their hands."

"I wish you wouldn't be crude, Mark," MaryJo said. "I sent the children off to school without letting them wake you by kissing you good-bye. They were very upset."

"Good children."

"Mark, they're expecting you at the office."

Mark closed his eyes and spoke in measured tones.

"You can tell them and tell them I'll come in when I damn well feel like it and if they can't cope with the problem themselves I'll fire them all as incompetents."

MaryJo was silent for a moment. "Mark, I can't say that."

"Word for word. I'm tired. I need a rest. My mind is doing funny things to me." And with that Mark remembered all the illusions of the day before, including the illusion of having children.

"There aren't any children," he said.

Her eyes grew wide. "What do you mean?"

He almost shouted at her, demanded to know what was going on, why she didn't just tell him the truth for a moment. But the lethargy and disinterest clamped down and he said nothing, just rolled back over and looked at the curtains as they drifted in and out with the air conditioning. Soon MaryJo left him, and he heard the sound of machinery starting up downstairs. The washer, the dryer, the dishwasher, the garbage disposer: it seemed that all the machines were going at once. He had never heard the sounds before—MaryJo never ran them in the evenings or on weekends, when he was home.

At noon he finally got up, but he didn't feel like showering and shaving, though any other day he would have felt dirty and uncomfortable until those rituals were done with. He just put on his robe and went downstairs. He planned to go in to breakfast, but instead he went into his study and opened the lid of the coffin.

It took him a bit of preparation, of course. There was some pacing back and forth before the coffin, and much stroking of the wood, but finally he put his thumbs under the lid and lifted.

The corpse looked stiff and awkward. A man, not particularly old, not particularly young. Hair of a determinedly average color. Except for the grayness of the skin color the body looked completely natural and so utterly average that Mark felt sure he might have seen the man a million times without remembering he had seen him at all. Yet he was unmistakably dead, not because of the cheap satin lining the coffin rather slackly, but because of the hunch of the shoulders, the jut of the chin. The man was not comfortable.

He smelled of embalming fluid.

Mark was holding the lid open with one hand, leaning on the coffin with the other. He was trembling. Yet he felt no excitement, no fear. The trembling was coming from his body, not from anything he could find within his thoughts. The trembling was because it was cold.

There was a soft sound or absence of sound at the door. He turned around abruptly. The lid dropped closed behind him. MaryJo was standing in the door, wearing a frilly housedress, her eyes wide with horror.

In that moment years fell away and to Mark she was twenty, a shy and somewhat awkward girl who was forever being surprised by the way the world actually worked. He waited for her to say, "But Mark, you cheated him." She had said it only once, but ever since then he had heard the words in his mind whenever he was closing a deal. It was the closest thing to a conscience he had in his business dealings. It was enough to get him a reputation as a very honest man.

"Mark," she said softly, as if struggling to keep control of herself, "Mark, I couldn't go on without you."

She sounded as if she were afraid something terrible was going to happen to him, and her hands were shaking. He took a step toward her. She lifted her hands, came to him, clung to him, and cried in a high whimper into his shoulder, "I couldn't. I just couldn't."

"You don't have to," he said, puzzled.

"I'm just not," she said between gentle sobs, "the kind of person who can live alone."

"But even if I, even if something happened to me, MaryJo, you'd have the—" He was going to say the children. Something was wrong with that, though, wasn't there? They loved no one better in the world than their children; no parents had ever been happier than they had been when their two were born. Yet he couldn't say it.

"I'd have what?" MaryJo asked. "Oh, Mark, I'd have nothing."

And then Mark remembered again (what's happening to me!) that they were childless, that to MaryJo, who was old-fashioned enough to regard motherhood as the main purpose for her existence, the fact that they had no hope of children was God's condemnation of her. The only thing that had pulled her through after the operation was Mark, was her fussing over his meaning-less and sometimes invented problems at the office or telling him endlessly the events of her lonely days. It was as if he were her anchor to reality, and only he kept her from going adrift in the eddies of her own fears. No wonder the poor girl (for at such times Mark could not think of her as completely adult) was distraught as she thought of Mark's death, and the damned coffin in the house did no good at all.

But I'm in no position to cope with this, Mark thought. I'm falling apart, I'm not only forgetting things, I'm remembering things that didn't happen. And what if I died? What if I suddenly had a stroke like my father had and died on the way to the hospital? What would happen to MaryJo?

She'd never lack for money. Between the business and the insurance, even the house would be paid off, with enough money to live like a queen on the interest. But would the insurance company arrange for someone to hold her patiently while she cried out her fears? Would they provide someone for her to waken in the

middle of the night because of the nameless terrors that
haunted her?

Her sobs turned into frantic hiccoughs and her fingers
dug more deeply into his back through the soft fabric
of his robe. See how she clings to me, he thought. She'll
never let me go, he thought, and then the blackness
came again and again he was falling backward into
nothing and again he did not care about anything. Did
not even know there was anything to care about.

Except for the fingers pressing into his back and the
weight he held in his arms. I do not mind losing the
world, he thought. I do not mind losing even my memories of the past. But these fingers. This woman. I cannot
lay this burden down because there is no one who can
pick it up again. If I mislay her she is lost.

And yet he longed for the darkness, resented her need
that held him. Surely there is a way out of this, he
thought. Surely a balance between two hungers that
leaves both satisfied. But still the hands held him. All
the world was silent and the silence was peace except
for the sharp, insistent fingers and he cried out in frus-
tration and the sound was still ringing in the room
when he opened his eyes and saw MaryJo standing
against a wall, leaning against the wall, looking at him
in terror.

"What's wrong?" she whispered.

"I'm losing," he answered. But he could not remember what he had thought to win.

And at that moment a door slammed in the house
and Amy came running with little loud feet through
the kitchen and into the study, flinging herself on her
mother and bellowing about the day at school and the
dog that chased her for the second time and how the
teacher told her she was the *best* reader in the second
grade but Darrel had spilled milk on her and could

she have a sandwich because she had dropped hers and stepped on it accidentally at lunch—

MaryJo looked at Mark cheerfully and winked and laughed. "Sounds like Amy's had a busy day, doesn't it, Mark?"

Mark could not smile. He just nodded as MaryJo straightened Amy's disheveled clothing and led her toward the kitchen.

"MaryJo," Mark said. "There's something I have to talk to you about."

"Can it wait?" MaryJo asked, not even pausing. Mark heard the cupboard door opening, heard the lid come off the peanut butter jar, heard Amy giggle and say, "Mommy, not so *thick*."

Mark didn't understand why he was so confused and terrified. Amy had had a sandwich after school ever since she had started going—even as an infant she had had seven meals a day, and never gained an ounce of fat. It wasn't what was happening in the kitchen that was bothering him, couldn't be. Yet he could not stop himself from crying out, "MaryJo! MaryJo, come here!"

"Is Daddy mad?" he heard Amy ask softly.

"No," MaryJo answered, and she bustled back into the room and impatiently said, "What's wrong, dear?"

"I just need—just need to have you in here for a minute."

"Really, Mark, that's not your style, is it? Amy needs to have a lot of attention right after school, it's the way she is. I wish you wouldn't stay home from work with nothing to do, Mark, you become quite impossible around the house." She smiled to show that she was only half serious and left again to go back to Amy.

For a moment Mark felt a terrible stab of jealousy that MaryJo was far more sensitive to Amy's needs than to his.

But that jealousy passed quickly, like the memory of the pain of MaryJo's fingers pressing into his back, and with a tremendous feeling of relief Mark didn't care about anything at all, and he turned around to the coffin, which fascinated him, and he opened the lid again and looked inside. It was as if the poor man had no face at all, Mark realized. As if death stole faces from people and made them anonymous even to themselves.

He ran his fingers back and forth across the satin and it felt cool and inviting. The rest of the room, the rest of the world receded into deep background. Only Mark and the coffin and the corpse remained and Mark felt very tired and very hot, as if life itself were a terrible friction making heat within him, and he took off his robe and pajamas and awkwardly climbed on a chair and stepped over the edge into the coffin and knelt and then lay down. There was no other corpse to share the slight space with him; nothing between his body and the cold satin, and as he lay on it it didn't get any warmer because at last the friction was slowing, was cooling, and he reached up and pulled down the lid and the world was dark and silent and there was no odor and no taste and no feel but the cold of the sheets.

"Why is the lid closed?" asked little Amy, holding her mother's hand.

"Because it's not the body we must remember," MaryJo said softly, with careful control, "but the way Daddy always was. We must remember him happy and laughing and loving us."

Amy looked puzzled. "But I remember he spanked me."

MaryJo nodded, smiling, something she had not done recently. "It's all right to remember that, too," MaryJo said, and then she took her daughter from the coffin back into the living room, where Amy, not realizing yet the terrible loss she had sustained, laughed and climbed on Grandpa.

David, his face serious and tear-stained because he did understand, came and put his hand in his mother's hand and held tightly to her. "We'll be fine," he said.

"Yes," MaryJo answered. "I think so."

And her mother whispered in her ear, "I don't know how you can stand it so bravely, my dear."

Tears came to MaryJo's eyes. "I'm not brave at all," she whispered back. "But the children. They depend on me so much. I can't let go when they're leaning on me."

"How terrible it would be," her mother said, nodding wisely, "if you had no children."

Inside the coffin, his last need fulfilled, Mark Tapworth heard it all, but could not hold it in his mind, for in his mind there was space or time for only one thought: consent. Everlasting consent to his life, to his death, to the world, and to the everlasting absence of the world. For now there were children.

DEEP BREATHING EXERCISES

—————

I F DALE YORGASON weren't so easily distracted, he
might never have noticed the breathing. But he was
on his way upstairs to change clothes, noticed the headline on the paper, and got deflected; instead of climbing
the stairs, he sat on them and began to read. He could
not even concentrate on that, however. He began to
hear all the sounds of the house. Brian, their two-year-
old son, was upstairs, breathing heavily in sleep. Colly,
his wife, was in the kitchen, kneading bread and also
breathing heavily.

Their breath was exactly in unison. Brian's rasping
breath upstairs, thick with the mucus of a child's sleep;
Colly's deep breaths as she labored with the dough.
It set Dale to thinking, the newspapers forgotten. He
wondered how often people did that—breathed perfectly together for minutes on end. He began to wonder
about coincidence.

And then, because he was easily distracted, he remembered that he had to change his clothes and went upstairs. When he came down in his jeans and sweatshirt, ready for a good game of outdoor basketball now that it was spring, Colly called to him. "I'm out of cinnamon, Dale!"

"I'll get it on the way home!"

"I need it *now*!" Colly called.

"We have two cars!" Dale yelled back, then closed the door. He briefly felt bad about not helping her out, but reminded himself that he was already running late and it wouldn't hurt her to take Brian with her and get outside the house; she never seemed to get out of the house anymore.

His team of friends from Allways Home Products, Inc., won the game, and he came home deliciously sweaty. No one was there. The bread dough had risen impossibly, was spread all over the counter and dropping in large chunks onto the floor. Colly had obviously been gone too long. He wondered what could have delayed her.

Then came the phone call from the police, and he did not have to wonder anymore. Colly had a habit of inadvertently running stop signs.

The funeral was well attended because Dale had a large family and was well liked at the office. He sat between his own parents and Colly's parents. The speakers droned on, and Dale, easily distracted, kept thinking of the fact that of all the mourners there, only a few were there in private grief. Only a few had actually known Colly, who preferred to avoid office functions and social gatherings; who stayed home with Brian most of the time being a perfect housewife and reading books and being, in the end, solitary. Most of the people at the funeral had come for Dale's sake, to comfort him. Am I comforted? he asked himself. Not by my friends—

they had little to say, were awkward and embarrassed. Only his father had had the right instinct, just embracing him and then talking about everything except Dale's wife and son who were dead, so mangled in the incident that the coffin was never opened for anyone. There was talk of the fishing in Lake Superior this summer; talk of the bastards at Continental Hardware who thought that the 65-year retirement rule ought to apply to the president of the company; talk of nothing at all. But it was good enough. It distracted Dale from his grief.

Now, however, he wondered whether he had really been a good husband for Colly. Had she really been happy, cooped up in the house all day? He had tried to get her out, get to meet people, and she had resisted. But in the end, as he wondered whether he knew her at all, he could not find an answer, not one he was sure of. And Brian—he had not known Brian at all. The boy was smart and quick, speaking in sentences when other children were still struggling with single words; but what had he and Dale ever had to talk about? All Brian's companionship had been with his mother; all Colly's companionship had been with Brian. In a way it was like their breathing—the last time Dale had heard them breathe—in unison, as if even the rhythms of their bodies were together. It pleased Dale somehow to think that they had drawn their last breath together, too, the unison continuing to the grave; now they would be lowered into the earth in perfect unison, sharing a coffin as they had shared every day since Brian's birth.

Dale's grief swept over him again, surprising him because he had thought he had cried as much as he possibly could, and now he discovered there were more tears waiting to flow. He was not sure whether he was crying because of the empty house he would come home to, or because he had always been somewhat closed off from his family; was the coffin, after all, just an expression of the way their relationship had always been? It was not a productive line of thought, and Dale let himself be distracted. He let himself notice that his parents were breathing together.

Their breaths were soft, hard to hear. But Dale heard, and looked at them, watched their chests rise and fall together. It unnerved him—was unison breathing more common than he had thought? He listened for others, but Colly's parents were not breathing together, and certainly Dale's breaths were at his own rhythm. Then Dale's mother looked at him, smiled, and nodded to him in an attempt at silent communication. Dale was not good at silent communication; meaningful pauses and knowing looks always left him baffled. They always made him want to check his fly. Another distraction, and he did not think of breathing again.

Until at the airport, when the plane was an hour late in arriving because of technical difficulties in Los Angeles. There was not much to talk to his parents about; even his father's chatter failed him, and they sat in silence most of the time, as did most of the other passengers. Even a stewardess and the pilot sat near them, waiting silently for the plane to arrive.

It was in one of the deeper silences that Dale noticed that his father and the pilot were both swinging their crossed legs in unison. Then he listened, and realized there was a strong sound in the gate waiting area, a rhythmic soughing of many of the passengers inhaling and exhaling together. Dale's mother and father, the pilot, the stewardess, several other passengers, all were breathing together. It unnerved him. How could this be? Brian and Colly had been mother and son; Dale's parents had been together for years. But why should half the people in the waiting area breathe together?

He pointed it out to his father.

"Kind of strange, but I think you're right," his father said, rather delighted with the odd event. Dale's father loved odd events.

And then the rhythm broke, and the plane taxied close to the windows, and the crowd stirred and got ready to board, even though the actual boarding was surely half an hour off.

The plane broke apart at landing. About half the people in the airplane survived. However, the entire crew and several passengers, including Dale's parents, were killed when the plane hit the ground.

It was then that Dale realized that the breathing was not a result of coincidence, or the people's closeness during their lives. It was a messenger of death; they breathed together *because* they were going to draw their last breath together. He said nothing about this thought to anyone else, but whenever he got distracted from other things, he tended to speculate on this. It was better than dwelling on the fact that he, a man to whom family had been very important, was now completely without family; that the only people with whom he was completely himself, completely at ease, were gone, and there was no more ease for him in the world. Much better to wonder whether his knowledge might be used to save lives. After all, he often thought, reasoning in a circular pattern that never seemed to end, if I notice this again, I should be able to alert someone, to warn someone, to save their lives. Yet if I were going to save their lives, would they then breathe in unison? If my parents had been warned, and changed flights, he thought, they wouldn't have died, and therefore wouldn't have breathed together, and so I wouldn't have been able to warn them, and so they *wouldn't* have changed flights, and so they *would* have died, and so they *would* have breathed in unison, and so I would have noticed and warned them. . . .

More than anything that had ever passed through his mind before, this thought engaged him, and he was not easily distracted from it. It began to hurt his work; he slowed down, made mistakes, because he concentrated only on breathing, listening constantly to the secretaries and other executives in his company, waiting for the fatal moment when they would breathe in unison.

He was eating alone in a restaurant when he heard it again. The sighs of breath came all together, from every table near him. It took him a few moments to be sure; then he leaped from the table and walked briskly outside. He did not stop to pay, for the breathing was still in unison at every table to the door of the restaurant.

The maître d', predictably, was annoyed at his leaving without paying, and called out to him. Dale did not answer. "Wait! You didn't pay!" cried the man, following Dale out into the street.

Dale did not know how far he had to go for safety from whatever danger faced everyone in the restaurant; he ended up having no choice in the matter. The maître d' stopped him on the sidewalk, only a few doors down from the restaurant, tried to pull him back toward the place, Dale resisting all the way.

"You can't leave without paying! What do you think you're doing?"

"I can't go back," Dale shouted. "I'll pay you! I'll pay you right here!" And he fumbled in his wallet for the money as a huge explosion knocked him and the maître d' to the ground. Flame erupted from the restaurant, and people screamed as the building began crumbling from the force of the explosion. It was impossible that anyone still inside the building could be alive.

The maître d', his eyes wide with horror, stood up as Dale did, and looked at him with dawning understanding. "You knew!" the maître d' said. "You knew!"

* * *

Dale was acquitted at the trial—phone calls from a radical group and the purchase of a large quantity of explosives in several states led to indictment and conviction of someone else. But at the trial enough was said to convince Dale and several psychiatrists that something was seriously wrong with him. He was voluntarily committed to an institution, where Dr. Howard Rumming spent hours in conversation with Dale, trying to understand his madness, his fixation on breathing as a sign of coming death.

"I'm sane in every other way, aren't I, Doctor?" Dale asked, again and again.

And repeatedly the doctor answered, "What is sanity? Who has it? How can I know?"

Dale soon found that the mental hospital was not an unpleasant place to be. It was a private institution, and a lot of money had gone into it; most of the people there were voluntary commitments, which meant that conditions had to remain excellent. It was one of the things that made Dale grateful for his father's wealth. In the hospital he was safe; the only contact with the outside world was on the television. Gradually, meeting people and becoming attached to them in the hospital, he began to relax, to lose his obsession with breathing, to stop listening quite so intently for the sound of inhalation and exhalation, the way that different people's breathing rhythms fit together. Gradually he began to be his old, distractable self.

"I'm nearly cured, Doctor," Dale announced one day in the middle of a game of backgammon.

The doctor sighed. "I know it, Dale. I have to admit it—I'm disappointed. Not in your cure, you understand. It's just that you've been a breath of fresh air, you should pardon the expression." They both laughed a little. "I get so tired of middle-aged women with fashionable nervous breakdowns."

Dale was gammoned—the dice were all against him. But he took it well, knowing that next time he was quite likely to win handily—he usually did. Then he and Dr. Rumming got up from their table and walked toward the front of the recreation room, where the television program had been interrupted by a special news bulletin. The people around the television looked disturbed; news was never allowed on the hospital television, and only a bulletin like this could creep in. Dr. Rumming intended to turn if off immediately, but then heard the words being said.

". . . from satellites fully capable of destroying every major city in the United States. The President was furnished with a list of fifty-four cities targeted by the orbiting missiles. One of these, said the communiqué, will be destroyed immediately to show that the threat is serious and will be carried out. Civil defense authorities have been notified, and citizens of the fifty-four cities will be on standby for immediate evacuation." There followed the normal parade of special reports and deep background, but the reporters were all afraid.

Dale's mind could not stay on the program, however, because he was distracted by something far more compelling. Every person in the room was breathing in perfect unison, including Dale. He tried to break out of the rhythm, and couldn't.

It's just my fear, Dale thought. Just the broadcast, making me think that I hear the breathing.

A Denver newsman came on the air then, overriding the network broadcast. "Denver, ladies and gentlemen, is one of the targeted cities. The city has asked us to inform you that orderly evacuation is to begin immediately. Obey all traffic laws, and drive east from the city if you live in the following neighborhoods. . . ."

Then the newsman stopped, and, breathing heavily, listened to something coming through his earphone.

The newsman was breathing in perfect unison with all the people in the room.

"Dale," Dr. Rumming said.

Dale only breathed, feeling death poised above him in the sky.

"Dale, can you hear the breathing?"

Dale heard the breathing.

The newsman spoke again. "Denver is definitely the target. The missiles have already been launched. Please leave immediately. Do not stop for any reason. It is estimated that we have less than—less than three minutes. My God," he said, and got up from his chair, breathing heavily, running out of the range of the camera. No one turned any equipment off in the station—the tube kept on showing the local news set, the empty chairs, the tables, the weather map.

"We can't get out in time," Dr. Rumming said to the inmates in the room. "We're near the center of Denver. Our only hope is to lie on the floor. Try to get under tables and chairs as much as possible." The inmates, terrified, complied with the voice of authority.

"So much for my cure," Dale said, his voice trembling. Rumming managed a half-smile. They lay together in the middle of the floor, leaving the furniture for everyone else because they knew that the furniture would do no good at all.

"You definitely don't belong here," Rumming told him. "I never met a saner man in all my life."

Dale was distracted, however. Instead of his impending death he thought of Colly and Brian in their coffin. He imagined the earth being swept away in a huge wind, and the coffin being ashed immediately in the white explosion from the sky. The barrier is coming down at last, Dale thought, and I will be with them as completely as it is possible to be. He thought of Brian learning to walk, crying when he fell; he remembered Colly saying, "Don't pick him up every time he cries, or he'll just learn that crying gets results." And so for three days Dale had listened to Brian cry and cry, and never lifted a hand to help the boy. Brian learned to walk quite well, and quickly. But now, suddenly, Dale felt again that irresistible impulse to pick him up, to put his pathetically red and weeping face on his shoulder, to say, That's all right, Daddy's holding you.

"That's all right, Daddy's holding you," Dale said aloud, softly. Then there was a flash of white so bright that it could be seen as easily through the walls as through the window, for there were no walls, and all the breath was drawn out of their bodies at once, their voices robbed from them so suddenly that they all involuntarily shouted and then, forever, were silent. Their shout was taken up in a violent wind that swept the sound, wrung from every throat in perfect unison, upward into the clouds forming over what had once been Denver.

And in the last moment, as the shout was drawn from his lungs and the heat took his eyes out of his face, Dale realized that despite all his foreknowledge, the only life he had ever saved was that of a maître d' hôtel, whose life, to Dale, didn't mean a thing.

FAT FARM

THE RECEPTIONIST WAS surprised that he was back so soon.

"Why, Mr. Barth, how glad I am to see you," she said.

"Surprised, you mean," Barth answered. His voice rumbled from the rolls of fat under his chin.

"Delighted."

"How long has it been?" Barth asked.

"Three years. How time flies."

The receptionist smiled, but Barth saw the awe and revulsion on her face as she glanced over his immense body. In her job she saw fat people every day. But Barth knew he was unusual. He was proud of being unusual.

"Back to the fat farm," he said, laughing.

The effort of laughing made him short of breath, and he gasped for air as she pushed a button and said, "Mr. Barth is back."

He did not bother to look for a chair. No chair could

hold him. He did lean against a wall, however. Standing was a labor he preferred to avoid.

Yet it was not shortness of breath or exhaustion at the slightest effort that had brought him back to Anderson's Fitness Center. He had often been fat before, and he rather relished the sensation of bulk, the impression he made as crowds parted for him. He pitied those who could only be slightly fat—short people, who were not able to bear the weight. At well over two meters, Barth could get gloriously fat, stunningly fat. He owned thirty wardrobes and took delight in changing from one to another as his belly and buttocks and thighs grew. At times he felt that if he grew large enough, he could take over the world, be the world. At the dinner table he was a conqueror to rival Genghis Khan.

It was not his fatness, then, that had brought him in. It was that at last the fat was interfering with his other pleasures. The girl he had been with the night before had tried and tried, but he was incapable—a sign that it was time to renew, refresh, reduce.

"I am a man of pleasure," he wheezed to the receptionist, whose name he never bothered to learn. She smiled back.

"Mr. Anderson will be here in a moment."

"Isn't it ironic," he said, "that a man such as I, who is capable of fulfilling every one of his desires, is never satisfied!" He gasped with laughter again. "Why haven't we ever slept together?" he asked.

She looked at him, irritation crossing her face. "You always ask that, Mr. Barth, on your way in. But you never ask it on your way out."

True enough. When he was on his way out of the Anderson Fitness Center, she never seemed as attractive as she had on his way in.

Anderson came in, effusively handsome, gushingly

warm, taking Barth's fleshy hand in his and pumping it with enthusiasm.

"One of my best customers," he said.

"The usual," Barth said.

"Of course," Anderson answered. "But the price *has* gone up."

"If you ever go out of business," Barth said, following Anderson into the inner rooms, "give me plenty of warning. I only let myself go this much because I know you're here."

"Oh," Anderson chuckled. "We'll never go out of business."

"I have no doubt you could support your whole organization on what you charge *me*."

"You're paying for much more than the simple service we perform. You're also paying for privacy. Our, shall we say, lack of government intervention."

"How many of the bastards do you bribe?"

"Very few, very few. Partly because so many high officials also need our service."

"No doubt."

"It isn't just weight gains that bring people to us, you know. It's cancer and aging and accidental disfigurement. You'd be surprised to learn who has had our service."

Barth doubted that he would. The couch was ready for him, immense and soft and angled so that it would be easy for him to get up again.

"Damn near got married this time," Barth said, by way of conversation.

Anderson turned to him in surprise.

"But you didn't?"

"Of course not. Started getting fat, and she couldn't cope."

"Did you tell her?"

"That I was getting fat? It was obvious."

"About us, I mean."

"I'm not a fool."

Anderson looked relieved. "Can't have rumors getting around among the thin and young, you know."

"Still, I think I'll look her up again, afterward. She did things to me a woman shouldn't be able to do. And I thought I was jaded."

Anderson placed a tight-fitting rubber cap over Barth's head.

"Think your key thought," Anderson reminded him.

Key thought. At first that had been such a comfort, to make sure that not one iota of his memory would be lost. Now it was boring, almost juvenile. Key thought. Do you have your own Captain Aardvark secret decoder ring? Be the first on your block. The only thing Barth had been the first on his block to do was reach puberty. He had also been the first on his block to reach one hundred fifty kilos.

How many times have I been here? he wondered as the tingling in his scalp began. *This is the eighth time. Eight times, and my fortune is larger than ever, the kind of wealth that takes on a life on its own. I can keep this up forever,* he thought, with relish. Forever at the supper table with neither worries nor restraints. "It's dangerous to gain so much weight," Lynette had said. "Heart attacks, you know." But the only things that Barth worried about were hemorrhoids and impotence. The former was a nuisance, but the latter made life unbearable and drove him back to Anderson.

Key thought. What else? Lynette, standing naked on the edge of the cliff with the wind blowing. She was courting death, and he admired her for it, almost hoped that she would find it. She despised safety precautions. Like clothing, they were restrictions to be cast aside. She had once talked him into playing tag with her on a construction site, racing along the girders in the darkness, until the police came and made them leave. That had been when Barth was still thin from his last time at Anderson's. But it was not Lynette on the girders that he held in his mind. It was Lynette, fragile and beautiful Lynette, daring the wind to snatch her from the cliff and break up her body on the rocks by the river.

Even that, Barth thought, *would be a kind of pleasure. A new kind of pleasure, to taste a grief so magnificently, so admirably earned.*

And then the tingling in his head stopped. Anderson came back in.

"Already?" Barth asked.

"We've streamlined the process." Anderson carefully peeled the cap from Barth's head, helped the immense man lift himself from the couch.

"I can't understand why it's illegal," Barth said. "Such a simple thing."

"Oh, there are reasons. Population control, that sort of thing. This is a kind of immortality, you know. But it's mostly the repugnance most people feel. They can't face the thought. You're a man of rare courage."

But it was not courage, Barth knew. It was pleasure. He eagerly anticipated seeing, and they did not make him wait.

"Mr. Barth, meet Mr. Barth."

It nearly broke his heart to see his own body young and strong and beautiful again, as it never had been the first time through his life. It was unquestionably himself, however, that they led into the room. Except that the belly was firm, the thighs well muscled but slender enough that they did not meet, even at the crotch. They brought him in naked, of course. Barth insisted on it.

He tried to remember the last time. Then *he* had been the one coming from the learning room, emerging to see the immense fat man that all his memories told him was himself. Barth remembered that it had been a double pleasure, to see the mountain he had made of himself, yet to view it from inside this beautiful young body.

"Come here," Barth said, his own voice arousing echoes of the last time, when it had been the other Barth who had said it. And just as that other had done the last time, he touched the naked young Barth, stroked the smooth and lovely skin, and finally embraced him.

And the young Barth embraced him back, for that was the way of it. No one loved Barth as much as Barth did, thin or fat, young or old. Life was a celebration of Barth; the sight of himself was his strongest nostalgia.

"What did I think of?" Barth asked.

The young Barth smiled into his eyes. "Lynette," he said. "Naked on a cliff. The wind blowing. And the thought of her thrown to her death."

"Will you go back to her?" Barth asked his young self eagerly.

"Perhaps. Or to someone like her." And Barth saw with delight that the mere thought of it had aroused his young self more than a little.

"He'll do," Barth said, and Anderson handed him the simple papers to sign—papers that would never be seen in a court of law because they attested to Barth's own compliance in and initiation of an act that was second only to murder in the lawbooks of every state.

"That's it, then," Anderson said, turning from the fat Barth to the young, thin one. "You're Mr. Barth now, in control of his wealth and his life. Your clothing is in the next room."

"I know where it is," the young Barth said with a smile, and his footsteps were buoyant as he left the room. He would dress quickly and leave the Fitness Center briskly, hardly noticing the rather plain-looking receptionist, except to take note of her wistful look after him, a tall, slender, beautiful man who had, only moments before, been lying mindless in storage, waiting to be given a mind and a memory, waiting for a fat man to move out of the way so he could fill his space.

In the memory room Barth sat on the edge of the couch, looking at the door, and then realized, with surprise, that he had no idea what came next.

"My memories run out here," Barth said to Anderson. "The agreement was—what was the agreement?"

"The agreement was tender care of you until you passed away."

"Ah, yes."

"The agreement isn't worth a damn thing," Anderson said, smiling.

Barth looked at him with surprise. "What do you mean?"

"There are two options, Barth. A needle within the next fifteen minutes. Or employment."

"What are you talking about?"

"You didn't think we'd waste time and effort feeding you the ridiculous amounts of food you require, did you?"

Barth felt himself sink inside. This was not what he had expected, though he had not honestly expected anything. Barth was not the kind to anticipate trouble. Life had never given him much trouble.

"A needle?"

"Cyanide, if you insist, though we'd rather be able to vivisect you and get as many useful body parts as we can. Your body's still fairly young. We can get incredible amounts of money for your pelvis and your glands, but they have to be taken from you alive."

"What are you talking about? This isn't what we agreed."

"I agreed to nothing with *you*, my friend," Anderson said, smiling. "I agreed with Barth. And Barth just left the room."

"Call him back! I insist—"

"Barth doesn't give a damn what happens to you."

And he knew that it was true.

"You said something about employment."

"Indeed."

"What kind of employment?"

Anderson shook his head. "It all depends," he said.

"On what?"

"On what kind of work turns up. There are several assignments every year that must be performed by a living human being, for which no volunteer can be found. No person, not even a criminal, can be compelled to do them."

"And I?"

"Will do them. Or one of them, rather, since you rarely get a second job."

"How can you do this? I'm a human being!"

Anderson shook his head. "The law says that there is only one possible Barth in all the world. And you aren't it. You're just a number. And a letter. The letter *H*."

"Why *H*?"

"Because you're such a disgusting glutton, my friend. Even our first customers haven't got past *C* yet."

Anderson left then, and Barth was alone in the room. Why hadn't he anticipated this? *Of course, of course,* he shouted to himself now. Of course they wouldn't keep him pleasantly alive. He wanted to get up and try to run. But walking was difficult for him; running would be impossible. He sat there, his belly pressing heavily on his thighs, which were spread wide by the fat. He stood, with great effort, and could only waddle because his legs were so far apart, so constrained in their movement.

This has happened every time, Barth thought. *Every damn time I've walked out of this place young and thin, I've left behind someone like me, and they've had their way, haven't they?* His hands trembled badly.

He wondered what he had decided before and knew immediately that there was no decision to make at all. Some fat people might hate themselves and choose death for the sake of having a thin version of themselves live on. But not Barth. Barth could never choose to cause himself any pain. And to obliterate even an illegal, clandestine version of himself—impossible. Whatever else he might be, he was still Barth. The man who walked out of the memory room a few minutes before had not taken over Barth's identity. He had only duplicated it. *They've stolen my soul with mirrors*, Barth told himself. *I have to get it back*.

"Anderson!" Barth shouted. "Anderson! I've made up my mind."

It was not Anderson who entered, of course. Barth would never see Anderson again. It would have been too tempting to try to kill him.

"Get to work, H!" the old man shouted from the other side of the field.

Barth leaned on his hoe a moment more, then got back to work, scraping weeds from between the potato plants. The calluses on his hands had long since shaped themselves to fit the wooden handle, and his muscles knew how to perform the work without Barth's having to think about it at all. Yet that made the labor no easier. When he first realized that they meant him to be a potato farmer, he had asked, "Is this my assignment? Is this *all*?" And they had laughed and told him no. "It's just preparation," they said, "to get you in shape." So for two years he had worked in the potato fields, and now he began to doubt that they would ever come back, that the potatoes would ever end.

The old man was watching, he knew. His gaze always burned worse than the sun. The old man was watching, and if Barth rested too long or too often, the old man would come to him, whip in hand, to scar him deeply, to hurt him to the soul.

He dug into the ground, chopping at a stubborn plant whose root seemed to cling to the foundation of the world. "Come up, damn you," he muttered. He thought his arms were too weak to strike harder, but he struck harder anyway. The root split, and the impact shattered him to the bone.

He was naked and brown to the point of blackness from the sun. The flesh hung loosely on him in great folds, a memory of the mountain he had been. Under the loose skin, however, he was tight and hard. It might have given him pleasure, for every muscle had been earned by hard labor and the pain of the lash. But there was no pleasure in it. The price was too high.

I'll kill myself, he often thought and thought again now with his arms trembling with exhaustion. *I'll kill myself so they can't use my body and can't use my soul.*

But he would never kill himself. Even now, Barth was incapable of ending it.

The farm he worked on was unfenced, but the time he had gotten away he had walked and walked and walked for three days and had not once seen any sign of human habitation other than an occasional jeep track in the sagebrush-and-grass desert. Then they found him and brought him back, weary and despairing, and forced him to finish a day's work in the field before letting him rest. And even then the lash had bitten deep, the old man laying it on with a relish that spoke of sadism or a deep, personal hatred.

But why should the old man hate me? Barth wondered. *I don't know him.* He finally decided that it was
because he had been so fat, so obviously soft, while the
old man was wiry to the point of being gaunt, his face
pinched by years of exposure to the sunlight. Yet the
old man's hatred had not diminished as the months
went by and the fat melted away in the sweat and
sunlight of the potato field.

A sharp sting across his back, the sound of slapping
leather on skin, and then an excruciating pain deep in
his muscles. He had paused too long. The old man had
come to him.

The old man said nothing. Just raised the lash again,
ready to strike. Barth lifted the hoe out of the ground,
to start work again. It occurred to him, as it had a
hundred times before, that the hoe could reach as far
as the whip, with as good effect. But, as a hundred times
before, Barth looked into the old man's eyes, and what
he saw there, while he did not understand it, was
enough to stop him. He could not strike back. He could
only endure.

The lash did not fall again. Instead he and the old
man just looked at each other. The sun burned where
blood was coming from his back. Flies buzzed near him.
He did not bother to brush them away.

Finally the old man broke the silence.

"H," he said.

Barth did not answer. Just waited.

"They've come for you. First job," said the old man.

First job. It took Barth a moment to realize the implications. The end of the potato fields. The end of the
sunlight. The end of the old man with the whip. The
end of the loneliness or, at least, of the boredom.

"Thank God," Barth said. His throat was dry.

"Go wash," the old man said.

Barth carried the hoe back to the shed. He remembered how heavy the hoe had seemed when he first arrived. How ten minutes in the sunlight had made him faint. Yet they had revived him in the field, and the old man had said, "Carry it back." So he had carried back the heavy, heavy hoe, feeling for all the world like Christ bearing his cross. Soon enough the others had gone, and the old man and he had been alone together, but the ritual with the hoe never changed. They got to the shed, and the old man carefully took the hoe from him and locked it away, so that Barth couldn't get it in the night and kill him with it.

And then into the house, where Barth bathed painfully and the old man put an excruciating disinfectant on his back. Barth had long since given up on the idea of an anesthetic. It wasn't in the old man's nature to use an anesthetic.

Clean clothes. A few minutes' wait. And then the helicopter. A young, businesslike man emerged from it, looking unfamiliar in detail but very familiar in general. He was an echo of all the businesslike young men and women who had dealt with him before. The young man came to him, unsmilingly, and said, "H?"

Barth nodded. It was the only name they used for him.

"You have an assignment."

"What is it?" Barth asked.

The young man did not answer. The old man, behind him, whispered, "They'll tell you soon enough. And then you'll wish you were back here, H. They'll tell you, and you'll pray for the potato fields."

But Barth doubted it. In two years there had not been a moment's pleasure. The food was hideous, and there was never enough. There were no women, and he was usually too tired to amuse himself. Just pain and labor and loneliness, all excruciating. He would leave that now. Anything would be better, anything at all.

"Whatever they assign you, though," the old man said, "it can't be any worse than my assignment."

Barth would have asked him what his assignment had been, but there was nothing in the old man's voice that invited the question, and there was nothing in their relationship in the past that would allow the question to be asked. Instead, they stood in silence as the young man reached into the helicopter and helped a man get out. An immensely fat man, stark-naked and white as the flesh of a potato, looking petrified. The old man strode purposefully toward him.

"Hello, I," the old man said.

"My name's Barth," the fat man answered, petulantly. The old man struck him hard across the mouth, hard enough that the tender lip split and blood dripped from where his teeth had cut into the skin.

"I," said the old man. "Your name is I."

The fat man nodded pitiably, but Barth—H—felt no pity for him. Two years this time. Only two damnable years and he was already in this condition. Barth could vaguely remember being proud of the mountain he had made of himself. But now he felt only contempt. Only a desire to go to the fat man, to scream in his face, "Why did you do it! Why did you let it happen again!"

It would have meant nothing. To I, as to H, it was the first time, the first betrayal. There had been no others in his memory.

Barth watched as the old man put a hoe in the fat man's hands and drove him out into the field. Two more young men got out of the helicopter. Barth knew what they would do, could almost see them helping the old man for a few days, until I finally learned the hopelessness of resistance and delay.

But Barth did not get to watch the replay of his own torture of two years before. The young man who had first emerged from the copter now led him to it, put him in a seat by a window, and sat beside him. The pilot speeded up the engines, and the copter began to rise.

"The bastard," Barth said, looking out the window at the old man as he slapped I across the face brutally.

The young man chuckled. Then he told Barth his assignment.

Barth clung to the window, looking out, feeling his life slip away from him even as the ground receded slowly. "I can't do it."

"There are worse assignments," the young man said.

Barth did not believe it.

"If I live," he said, "if I live, I want to come back here."

"Love it that much?"

"To kill him."

The young man looked at him blankly.

"The old man," Barth explained, then realized that the young man was ultimately incapable of understanding anything. He looked back out the window. The old man looked very small next to the huge lump of white flesh beside him. Barth felt a terrible loathing for I. A terrible despair in knowing that nothing could possibly be learned, that again and again his selves would replay this hideous scenario.

Somewhere, the man who would be J was dancing, was playing polo, was seducing and perverting and being delighted by every woman and boy and, God knows, sheep that he could find; somewhere the man who would be J dined.

I bent immensely in the sunlight and tried, clumsily, to use the hoe. Then, losing his balance, he fell over into the dirt, writhing. The old man raised his whip.

The helicopter turned then, so that Barth could see nothing but sky from his window. He never saw the whip fall. But he imagined the whip falling. Imagined and relished it, longed to feel the heaviness of the blow flowing from his own arm. *Hit him again!* he cried out inside himself. *Hit him for me!* And inside himself he made the whip fall a dozen times more.

"What are you thinking?" the young man asked, smiling, as if he knew the punch line of a joke.

"I was thinking," Barth said, "that the old man can't possibly hate him as much as I do."

Apparently that was the punch line. The young man laughed uproariously. Barth did not understand the joke, but somehow he was certain that he was the butt of it. He wanted to strike out but dared not.

Perhaps the young man saw the tension in Barth's body, or perhaps he merely wanted to explain. He stopped laughing but could not repress his smile, which penetrated Barth far more deeply than the laugh.

"But don't you see?" the young man asked. "Don't you know who the old man is?"

Barth didn't know.

"What do you think we did with A?" And the young man laughed again.

There are worse assignments than mine, Barth realized. And the worst of all would be to spend day after day, month after month, supervising that contemptible animal that he could not deny was himself.

The scar on his back bled a little, and the blood stuck to the seat when it dried.

CLOSING THE TIMELID

───────

GEMINI LAY BACK in his cushioned chair and slid the box over his head. It was pitch black inside, except the light coming from down around his shoulders.

"All right, I'm pulling us over," said Orion. Gemini braced himself. He heard the clicking of a switch (or someone's teeth clicking shut in surprise?) and the timelid closed down on him, shut out the light, and green and orange and another, nameless color beyond purple danced at the edges of his eyes.

And he stood, abruptly, in thick grass at the side of a road. A branch full of leaves brushed heavily against his back with the breeze. He moved forward, looking for—

The road, just as Orion had said. About a minute to wait, then.

Gemini slid awkwardly down the embankment, covering his hands with dirt. To his surprise it was moist and soft, clinging. He had expected it to be hard. That's what you get for believing pictures in the encyclopedia, he thought. And the ground gave gently under his feet.

He glanced behind him. Two furrows down the bank showed his path. I have a mark in this world after all, he thought. It'll make no difference, but there is a sign of me in this time when men could still leave signs.

Then dazzling lights far up the road. The truck was coming. Gemini sniffed the air. He couldn't smell anything—and yet the books all stressed how smelly gasoline engines had been. Perhaps it was too far.

Then the lights swerved away. The curve. In a moment it would be here, turning just the wrong way on the curving mountain road until it would be too late.

Gemini stepped out into the road, a shiver of anticipation running through him. Oh, he had been under the timelid several times before. Like everyone, he had seen the major events. Michelangelo doing the Sistine Chapel. Handel writing the *Messiah* (everyone strictly forbidden to hum *any* tunes). The premiere performance of *Love's Labour's Lost*. And a few offbeat things that his hobby of history had sent him to: the assassination of John F. Kennedy, a politician; the meeting between Lorenzo d'Medici and the King of Naples; Jeanne d'Arc's death by fire—grisly.

And now, at last, to experience in the past something he was utterly unable to live through in the present.

Death.

And the truck careened around the corner, the lights sweeping the far embankment and then swerving in, brilliantly lighting Gemini for one instant before he leaped up and in, toward the glass (how horrified the face of the driver, how bright the lights, how harsh the metal) and then

agony. Ah, agony in a tearing that made him feel, for

the first time, every particle of his body as it screamed in pain. Bones shouting as they splintered like old wood under a sledgehammer. Flesh and fat slithering like jelly up and down and sideways. Blood skittering madly over the surface of the truck. Eyes popping open as the brain and skull crushed forward, demanding to be let through, let by, let fly. No no no no no, cried Gemini inside the last fragment of his mind. No no no no no, make it stop!

And green and orange and more-than-purple dazzled the sides of his vision. A twist of his insides, a shudder of his mind, and he was back, snatched from death by the inexorable mathematics of the timelid. He felt his whole, unmarred body rushing back, felt every particle, yes, as clearly as when it had been hit by the truck, but now with pleasure—pleasure so complete that he didn't even notice the mere orgasm his body added to the general symphony of joy.

The timelid lifted. The box was slid back. And Gemini lay gasping, sweating, yet laughing and crying and longing to sing.

What was it like? The others asked eagerly, crowding around. What is it like, what is it, is it like—

"It's like nothing. It's." Gemini had no words. "It's like everything God promised the righteous and Satan promised the sinners rolled into one." He tried to explain about the delicious agony, the joy passing all joys, the—

"Is it better than fairy dust?" asked one man, young and shy, and Gemini realized that the reason he was so retiring was that he was undoubtedly dusting tonight.

"After this," Gemini said, "dusting is no better than going to the bathroom."

Everyone laughed, chattered, volunteered to be next ("Orion knows how to throw a party"), as Gemini left the chair and the timelid and found Orion a few meters away at the controls.

"Did you like the ride?" Orion asked, smiling gently at his friend.

Gemini shook his head. "Never again," he said.

Orion looked disturbed for a moment, worried. "That bad for you?"

"Not bad. Strong. I'll never forget it, I've never felt so—alive, Orion. Who would have thought it. Death being so—"

"Bright," Orion said, supplying the word. His hair hung loosely and clean over his forehead—he shook it out of his eyes. "The second time is better. You have more time to appreciate the dying."

Gemini shook his head. "Once is enough for me. Life will never be bland again." He laughed. "Well, time for somebody else, yes?"

Harmony had already lain down on the chair. She had removed her clothing, much to the titillation of the other party-goers, saying, "I want nothing between me and the cold metal." Orion made her wait, though, while he corrected the setting. While he worked, Gemini thought of a question. "How many times have you done this, Orion?"

"Often enough," the man answered, studying the holographic model of the timeclip. And Gemini wondered then if death could not, perhaps, be as addictive as fairy dust, or cresting, or pitching in.

Rod Bingley finally brought the truck to a halt, gasping back the shock and horror. The eyes were still resting there in the gore on the windshield. Only they seemed real. The rest was road-splashing, mud flipped by the weather and the tires.

Rod flung open the door and ran around the front of the truck, hoping to do—what? There was no hope that the man was alive. But perhaps some identification. A nuthouse freak, turned loose in weird white clothes to wander the mountain roads? But there was no hospital near here.

And there was no body on the front of his truck.

He ran his hand across the shiny metal, the clean windshield. A few bugs on the grill.

Had this dent in the metal been there before? Rod couldn't remember. He looked all around the truck. Not a sign of anything. Had he imagined it?

He must have. But it seemed so real. And he hadn't drunk anything, hadn't taken any uppers—no trucker in his right mind *ever* took stay-awakes. He shook his head. He felt creepy. *Watched*. He glanced back over his shoulder. Nothing but the trees bending slightly in the wind. Not even an animal. Some moths already gathering in the headlights. That's all.

Ashamed of himself for being afraid at nothing, he nevertheless jumped into the cab quickly and slammed the door shut behind him and locked it. The key turned in the starter. And he had to force himself to look up through that windshield. He half-expected to see those eyes again.

The windshield was clear. And because he had a deadline to meet, he pressed on. The road curved away infinitely before him.

He drove more quickly, determined to get back to civilization before he had another hallucination.

And as he rounded a curve, his lights sweeping the trees on the far side of the road, he thought he glimpsed a flash of white to the right, in the middle of the road.

The lights caught her just before the truck did, a beautiful girl, naked and voluptuous and eager. Madly eager, standing there, legs broadly apart, arms wide. She dipped, then jumped up as the truck caught her, even as Rod smashed his foot into the brake, swerved the truck to the side. Because he swerved she ended up, not centered, but caught on the left side, directly in front of Rod, one of her arms flapping crazily around the edge of the cab, the hand rapping on the glass of the side window. She, too, splashed.

Rod whimpered as the truck again came to a halt. The hand had dropped loosely down to the woman's side, so it no longer blocked the door. Rod got out quickly, swung himself around the open door, and touched her.

Body warm. Hand real. He touched the buttock nearest him. It gave softly, sweetly, but under it Rod could feel that the pelvis was shattered. And then the body slopped free of the front of the truck, slid to the oil-and-gravel surface of the road

and disappeared.

Rod took it calmly for a moment. She fell from the front of the truck, and then there was nothing there. Except a faint (and new, definitely new!) crack in the windshield, there was no sign of her.

Rodney screamed.

The sound echoed from the cliff on the other side of the chasm. The trees seemed to swell the sound, making it louder among the trunks. An owl hooted back.

And finally, Rod got back into the truck and drove again, slowly, but erratically, wondering what, please God tell me what the hell's the matter with my mind.

Harmony rolled off the couch, panting and shuddering violently.

"Is it better than sex?" one of the men asked her. One who had doubtless tried, but failed, to get into her bed.

"It *is* sex," she answered. "But it's better than sex with *you*."

Everyone laughed. What a wonderful party. Who could top this? The would-be hosts and hostesses despaired, even as they clamored for a chance at the timelid.

But the crambox opened then, buzzing with the police override. "We're busted!" somebody shrieked gaily, and everyone laughed and clapped.

The policeman was young, and she seemed unused to the forceshield, walking awkwardly as she stepped into the middle of the happy room.

"Orion Overweed?" she asked, looking around.

"I," answered Orion, from where he sat at the controls, looking wary, Gemini beside him.

"Officer Mercy Manwool, Los Angeles Timesquad."

"Oh no," somebody muttered.

"You have no jurisdiction here," Orion said.

"We have a reciprocal enforcement agreement with the Canadian Chronospot Corporation. And we have reason to believe you are interfering with timetracks in the eighth decade of the twentieth century." She smiled curtly. "We have witnessed two suicides, and by making a careful check of your recent use of your private timelid, we have found several others. Apparently you have a new way to pass the time, Mr. Overweed."

Orion shrugged. "It's merely a passing fancy. But I am not interfering with timetracks."

She walked over to the controls and reached unerringly for the coldswitch. Orion immediately snagged her wrist with his hand. Gemini was surprised to see how the muscles of his forearm bulged with strength. Had he been playing some kind of *sport*? It would be just like Orion, of course, behaving like one of the lower orders—

"A warrant," Orion said.

She withdrew her arm. "I have an official complaint from the Timesquad's observation team. That is sufficient. I must interrupt your activity."

"According to law," Orion said, "you must show cause. Nothing we have done tonight will in any way change history."

"That truck is not robot-driven," she said, her voice growing strident. "There's a man in there. You are changing his life."

Orion only laughed. "Your observers haven't done their homework. I have. Look."

He turned to the control and played a speeded-up sequence, focused always on the shadow image of a truck speeding down a mountain road. The truck made turn after turn, and since the hologram was centered perpetually on the truck, it made the surrounding scenery dance past in a jerky rush, swinging left and right, up and down as the truck banked for turns or struck bumps.

And then, near the bottom of the chasm, between mountains, the truck got on a long, slow curve that led across the river on a slender bridge.

But the bridge wasn't there.

And the truck, unable to stop, skidded and swerved off the end of the truncated road, hung in the air over the chasm, then toppled, tumbled, banging against first this side, then that side of the ravine. It wedged between two outcroppings of rock more than ten meters above the water. The cab of the truck was crushed completely.

"He dies," Orion said. "Which means that anything we do with him before his death and after his last possible contact with another human being is legal. According to the code."

The policeman turned red with anger.

"I saw your little games with airplanes and sinking ships. But this is cruelty, Mr. Overweed."

"Cruelty to a dead man is, by definition, not cruelty. I don't change history. And Mr. Rodney Bingley is dead, has been for more than four centuries. I am doing no harm to any living man. And you owe me an apology."

Officer Mercy Manwool shook her head. "I think you're as bad as the Romans, who threw people into circuses to be torn by lions—"

"I know about the Romans," Orion said coldly, "and I know whom they threw. In this case, however, I am throwing my friends. And retrieving them very safely through the full retrieval and reassembly feature of the Hamburger Safety Device built inextricably into every timelid. And you owe me an apology."

She drew herself erect. "The Los Angeles Timesquad officially apologizes for making improper allegations about the activities of Orion Overweed."

Orion grinned. "Not exactly heartfelt, but I accept it. And while you're here, may I offer you a drink?"

"Nonalcoholic," she said instantly, and then looked away from him at Gemini, who was watching her with sad but intent eyes. Orion went for glasses and to try to find something nonalcoholic in the house.

"You performed superbly," Gemini said.

"And you, Gemini," she said softly (voicelessly), "were the first subject to travel."

Gemini shrugged. "Nobody said anything about my not taking part."

She turned her back on him. Orion came back with the drink. He laughed. "Coca-Cola," he said. "I had to import it all the way from Brazil. They still drink it there, you know. Original recipe." She took it and drank.

Orion sat back at the controls.

"Next!" he shouted, and a man and woman jumped on the couch together, laughing as the others slid the box over their heads.

Rod had lost count. At first he had tried to count the curves. Then the white lines in the road, until a new asphalt surface covered them. Then stars. But the only number that stuck in his head was nine.

9

NINE

Oh God, he prayed silently, what is happening to me, what is happening to me, change this night, let me wake up, whatever is happening to me make it *stop*.

A gray-haired man was standing beside the road, urinating. Rod slowed to a crawl. Slowed until he was barely moving. Crept past the man so slowly that if he had even twitched Rod could have stopped the truck. But the gray-haired man only finished, dropped his robe, and waved gaily to Rod. At that moment Rod heaved a sigh of relief and sped up.

Dropped his robe. The man was wearing a robe. Except for this gory night men did not wear *robes*. And at that moment he caught through his side mirror the white flash of the man throwing himself under the rear tires. Rod slammed on the brake and leaned his head against the steering wheel and wept loud, wracking sobs that shook the whole cab, that set the truck rocking slightly on its heavy-duty springs.

For in every death Rod saw the face of his wife after the traffic accident (not my fault!) that had killed her instantly and yet left Rod to walk away from the wreck without a scratch on him.

I was not supposed to live, he thought at the time, and thought now. I was not supposed to live, and now

God is telling me that I am a murderer with my wheels and my motor and my steering wheel.

And he looked up from the wheel.

Orion was still laughing at Hector's account of how he fooled the truck driver into speeding up.

"He thought I was conking into the bushes at the side of the road!" he howled again, and Orion burst into a fresh peal of laughter at his friend.

"And then a backflip into the road, under his tires! How I wish I could see it!" Orion shouted. The other guests were laughing, too. Except Gemini and Officer Manwool.

"You can see it, of course," Manwool said softly.

Her words penetrated through the noise, and Orion shook his head. "Only on the holo. And that's not very good, not a good image at all."

"It'll do," she said.

And Gemini, behind Orion, murmured, "Why not, Orry?"

The sound of the old term of endearment was startling to Orion, but oddly comforting. Did Gemini, then, treasure those memories as Orion did? Orion turned slowly, looked into Gemini's sad, deep eyes. "Would you like to see it on the holo?" he asked.

Gemini only smiled. Or rather, twitched his lips into that momentary piece of a smile that Orion knew from so many years before (only forty years; but forty years was back into my childhood, when I was only thirty and Gemini was—what?—fifteen. Helot to my Spartan; Slav to my Hun) and Orion smiled back. His fingers danced over the controls.

Many of the guests gathered around, although others, bored with the coming and going in the timelid, however extravagant it might be as a party entertainment ("Enough energy to light all of Mexico for an hour," said the one with the giddy laugh who had already promised her body to four men and a woman and was now giving it to another who would not wait), occupied themselves with something decadent and delightful and distracting in the darker corners of the room.

The holo flashed on. The truck crept slowly down the road, its holographic image flickering.

"Why does it do that?" someone asked, and Orion answered mechanically, "There aren't as many chronons as there are photons, and they have a lot more area to cover."

And then the image of a man flickering by the side of the road. Everyone laughed as they realized it was Hector, conking away with all his heart. Then another laugh as he dropped his robe and waved. The truck sped up, and then a backflip by the manfigure, under the wheels. The body flopped under the doubled back tires, then lay limp and shattered in the road as the truck came to a stop only a few meters ahead. A few moments later, the body disappeared.

"Brilliantly done, Hector!" Orion shouted again. "Better than you told it!" Everyone applauded in agreement, and Orion reached over to flip off the holo. But Officer Manwool stopped him.

"Don't turn it off, Mr. Overweed," she said. "Freeze it, and move the image."

Orion looked at her for a moment, then shrugged and did as she said. He expanded the view, so that the truck shrank. And then he suddenly stiffened, as did the guests close enough and interested enough to notice. Not more than ten meters in front of the truck was the ravine, where the broken bridge waited.

"He can see it," somebody gasped. And Officer Manwool slipped a lovecord around Orion's wrist, pulled it taut, and fastened the loose end to her workbelt.

"Orion Overweed, you're under arrest. That man can

see the ravine. He will not die. He was brought to a stop in plenty of time to notice the certain death ahead of him. He will live—with a knowledge of whatever he saw tonight. And already you have altered the future, the present, and all the past from his time until the present."

And for the first time in all his life, Orion realized that he had reason to be afraid.

"But that's a capital offense," he said lamely.

"I only wish it included torture," Officer Manwool said heatedly, "the kind of torture you put that poor truck driver through!"

And then she started to pull Orion out of the room.

Rod Bingley lifted his eyes from the steering wheel and stared uncomprehendingly at the road ahead. The truck's light illuminated the road clearly for many meters. And for five seconds or thirty minutes or some other length of time that was both brief and infinite he did not understand what it meant.

He got out of the cab and walked to the edge of the ravine, looking down. For a few minutes he felt relieved.

Then he walked back to the truck and counted the wounds in the cab. The dents on the grill and the smooth metal. Three cracks in the windshield.

He walked back to where the man had been urinating. Sure enough, though there was no urine, there was an indentation in the ground where the hot liquid had struck, speckles in the dirt where it had splashed.

And in the fresh asphalt, laid, surely, that morning (but then why no warning signs on the bridge? Perhaps the wind tonight blew them over), his tire tracks showed clearly. Except for a manwidth stretch where the left rear tires had left no print at all.

And Rodney remembered the dead, smashed faces,

especially the bright and livid eyes among the blood and broken bone. They all looked like Rachel to him. Rachel who had wanted him to—to what? Couldn't even remember the dreams anymore?

He got back into the cab and gripped the steering wheel. His head spun and ached, but he felt himself on the verge of a marvelous conclusion, a simple answer to all of this. There was evidence, yes, even though the bodies were gone, there was evidence that he had hit those people. He had not imagined it.

They must, then, be (he stumbled over the word, even in his mind, laughed at himself as he concluded:) angels. Jesus sent them, he knew it, as his mother had taught him, destroying angels teaching him the death that he had brought to his wife while daring, himself, to walk away scatheless.

It was time to even up the debt.

He started the engine and drove, slowly, deliberately toward the end of the road. And as the front tires bumped off and a sickening moment passed when he feared that the truck would be too heavy for the driving wheels to push along the ground, he clasped his hands in front of his face and prayed, aloud: "Forward!"

And then the truck slid forward, tipped downward, hung in the air, and fell. His body pressed into the back of the truck. His clasped hands struck his face. He meant to say, "Into thy hands I commend my spirit," but instead he screamed, "No no no no no," in an infinite negation of death that, after all, didn't do a bit of good once he was committed into the gentle, unyielding hands of the ravine. They clasped and enfolded him, pressed him tightly, closed his eyes and pillowed his head between the gas tank and the granite.

"Wait," Gemini said.

"Why the hell should we?" Officer Manwool said,

stopping at the door with Orion following docilely on the end of the lovecord. Orion, too, stopped, and looked at the policeman with the adoring expression all lovecord captives wore.

"Give the man a break," Gemini said.

"He doesn't deserve one," she said. "And neither do you."

"I say give the man a break. At least wait for the proof."

She snorted. "What more proof does he need, Gemini? A signed statement from Rodney Bingley that Orion Overweed is a bloody hitler?"

Gemini smiled and spread his hands. "We didn't actually *see* what Rodney did next, did we? Maybe he was struck by lightning two hours later, before he saw anybody—I mean, you're required to show that damage did happen. And I don't feel any change to the present—"

"You know that changes aren't felt. They aren't even known, since we wouldn't remember anything other than how things actually happened!"

"At least," Gemini said, "watch what happens and see whom Rodney tells."

So she led Orion back to the controls, and at her instructions Orion lovingly started the holo moving again.

And they all watched as Rodney Bingley walked to the edge of the ravine, then walked back to the truck, drove it to the edge and over into the chasm, and died on the rocks.

As it happened, Hector hooted in joy. "He died after all! Orion didn't change a damned thing, not one damned thing!"

Manwool turned on him in disgust. "You make me sick," she said.

"The man's dead," Hector said in glee. "So get that stupid string off Orion or I'll sue for a writ of—"

"Go pucker in a corner," she said, and several of the women pretended to be shocked. Manwool loosened the lovecord and slid it off Orion's wrist. Immediately he turned on her, snarling. "Get out of here! Get out! Get out!"

He followed her to the door of the crambox. Gemini was not the only one who wondered if he would hit her. But Orion kept his control, and she left unharmed.

Orion stumbled back from the crambox rubbing his arms as if with soap, as if trying to scrape them clean from contact with the lovecord. "That thing ought to be outlawed. I actually loved her. I actually loved that stinking, bloody, son-of-a-bitching cop!" And he shuddered so violently that several of the guests laughed and the spell was broken.

Orion managed a smile and the guests went back to amusing themselves. With the sensitivity that even the insensitive and jaded sometimes exhibit, they left him alone with Gemini at the controls of the timelid.

Gemini reached out and brushed a strand of hair out of Orion's eyes. "Get a comb someday," he said. Orion smiled and gently stroked Gemini's hand. Gemini slowly removed his hand from Orion's reach. "Sorry, Orry," Gemini said, "but not anymore."

Orion pretended to shrug. "I know," he said. "Not even for old times' sake." He laughed softly. "That stupid string made me love her. They shouldn't even do that to criminals."

He played with the controls of the holo, which was still on. The image zoomed in; the cab of the truck grew larger and larger. The chronons were too scattered and the image began to blur and fade. Orion stopped it.

By ducking slightly and looking through a window into the cab, Orion and Gemini could see the exact place where the outcropping of rock crushed Rod Bingley's head against the gas tank. Details, of course, were indecipherable.

"I wonder," Orion finally said, "if it's any different."

"What's any different?" Gemini asked.

"Death. If it's any different when you don't wake up right afterward."

A silence.

Then the sound of Gemini's soft laughter.

"What's funny?" Orion asked.

"You," the younger man answered. "Only one thing left that you haven't tried, isn't there?"

"How could I do it?" Orion asked, half-seriously (only half?). "They'd only clone me back."

"Simple enough," Gemini said. "All you need is a friend who's willing to turn off the machine while you're on the far end. Nothing is left. And you can take care of the actual suicide yourself."

"Suicide," Orion said with a smile. "Trust you to use the policeman's term."

And that night, as the other guests slept off the alcohol in beds or other convenient places, Orion lay on the chair and pulled the box over his head. And with Gemini's last kiss on his cheek and Gemini's left hand on the controls, Orion said, "All right. Pull me over."

After a few minutes Gemini was alone in the room. He did not even pause to reflect before he went to the breaker box and shut off all the power for a critical few seconds. Then he returned, sat alone in the room with the disconnected machine and the empty chair. The crambox soon buzzed with the police override, and Mercy Manwool stepped out. She went straight to Gemini, embraced him. He kissed her, hard.

"Done?" she asked.

He nodded.

"The bastard didn't deserve to live," she said.

Gemini shook his head. "You didn't get your justice, my dear Mercy."

"Isn't he dead?"

"Oh yes, that. Well, it's what he wanted, you know. I told him what I planned. And he asked me to do it."

She looked at him angrily. "You would. And then tell *me* about it, so I wouldn't get any joy out of this at all." Gemini only shrugged.

Manwool turned away from him, walked to the timelid. She ran her fingers along the box. Then she detached her laser from her belt and slowly melted the timelid until it was a mass of hot plastic on a metal stand. The few metal components had even melted a little, bending to be just a little out of shape.

"Screw the past anyway," she said. "Why can't it stay where it belongs?"

FREEWAY GAMES

EXCEPT FOR DONNER PASS, everything on the road between San Francisco and Salt Lake City was boring. Stanley had driven the road a dozen deadly times until he was sure he knew Nevada by heart: an endless road winding among hills covered with sagebrush. "When God got through making scenery," Stanley often said, "there was a lot of land left over in Nevada, and God said, 'Aw, to hell with it,' and that's where Nevada's been ever since."

Today Stanley was relaxed, there was no rush for him to get back to Salt Lake, and so, to ease the boredom, he began playing freeway games.

He played Blue Angels first. On the upslope of the Sierra Nevadas he found two cars riding side by side at fifty miles an hour. He pulled his Datsun 260Z into formation beside them. At fifty miles an hour they cruised along, blocking all the lanes of the freeway. Traffic began piling up behind them.

The game was successful—the other two drivers got into the spirit of the thing. When the middle car drifted forward, Stanley eased back to stay even with the driver on the right, so that they drove down the freeway in an arrowhead formation. They made diagonals, funnels; danced around each other for half an hour; and whenever one of them pulled slightly ahead, the frantically angry drivers behind them jockeyed behind the leading car.

Finally, Stanley tired of the game, despite the fun of the honks and flashing lights behind them. He honked twice, and waved jauntily to the driver beside him, then pressed on the accelerator and leaped forward at seventy miles an hour, soon dropping back to sixty as dozens of other cars, their drivers trying to make up for lost time (or trying to compensate for long confinement), passed by going much faster. Many paused to drive beside him, honking, glaring, and making obscene gestures. Stanley grinned at them all.

He got bored again east of Reno.

This time he decided to play Follow. A yellow AM Hornet was just ahead of him on the highway, going fifty-eight to sixty miles per hour. A good speed. Stanley settled in behind the car, about three lengths behind, and followed. The driver was a woman, with dark hair that danced in the erratic wind that came through her open windows. Stanley wondered how long it would take her to notice that she was being followed.

Two songs on the radio (Stanley's measure of time while traveling), and halfway through a commercial for hair spray—and she began to pull away. Stanley prided himself on quick reflexes. She didn't even gain a car length; even when she reached seventy, he stayed behind her.

He hummed along with an old Billy Joel song even as the Reno radio station began to fade. He hunted for another station, but found only country and western, which he loathed. So in silence he followed as the woman in the Hornet slowed down.

She went thirty miles an hour, and still he didn't pass. Stanley chuckled. At this point, he was sure she was imagining the worst. A rapist, a thief, a kidnapper, determined to destroy her. She kept on looking in her rearview mirror.

"Don't worry, little lady," Stanley said, "I'm just a Salt Lake City boy who's having fun." She slowed down to twenty, and he stayed behind her; she sped up abruptly until she was going fifty, but her Hornet couldn't possibly out-accelerate his Z.

"I made forty thousand dollars for the company," he sang in the silence of his car, "and that's six thousand dollars for me."

The Hornet came up behind a truck that was having trouble getting up a hill. There was a passing lane, but the Hornet didn't use it at first, hoping, apparently, that Stanley would pass. Stanley didn't pass. So the Hornet pulled out, got even with the nose of the truck, then rode parallel with the truck all the rest of the way up the hill.

"Ah," Stanley said, "playing Blue Angels with the Pacific Intermountain Express." He followed her closely.

At the top of the hill, the passing lane ended. At the last possible moment the Hornet pulled in front of the truck—and stayed only a few yards ahead of it. There was no room for Stanley, and now on a two-lane road a car was coming straight at him.

"What a bitch!" Stanley mumbled. In a split second, because when angry Stanley doesn't like to give in, he decided that she wasn't going to outsmart *him*. He nosed into the space between the Hornet and the truck anyway.

There wasn't room. The truck driver leaned on his horn and braked; the woman, afraid, pulled forward. Stanley got out of the way just as the oncoming car, its driver a father with a wife and several rowdy children looking petrified at the accident that had nearly happened, passed on the left.

"Think you're smart, don't you, bitch? But Stanley Howard's feeling rich." Nonsense, nonsense, but it sounded good and he sang it in several keys as he followed the woman, who was now going a steady sixty-five, two car-lengths behind. The Hornet had Utah plates—she was going to be on that road a long time.

Stanley's mind wandered. From thoughts of Utah plates to a memory of eating at Alioto's and on to his critical decision that no matter how close you put Alioto's to the wharf, the fish there wasn't any better than the fish at Bratten's in Salt Lake. He decided that he would have to eat there soon, to make sure his impression was correct; he wondered whether he should bother taking Liz out again, since she so obviously wasn't interested; speculated on whether Genevieve would say yes if he asked her.

And the Hornet wasn't in front of him anymore.

He was only going forty-five, and the PIE truck was catching up to him on a straight section of the road. There were curves into a mountain pass up ahead—she must have gone faster when he wasn't noticing. But he sped up, sped even faster, and didn't see her. She must have pulled off somewhere, and Stanley chuckled to think of her panting, her heart beating fast, as she watched Stanley drive on by. What a relief that must have been, Stanley thought. Poor lady. What a nasty game. And he giggled with delight, silently, his chest and stomach shaking but making no sound.

He stopped for gas in Elko, had a package of cupcakes from the vending machine in the gas station, and was

leaning on his car when he watched the Hornet go by.
He waved, but the woman didn't see him. He did notice, however, that she pulled into an Amoco station
not far up the road.

It was just a whim. I'm taking this too far, he thought,
even as he waited in his car for her to pull out of the
gas station. She pulled out. For just a moment Stanley
hesitated, decided not to go on with the chase, then
pulled out and drove along the main street of Elko a
few blocks behind the Hornet. The woman stopped at
a light. When it turned green, Stanley was right behind
her. He saw her look in her rearview mirror again,
stiffen; her eyes were afraid.

"Don't worry, lady," he said. "I'm not following you
this time. Just going my own sweet way home."

The woman abruptly, without signalling, pulled into
a parking place. Stanley calmly drove on. "See?" he
said. "Not following. Not following."

A few miles outside Elko, he pulled off the road. He
knew why he was waiting. He denied it to himself. Just
resting, he told himself. Just sitting here because I'm
in no hurry to get back to Salt Lake City. But it was
hot and uncomfortable, and with the car stopped, there
wasn't the slightest breeze coming through the windows of the Z. This is stupid, he told himself. Why
persecute the poor woman anymore? he asked himself.
Why the hell am I still sitting here?

He was still sitting there when she passed him. She
saw him. She sped up. Stanley put the car in gear, drove
out into the road from the shoulder, caught up with her
quickly, and settled in behind her. "I am a shithead,"
he announced to himself. "I am the meanest asshole
on the highway. I ought to be shot." He meant it. But
he stayed behind her, cursing himself all the way.

In the silence of his car (the noise of the wind did
not count as sound; the engine noise was silent to his

accustomed ears), he recited the speeds as they drove. "Fifty-five, sixty, sixty-five on a curve, are we out of our minds, young lady? Seventy—ah, ho, now, look for a Nevada state trooper anywhere along here." They took curves at ridiculous speeds; she stopped abruptly occasionally; always Stanley's reflexes were quick, and he stayed a few car lengths behind her.

"I really am a nice person, young lady," he said to the woman in the car, who was pretty, he realized as he remembered the face he saw when she passed him back in Elko. "If you met me in Salt Lake City, you'd like me. I might ask you out for a date sometime. And if you aren't some tight-assed little Mormon girl, we might get it on. You know? I'm a nice person."

She was pretty, and as he drove along behind her ("What? Eighty-five? I never thought a Hornet could go eighty-five"), he began to fantasize. He imagined her running out of gas, panicking because now, on some lonely stretch of road, she would be at the mercy of the crazy man following her. But in his fantasy, when he stopped it was she who had a gun, she who was in control of the situation. She held the gun on him, forced him to give her his car keys, and then she made him strip, took his clothes and stuffed them in the back of the Z, and took off in his car. "It's you that's dangerous, lady," he said. He replayed the fantasy several times, and each time she spent more time with him before she left him naked by the road with an out-of-gas Hornet and horny as hell.

Stanley realized the direction his fantasies had taken him. "I've been too lonely too long," he said. "Too lonely too long, and Liz won't unzip anything without a license." The word *lonely* made him laugh, thinking of tacky poetry. He sang: "Bury me not on the lone prairie where the coyotes howl and wind blows free."

For hours he followed the woman. By now he was

sure she realized it was a game. By now she must know he meant no harm. He had done nothing to try to get her to pull over. He was just tagging along. "Like a friendly dog," he said. "Arf. Woof. Growrrr." And he fantasized again until suddenly the lights of Wendover were dazzling, and he realized it was dark. He switched on his lights. When he did, the Hornet sped up, its taillights bright for a moment, then ordinary among the lights and signs saying that this was the last chance to lose money before getting to Utah.

Just inside Wendover, a police car was pulled to the side of the road, its lights flashing. Some poor sap caught speeding. Stanley expected the woman to be smart, to pull over behind the policeman, while Stanley moved on over the border, out of Nevada jurisdiction.

The Hornet, however, went right by the policeman, sped up, in fact, and Stanley was puzzled for a moment. Was the woman crazy? She must be scared out of her wits by now, and here was a chance for relief and rescue, and she ignored it. Of course, Stanley reasoned, as he followed the Hornet out of Wendover and down to the long straight stretch of the highway over the Salt Flats, of course she didn't stop. Poor lady was so conscious of having broken the law speeding that she was *afraid* of cops.

Crazy. People do crazy things under pressure, Stanley decided.

The highway stretched out straight in the blackness. No moon. Some starlight, but there were no landmarks on either side of the road, and so the cars barreled on as if in a tunnel, with only a hypnotic line to the left and headlights behind and taillights ahead.

How much gas would the tank of a Hornet hold? The Salt Flats went a long way before the first gas station, and what with daylight saving time it must be ten-thirty, eleven o'clock, maybe only ten, but some of

those gas stations would be closing up now. Stanley's
Z could get home to Salt Lake with gas to spare after a
fill-up in Elko, but the Hornet might run out of gas.

Stanley remembered his daydreams of the afternoon
and now translated them into night, into her panic in
the darkness, the gun flashing in his headlights. This
lady was armed and dangerous. She was carrying drugs
into Utah, and thought he was from the mob. She probably thought he was planning to get her on the lonely
Salt Flats, miles from anywhere. She was probably
checking the clip of her gun.

Eighty-five, said the speedometer.

"Going pretty fast, lady," he said.

Ninety, said the speedometer.

Of course, Stanley realized. She *is* running out of gas.
She wants to get going as fast as she can, outrun me,
but at least have enough momentum to coast when she
runs out.

Nonsense, thought Stanley. It's dark, and the poor
lady is scared out of her wits. I've got to stop this. This
is dangerous. It's dark and it's dangerous and this stupid
game has gone on for four hundred miles. I never meant
it to go on this long.

Stanley passed the road signs that told him, habitu-
ated as he was to this drive, that the first big curve was
coming up. A lot of people unfamiliar with the Salt
Flats thought it went straight as an arrow all the way.
But there was a curve where there was no reason to
have a curve, before the mountains, before anything.
And in typical Utah Highway Department fashion, the
Curve sign was posted right in the middle of the turn.
Instinctively, Stanley slowed down.

The woman in the Hornet did not.

In his headlights Stanley saw the Hornet slide off the
road. He screeched on his brakes; as he went past, he
saw the Hornet bounce on its nose, flip over and bounce

on its tail, then topple back and land flat on the roof. For a moment the car lay there. Stanley got his car stopped, looked back over his shoulder. The Hornet erupted in flames.

Stanley stayed there for only a minute or so, gasping, shuddering. In horror. In horror, he insisted to himself, saying, "What have I done! My God, what have I done," but knowing even as he pretended to be appalled that he was having an orgasm, that the shuddering of his body was the most powerful ejaculation he had ever had, that he had been trying to get up the Hornet's ass all the way from Reno and finally, finally, he had come.

He drove on. He drove for twenty minutes and came to a gas station with a pay phone. He got out of the car stiffly, his pants sticky and wet, and fumbled in his sticky pocket for a sticky dime, which he put in the phone. He dialed the emergency number.

"I—I passed a car on the Salt Flats. In flames. About fifteen miles before this Chevron station. Flames."

He hung up. He drove on. A few minutes later he saw a patrol car, lights whirling, speeding past going the other way. From Salt Lake City out into the desert. And still later he saw an ambulance and a fire truck go by. Stanley gripped the wheel tightly. They would know. They would see his skid marks. Someone would tell about the Z that was following the Hornet from Reno until the woman in the Hornet died in Utah.

But even as he worried, he knew that no one would know. He hadn't touched her. There wasn't a mark on his car.

The highway turned into a six-lane street with motels and shabby diners on either side. He went under the freeway, over the railroad tracks, and followed North Temple street up to Second Avenue, the school on the left, the Slow signs, everything normal, everything as he had left it, everything as it always had been when

he came home from a long trip. To L Street, to the
Chateau LeMans apartments; he parked in the under-
ground garage, got out. All the doors opened to his key.
His room was undisturbed.

What the hell do I expect? he asked himself. Sirens
heading my way? Five detectives in my living room
waiting to grill me?

The woman, the woman had died. He tried to feel
terrible. But all that he could remember, all that was
important in his mind, was the shuddering of his body,
the feeling that the orgasm would never end. There was
nothing. Nothing like that in the world.

He went to sleep quickly, slept easily. Murderer? he
asked himself as he drifted off.

But the word was taken by his mind and driven into
a part of his memory where Stanley could not retrieve
it. Can't live with that. Can't live with that. And so he
didn't.

Stanley found himself avoiding looking at the paper the
next morning, and so he forced himself to look. It
wasn't front-page news. It was buried back in the local
news section. Her name was Alix Humphreys. She was
twenty-two and single, working as a secretary to some
law firm. Her picture showed her as a young, attractive
girl.

"The driver apparently fell asleep at the wheel, according to police investigators. The vehicle was going
faster than eighty miles per hour when the mishap occurred."

Mishap.

Hell of a word for the flames.

Yet, Stanley went to work just as he always did,
flirted with the secretaries just as he always did, and
even drove his car, just as he always did, carefully and
politely on the road.

It wasn't long, however, before he began playing freeway games again. On his way up to Logan, he played Follow, and a woman in a Honda Civic smashed head-on into a pickup truck as she foolishly tried to pass a semitruck at the crest of a hill in Sardine Canyon. The police reports didn't mention (and no one knew) that she was trying to get away from a Datsun 260Z that had relentlessly followed her for eighty miles. Her name was Donna Weeks, and she had two children and a husband who had been expecting her back in Logan that evening. They couldn't get all her body out of the car.

On a hop over to Denver, a seventeen-year-old skier went out of control on a snowy road, her VW smashing into a mountain, bouncing off, and tumbling down a cliff. One of the skis on the back of her bug, incredibly enough, was unbroken. The other was splintered into kindling. Her head went through the windshield. Her body didn't.

The roads between Cameron trading post and Page, Arizona, were the worst in the world. It surprised no one when an eighteen-year-old blond model from Phoenix was killed when she smashed into the back of a van parked beside the road. She had been going more than a hundred miles an hour, which her friends said did not surprise them, she had always sped, especially when driving at night. A child in the van was killed in his sleep, and the family was hospitalized. There was no mention of a Datsun with Utah plates.

And Stanley began to remember more often. There wasn't room in the secret places of his mind to hold all of this. He clipped their faces out of the paper. He dreamed of them at night. In his dreams they always threatened him, always deserved the end they got. Every dream ended with orgasm. But never as strong a convulsion as the ecstacy when the collision came on the highway.

Check. And mate.

Aim, and fire.

Eighteen, seven, twenty-three, hike.

Games, all games, and the moment of truth.

"I'm sick." He sucked the end of his Bic four-color pen. "I need help."

The phone rang.

"Stan? It's Liz."

Hi, Liz.

"Stan, aren't you going to answer me?"

Go to hell, Liz.

"Stan, what kind of game is this? You don't call for nine months, and now you just sit there while I'm trying to talk to you?"

Come to bed, Liz.

"That *is* you, isn't it?"

"Yeah, it's me."

"Well, why didn't you answer me? Stan, you scared me. That really scared me."

"I'm sorry."

"Stan, what happened? Why haven't you called?"

"I needed you too much." Melodramatic, melodramatic. But true.

"Stan, I know. I was being a bitch."

"No, no, not really. I was being too demanding."

"Stan, I miss you. I want to be with you."

"I miss you, too, Liz. I've really needed you these last few months."

She droned on as Stanley sang silently, "Oh, bury me not on the lone prairie, where the coyotes howl—"

"Tonight? My apartment?"

"You mean you'll let me past the sacred chain lock?"

"Stanley. Don't be mean. I miss you."

"I'll be there."

"I love you."

"Me, too."

After this many months, Stanley was not sure, not sure at all. But Liz was a straw to grasp at. "I drown," Stanley said. "I die. *Morior. Moriar. Mortuus sum.*"

Back when he had been dating Liz, back when they had been together, Stanley hadn't played these freeway games. Stanley hadn't watched these women die. Stanley hadn't had to hide from himself in his sleep. "*Caedo. Caedam. Cecidi.*"

Wrong, wrong. He had been dating Liz the first time. He had only stopped after—after. Liz had nothing to do with it. Nothing would help. "*Despero. Desperabo. Desperavi.*"

And because it was the last thing he wanted to do, he got up, got dressed, went out to his car, and drove out onto the freeway. He got behind a woman in a red Audi. And he followed her.

She was young, but she was a good driver. He tailed her from Sixth South to the place where the freeway forks, I-15 continuing south, I-80 veering east. She stayed in the right-hand lane until the last moment, then swerved across two lanes of traffic and got onto I-80. Stanley did not think of letting her go. He, too, cut across traffic. A bus honked loudly; there was a screeching of brakes; Stanley's Z was on two wheels and he lost control; a lightpost loomed, then passed.

And Stanley was on I-80, following a few hundred yards behind the Audi. He quickly closed the gap. This woman was smart, Stanley said to himself. "You're smart, lady. You won't let me get away with anything. Nobody today. Nobody today." He meant to say nobody dies today, and he knew that was what he was really saying (hoping; denying), but he did not let himself say it. He spoke as if a microphone hung over his head, recording his words for posterity.

The Audi wove through traffic, averaging seventy-five. Stanley followed close behind. Occasionally, a gap in the traffic closed before he could use it; he found another. But he was a dozen cars behind when she cut off and took the last exit before I-80 plunged upward into Parley's Canyon. She was going south on I-215, and Stanley followed, though he had to brake violently to make the tight curve that led from one freeway to the other.

She drove rapidly down I-215 until it ended, turned into a narrow two-lane road winding along the foot of the mountain. As usual, a gravel truck was going thirty miles an hour, shambling along shedding stones like dandruff onto the road. The Audi pulled behind the gravel truck, and Stanley's Z pulled behind the Audi.

The woman was smart. She didn't try to pass. Not on that road.

When they reached the intersection with the road going up Big Cottonwood Canyon to the ski resorts (closed now in the spring, so there was no traffic), she seemed to be planning to turn right, to take Fort Union Boulevard back to the freeway. Instead, she turned left. But Stanley had been anticipating the move, and he turned left, too.

They were not far up the winding canyon road before it occurred to Stanley that this road led to nowhere. At Snowbird it was a dead end, a loop that turned around and headed back down. This woman, who had seemed so smart, was making a very stupid move.

And then he thought, I might catch her. He said, "I might catch you, girl. Better watch out."

What he would do if he caught her he wasn't sure. She must have a gun. She must be armed, or she wouldn't be daring him like this.

She took the curves at ridiculous speeds, and Stanley was pressed to the limit of his driving skills to stay up with her. This was the most difficult game of Follow he had ever played. But it might end too quickly—on any of these curves she might smash up, might meet a car coming the other way. Be careful, he thought. Be careful, be careful, it's just a game, don't be afraid, don't panic.

Panic? The moment this woman had realized she was being followed, she had sped and dodged, leading him on a merry chase. None of the confusion the others had shown. This was a live one. When he caught her, she'd know what to do. She'd know. *"Veniebam. Veniam. Venies."* He laughed at his joke.

Then he stopped laughing abruptly, swung the wheel hard to the right, jamming on the brake. He had seen just a flash of red going up a side road. Just a flash, but it was enough. This bitch in the red Audi thought she'd fool him. Thought she could ditch into a side road and he'd go on by.

He skidded in the gravel of the shoulder, but regained control and charged up the narrow dirt road. The Audi was stopped a few hundred yards from the entrance.

Stopped.

At last.

He pulled in behind her, even had his fingers on the door handle. But she had not meant to stop, apparently. She had only meant to pull out of sight till he went by. He had been too smart for her. He had seen. And now she was caught on a terribly lonely mountain road, still moist from the melting snow, with only trees around, in weather too warm for skiers, too cold for hikers. She had thought to trick him, and now he had trapped her.

She drove off. He followed. On the bumpy dirt road, twenty miles an hour was uncomfortably fast. She went thirty. His shocks were being shot to hell, but this was one that wouldn't get away. She wouldn't get away from Stanley. Her Audi was voluptuous with promises.

After interminable jolting progress up the side canyon, the mountains suddenly opened out into a small valley. The road, for a while, was flat, though certainly not straight. And the Audi sped up to forty incredible miles an hour. She wasn't giving up. And she was a damned good driver. But Stanley was a damned good driver, too. "I should quit now," he said to the invisible microphone in his car. But he didn't quit. He didn't quit and he didn't quit.

The road quit.

He came around a tree-lined curve and suddenly there was no road. Just a gap in the trees and, a few hundred yards away, the other side of a ravine. To the right, out of the corner of his eye, he saw where the road made a hairpin turn, saw the Audi stopped there, saw, he thought, a face looking at him in horror. And because of that face he turned to look, tried to look over his shoulder, desperate to see the face, desperate not to watch as the trees bent gracefully toward him and the rocks rose up and enlarged and engorged, and he impaled himself, himself and his Datsun 260Z on a rock that arched upward and shuddered as he swallowed its tip.

She sat in the Audi, shaking, her body heaving in great sobs of relief and shock at what had happened. Relief and shock, yes. But by now she knew that the shuddering was more than that. It was also ecstacy.

This has to stop, she cried out silently to herself. Four, four, four. "Four is enough," she said, beating on the steering wheel. Then she got control of herself, and the orgasm passed except for the trembling in her thighs and occasional cramps, and she jockeyed the car until it was turned around, and she headed back down the canyon to Salt Lake City, where she was already an hour late.

A Sepulchre of Songs

S HE WAS LOSING her mind during the rain. For four
  weeks it came down nearly every day, and the
people at the Millard County Rest Home didn't take
any of the patients outside. It bothered them all, of
course, and made life especially hellish for the nurses,
everyone complaining to them constantly and demanding to be entertained.

Elaine didn't demand entertainment, however. She
never seemed to demand much of anything. But the
rain hurt her worse than anyone. Perhaps because she
was only fifteen, the only child in an institution de-
voted to adult misery. More likely because she de-
pended more than most on the hours spent outside;
certainly she took more pleasure from them. They
would lift her into her chair, prop her up with pillows
so her body would stay straight, and then race down
the corridor to the glass doors, Elaine calling, "Faster,

faster," as they pushed her until finally they were out-side. They told me she never really said anything out there. Just sat quietly in her chair on the lawn, watch-ing everything. And then later in the day they would wheel her back in.

I often saw her being wheeled in—early, because I was there, though she never complained about my vis-its' cutting into her hours outside. As I watched her being pushed toward the rest home, she would smile at me so exuberantly that my mind invented arms for her, waving madly to match her childishly delighted face; I imagined legs pumping, imagined her running across the grass, breasting the air like great waves. But there were the pillows where arms should be, keeping her from falling to the side, and the belt around her middle kept her from pitching forward, since she had no legs to balance with.

It rained four weeks, and I nearly lost her.

My job was one of the worst in the state, touring six rest homes in as many counties, visiting each of them every week. I "did therapy" wherever the rest home administrators thought therapy was needed. I never figured out how they decided—all the patients were mad to one degree or another, most with the helpless insanity of age, the rest with the anguish of the invalid and the crippled.

You don't end up as a state-employed therapist if you had much ability in college. I sometimes pretend that I didn't distinguish myself in graduate school because I marched to a different drummer. But I didn't. As one kind professor gently and brutally told me, I wasn't cut out for science. But I was sure I was cut out for the art of therapy. Ever since I comforted my mother during her final year of cancer I had believed I had a knack for helping people get straight in their minds. I was everybody's confidant.

Somehow I had never supposed, though, that I would end up trying to help the hopeless in a part of the state where even the healthy didn't have much to live for. Yet that's all I had the credentials for, and when I (so maturely) told myself I was over the initial disappointment, I made the best of it.

Elaine was the best of it.

"Raining raining raining," was the greeting I got when I visited her on the third day of the wet spell.

"Don't I know it?" I said. "My hair's soaking wet."

"Wish mine was," Elaine answered.

"No, you don't. You'd get sick."

"Not me," she said.

"Well, Mr. Woodbury told me you're depressed. I'm supposed to make you happy."

"Make it stop raining."

"Do I look like God?"

"I thought maybe you were in disguise. *I'm* in disguise," she said. It was one of our regular games. "I'm really a large Texas armadillo who was granted one wish. I wished to be a human being. But there wasn't enough of the armadillo to make a full human being; so here I am." She smiled. I smiled back.

Actually, she had been five years old when an oil truck exploded right in front of her parents' car, killing both of them and blowing her arms and legs right off. That she survived was a miracle. That she had to keep on living was unimaginable cruelty. That she managed to be a reasonably happy person, a favorite of the nurses—that I don't understand in the least. Maybe it was because she had nothing else to do. There aren't many ways that a person with no arms or legs can kill herself.

"I want to go outside," she said, turning her head away from me to look out the window.

Outside wasn't much. A few trees, a lawn, and beyond that a fence, not to keep the inmates in but to keep out the seamier residents of a rather seamy town. But there were low hills in the distance, and the birds usually seemed cheerful. Now, of course, the rain had driven both birds and hills into hiding. There was no wind, and so the trees didn't even sway. The rain just came straight down.

"Outer space is like the rain," she said. "It sounds like that out there, just a low drizzling sound in the background of everything."

"Not really," I said. "There's no sound out there at all."

"How do *you* know?" she asked.

"There's no air. Can't be any sound without air."

She looked at me scornfully. "Just as I thought. You don't *really* know. You've never *been* there, have you?"

"Are you trying to pick a fight?"

She started to answer, caught herself, and nodded. "Damned rain."

"At least you don't have to drive in it," I said. But her eyes got wistful, and I knew I had taken the banter too far. "Hey," I said. "First clear day I'll take you out driving."

"It's hormones," she said.

"What's hormones?"

"I'm fifteen. It always bothered me when I had to stay in. But I want to scream. My muscles are all bunched up, my stomach is all tight, I want to go outside and *scream*. It's hormones."

"What about your friends?" I asked.

"Are you kidding? They're all out there, playing in the rain."

"*All* of them?"

"Except Grunty, of course. He'd dissolve."

"And where's Grunty?"

"In the freezer, of course."

"Someday the nurses are going to mistake him for ice cream and serve him to the guests."

She didn't smile. She just nodded, and I knew that I wasn't getting anywhere. She really was depressed.

I asked her whether she wanted something.

"No pills," she said. "They make me sleep all the time."

"If I gave you uppers, it would make you climb the walls."

"Neat trick," she said.

"It's that strong. So do you want something to take your mind off the rain and these four ugly yellow walls?"

She shook her head. "I'm trying not to sleep."

"Why not?"

She just shook her head again. "Can't sleep. Can't let myself sleep too much."

I asked again.

"Because," she said, "I might not wake up." She said it rather sternly, and I knew I shouldn't ask anymore. She didn't often get impatient with me, but I knew this time I was coming perilously close to overstaying my welcome.

"Got to go," I said. "You *will* wake up." And then I left, and I didn't see her for a week, and to tell the truth I didn't think of her much that week, what with the rain and a suicide in Ford County that really got to me, since she was fairly young and had a lot to live for, in my opinion. She disagreed and won the argument the hard way.

Weekends I live in a trailer in Piedmont. I live alone. The place is spotlessly clean because cleaning is something I do religiously. Besides, I tell myself, I might want to bring a woman home with me one night. Some nights I even do, and some nights I even enjoy it, but I always get restless and irritable when they start trying to get me to change my work schedule or take them along to the motels I live in or, once only, get the trailer-park manager to let them into my trailer when I'm gone. To keep things cozy for me. I'm not interested in "cozy." This is probably because of my mother's death; her cancer and my responsibilities as housekeeper for my father probably explain why I am a neat house-keeper. Therapist, therap thyself. The days passed in rain and highways and depressing people depressed out of their minds; the nights passed in television and sand-wiches and motel bedsheets at state expense; and then it was time to go to the Millard County Rest Home again, where Elaine was waiting. It was then that I thought of her and realized that the rain had been going on for more than a week, and the poor girl must be almost out of her mind. I bought a cassette of Copland conducting Copland. She insisted on cassettes, because they stopped. Eight-tracks went on and on until she couldn't think.

"Where have you been?" she demanded.

"Locked in a cage by a cruel duke in Transylvania. It was only four feet high, suspended over a pond filled with crocodiles. I got out by picking the lock with my teeth. Luckily, the crocodiles weren't hungry. Where have *you* been?"

"I mean it. Don't you keep a schedule?"

"I'm right on my schedule, Elaine. This is Wednes-day. I was here last Wednesday. This year Christmas falls on a Wednesday, and I'll be here on Christmas."

"It feels like a year."

"Only ten months. Till Christmas. Elaine, you aren't being any fun."

She wasn't in the mood for fun. There were tears in her eyes. "I can't stand much more," she said.

"I'm sorry."

"I'm afraid."

And she *was* afraid. Her voice trembled.

"At night, and in the daytime, whenever I sleep. I'm just the right size."

"For what?"

"What do you mean?"

"You said you were just the right size."

"I did? Oh, I don't know what I meant. I'm going crazy. That's what you're here for, isn't it? To keep me sane. It's the rain. I can't do anything, I can't see anything, and all I can hear most of the time is the hissing of the rain."

"Like outer space," I said, remembering what she had said the last time.

She apparently didn't remember our discussion. She looked startled. "How did you know?" she asked.

"You told me."

"There isn't any sound in outer space," she said.

"Oh," I answered.

"There's no air out there."

"I knew that."

"Then why did you say, 'Oh, of course'? The engines. You can hear them all over the ship. It's a drone, all the time. That's just like the rain. Only after a while you can't hear it anymore. It becomes like silence. Anansa told me."

Another imaginary friend. Her file said that she had kept her imaginary friends long after most children give them up. That was why I had first been assigned to see her, to get rid of the friends. Grunty, the ice pig; Howard, the boy who beat up everybody; Sue Ann, who would bring her dolls and play with them for her, making them do what Elaine said for them to do; Fuchsia, who lived among the flowers and was only inches high. There were others. After a few sessions with her I saw

that she knew that they weren't real. But they passed
time for her. They stepped outside her body and did
things she could never do. I felt they did her no harm
at all, and destroying that imaginary world for her
would only make her lonelier and more unhappy. She
was sane, that was certain. And yet I kept seeing her,
not entirely because I liked her so much. Partly because
I wondered whether she had been pretending when she
told me she knew her friends weren't real. Anansa was
a new one.

"Who's Anansa?"

"Oh, you don't want to know." She didn't want to
talk about her; that was obvious.

"I want to know."

She turned away. "I can't make you go away, but I
wish you would. When you get nosy."

"It's my job."

"Job!" She sounded contemptuous. "I see all of you,
running around on your healthy legs, doing all your
jobs."

What could I say to her? "It's how we stay alive," I
said. "I do my best."

Then she got a strange look on her face; *I've got a
secret*, she seemed to say, *and I want you to pry it out
of me*. "Maybe I can get a job, too."

"Maybe," I said. I tried to think of something she
could do.

"There's always music," she said.

I misunderstood. "There aren't many instruments
you can play. That's the way it is." Dose of reality and
all that.

"Don't be stupid."

"Okay. Never again."

"I meant that there's always the music. On my job."

"And what job is this?"

"Wouldn't you like to know?" she said, rolling her

eyes mysteriously and turning toward the window. I imagined her as a normal fifteen-year-old girl. Ordinarily I would have interpreted this as flirting. But there was something else under all this. A feeling of desperation. She was right. I really would like to know. I made a rather logical guess. I put together the two secrets she was trying to get me to figure out today.

"What kind of job is Anansa going to give you?"

She looked at me, startled. "So it's true then."

"What's true?"

"It's so frightening. I keep telling myself it's a dream. But it isn't, is it?"

"What, Anansa?"

"You think she's just one of my friends, don't you. But they're not in my dreams, not like this. Anansa—"

"What about Anansa?"

"She sings to me. In my sleep."

My trained psychologist's mind immediately conjured up mother figures. "Of course," I said.

"She's in space, and she sings to me. You wouldn't believe the songs."

It reminded me. I pulled out the cassette I had bought for her.

"Thank you," she said.

"You're welcome. Want to hear it?"

She nodded. I put it on the cassette player. *Appalachian Spring*. She moved her head to the music. I imagined her as a dancer. She felt the music very well.

But after a few minutes she stopped moving and started to cry.

"It's not the same," she said.

"You've heard it before?"

"Turn it off. Turn it *off*!"

I turned it off. "Sorry," I said. "Thought you'd like it."

"Guilt, nothing but guilt," she said. "You always feel guilty, don't you?"

"Pretty nearly always," I admitted cheerfully. A lot of my patients threw psychological jargon in my face. Or soap-opera language.

"*I'm* sorry," she said. "It's just—it's just not the music. Not *the* music. Now that I've heard it, everything is so dark compared to it. Like the rain, all gray and heavy and dim, as if the composer is trying to see the hills but the rain is always in the way. For a few minutes I thought he was getting it right."

"Anansa's music?"

She nodded. "I know you don't believe me. But I hear her when I'm asleep. She tells me that's the only time she can communicate with me. It's not talking. It's all her songs. She's out there, in her starship, singing. And at night I hear her."

"Why you?"

"You mean, Why only me?" She laughed. "Because of what I am. You told me yourself. Because I can't run around, I live in my imagination. She say that the threads between minds are very thin and hard to hold. But mine she can hold, because I live completely in my mind. She holds on to me. When I go to sleep, I can't escape her now anymore at all."

"Escape? I thought you liked her."

"I don't know what I like. I like—I like the music. But Anansa wants me. She wants to have me—she wants to give me a job."

"What's the singing like?" When she said *job*, she trembled and closed up; I referred back to something that she had been willing to talk about, to keep the floundering conversation going.

"It's not like anything. She's there in space, and it's black, just the humming of the engines like the sound of rain, and she reaches into the dust out there and draws in the songs. She reaches out her—out her fingers, or her ears, I don't know; it isn't clear. She reaches out and draws in the dust and the songs and turns them into the music that I hear. It's powerful. She says it's her songs that drive her between the stars."

"Is she alone?"

Elaine nodded. "She wants me."

"Wants you. How can she have you, with you here and her out there?"

Elaine licked her lips. "I don't want to talk about it," she said in a way that told me she was on the verge of telling me.

"I wish you would. I really wish you'd tell me."

"She says—she says that she can take me. She says that if I can learn the songs, she can pull me out of my body and take me there and give me arms and legs and fingers and I can run and dance and—"

She broke down, crying.

I patted her on the only place that she permitted, her soft little belly. She refused to be hugged. I had tried it years before, and she had screamed at me to stop it. One of the nurses told me it was because her mother had always hugged her, and Elaine wanted to hug back. And couldn't.

"It's a lovely dream, Elaine."

"It's a terrible dream. Don't you see? I'll be like *her*."

"And what's she like?"

"She's the ship. She's the starship. And she wants me with her, to be the starship with her. And sing our way through space together for thousands and thousands of years."

"It's just a dream, Elaine. You don't have to be afraid of it."

"They did it to her. They cut off her arms and legs and put her into the machines."

"But no one's going to put you into a machine."

"I want to go outside," she said.

"You can't. It's raining."

"Damn the rain."

"I do, every day."

"I'm not joking! She pulls me all the time now, even when I'm awake. She keeps pulling at me and making me fall asleep, and she sings to me, and I feel her pulling and pulling. If I could just go outside, I could hold on. I feel like I could hold on, if I could just—"

"Hey, relax. Let me give you a—"

"No! I don't want to sleep!"

"Listen, Elaine. It's just a dream. You can't let it get to you like this. It's just the rain keeping you here. It makes you sleepy, and so you keep dreaming this. But don't fight it. It's a beautiful dream in a way. Why not go with it?"

She looked at me with terror in her eyes.

"You don't mean that. You don't want me to go."

"No. Of course I don't want you to go anywhere. But you won't, don't you see? It's a dream, floating out there between the stars—"

"She's not floating. She's ramming her way through space so fast it makes me dizzy whenever she shows me."

"Then be dizzy. Think of it as your mind finding a way for you to run."

"You don't understand, Mr. Therapist. I thought you'd understand."

"I'm trying to."

"If I go with her, then I'll be dead."

I asked her nurse, "Who's been reading to her?"

"We all do, and volunteers from town. They like her. She always has someone to read to her."

"You'd better supervise them more carefully. Somebody's been putting ideas in her head. About spaceships and dust and singing between the stars. It's scared her pretty bad."

The nurse frowned. "We approve everything they read. She's been reading that kind of thing for years. It's never done her any harm before. Why now?"

"The rain, I guess. Cooped up in here, she's losing touch with reality."

The nurse nodded sympathetically and said, "I know. When she's asleep, she's doing the strangest things now."

"Like what? What kind of things?"

"Oh, singing these horrible songs."

"What are the words?"

"There aren't any words. She just sort of hums. Only the melodies are awful. Not even like music. And her voice gets funny and raspy. She's completely asleep. She sleeps a lot now. Mercifully, I think. She's always gotten impatient when she can't go outside."

The nurse obviously liked Elaine. It would be hard not to feel sorry for her, but Elaine insisted on being liked, and people liked her, those that could get over the horrible flatness of the sheets all around her trunk. "Listen," I said. "Can we bundle her up or something? Get her outside in spite of the rain?"

The nurse shook her head. "It isn't just the rain. It's cold out there. And the explosion that made her like she is—it messed her up inside. She isn't put together right. She doesn't have the strength to fight off any kind of disease at all. You understand—there's a good chance that exposure to that kind of weather would kill her eventually. And I won't take a chance on that."

"I'm going to be visiting her more often, then," I said. "As often as I can. She's got something going on in her head that's scaring her half to death. She thinks she's going to die."

"Oh, the poor darling," the nurse said. "Why would she think that?"

"Doesn't matter. One of her imaginary friends may be getting out of hand."

"I thought you said they were harmless."

"They were."

When I left the Millard County Rest Home that night, I stopped back in Elaine's room. She was asleep, and I heard her song. It was eerie. I could hear, now and then, themes from the bit of Copland music she had listened to. But it was distorted, and most of the music was unrecognizable—wasn't even music. Her voice was high and strange, and then suddenly it would change, would become low and raspy, and for a moment I clearly heard in her voice the sound of a vast engine coming through walls of metal, carried on slender metal rods, the sound of a great roar being swallowed up by a vast cushion of nothing. I pictured Elaine with wires coming out of her shoulders and hips, with her head encased in metal and her eyes closed in sleep, like her imaginary Anansa, piloting the starship as if it were her own body. I could see that this would be attractive to Elaine, in a way. After all, she hadn't been born this way. She had memories of running and playing, memories of feeding herself and dressing herself, perhaps even of learning to read, of sounding out the words as her fingers touched each letter. Even the false arms of a spaceship would be something to fill the great void.

Children's centers are not inside their bodies; their centers are outside, at the point where the fingers of the left hand and the fingers of the right hand meet. What they touch is where they live; what they see is their self. And Elaine had lost herself in an explosion before she had the chance to move inside. With this strange dream of Anansa she was getting a self back.

But a repellent self, for all that. I walked in and sat

by Elaine's bed, listening to her sing. Her body moved slightly, her back arching a little with the melody. High and light; low and rasping. The sounds alternated, and I wondered what they meant. What was going on inside her to make this music come out?

If I go with her, then I'll be dead.

Of course she was afraid. I looked at the lump of flesh that filled the bed shapelessly below where her head emerged from the covers. I tried to change my perspective, to see her body as she saw it, from above. It almost disappeared then, with the foreshortening and the height of her ribs making her stomach and hint of hips vanish into insignificance. Yet this was all she had, and if she believed—and certainly she seemed to—that surrendering to the fantasy of Anansa would mean the death of this pitiful body, is death any less frightening to those who have not been able to fully live? I doubt it. At least for Elaine, what life she had lived had been joyful. She would not willingly trade it for a life of music and metal arms, locked in her own mind.

Except for the rain. Except that nothing was so real to her as the outside, as the trees and birds and distant hills, and as the breeze touching her with a violence she permitted to no living person. And with that reality, the good part of her life, cut off from her by the rain, how long could she hold out against the incessant pulling of Anansa and her promise of arms and legs and eternal song?

I reached up, on a whim, and very gently lifted her eyelids.

Her eyes remained open, staring at the ceiling, not blinking.

I closed her eyes, and they remained closed.

I turned her head, and it stayed turned. She did not wake up. Just kept singing as if I had done nothing to her at all.

Catatonia, or the beginning of catalepsy. *She's losing her mind,* I thought, *and if I don't bring her back, keep her here somehow, Anansa will win, and the rest home will be caring for a lump of mindless flesh for the next however many years they can keep this remnant of Elaine alive.*

"I'll be back on Saturday," I told the administrator.

"Why so soon?"

"Elaine is going through a crisis of some kind," I explained. *An imaginary woman from space wants to carry her off*—that I didn't say. "Have the nurses keep her awake as much as they can. Read to her, play with her, talk to her. Her normal hours at night are enough. Avoid naps."

"Why?"

"I'm afraid for her, that's all. She could go catatonic on us at any time, I think. Her sleeping isn't normal. I want to have her watched all the time."

"This is really serious?"

"This is really serious."

On Friday it looked as if the clouds were breaking, but after only a few minutes of sunshine a huge new bank of clouds swept down from the northwest, and it was worse than before. I finished my work rather carelessly, stopping a sentence in the middle several times. One of my patients was annoyed with me. She squinted at me. "You're not paid to think about your woman troubles when you're talking to me." I apologized and tried to pay attention. She was a talker; my attention always wandered. But she was right in a way. I couldn't stop thinking of Elaine. And my patient's saying that about woman troubles must have triggered something in my mind. After all, my relationship with Elaine was the longest and closest I had had with a woman in many years. If you could think of Elaine as a woman.

On Saturday I drove back to Millard County and found the nurses rather distraught. They didn't realize how much she was sleeping until they tried to stop her, they all said. She was dozing off for two or three naps in the mornings, even more in the afternoons. She went to sleep at night at seven-thirty and slept at least twelve hours. "Singing all the time. It's awful. Even at night she keeps it up. Singing and singing."

But she was awake when I went in to see her.

"I stayed awake for you."

"Thanks," I said.

"A Saturday visit. I must really be going bonkers."

"Actually, no. But I don't like how sleepy you are."

She smiled wanly. "It isn't my idea."

I think my smile was more cheerful than hers. "And I think it's all in your head."

"Think what you like, Doctor."

"I'm not a doctor. My degree says I'm a master."

"How deep is the water outside?"

"Deep?"

"All this rain. Surely it's enough to keep a few dozen arks afloat. Is God destroying the world?"

"Unfortunately, no. Though He has killed the engines on a few cars that went a little fast through the puddles."

"How long would it have to rain to fill up the world?"

"The world is round. It would all drip off the bottom."

She laughed. It was good to hear her laugh, but it ended too abruptly, and she looked at me fearfully. "I'm going, you know."

"You are?"

"I'm just the right size. She's measured me, and I'll fit perfectly. She has just the place for me. It's a good place, where I can hear the music of the dust for myself, and learn to sing it. I'd have the directional engines."

I shook my head. "Grunty the ice pig was cute. This isn't cute, Elaine."

"Did I ever say I thought Anansa was cute? Grunty the ice pig was real, you know. My father made him out of crushed ice for a luau. He melted before they got the pig out of the ground. I don't make my friends up."

"Fuchsia the flower girl?"

"My mother would pinch blossoms off the fuchsia by our front door. We played with them like dolls in the grass."

"But not Anansa."

"Anansa came into my mind when I was asleep. She found me. I didn't make her up."

"Don't you see, Elaine, that's how the real hallucinations come? They feel like reality."

She shook her head. "I know all that. I've had the nurses read me psychology books. Anansa is—Anansa is other. She couldn't come out of my head. She's something else. She's real. I've heard her music. It isn't plain, like Copland. It isn't false."

"Elaine, when you were asleep on Wednesday, you were becoming catatonic."

"I know."

"You know?"

"I felt you touch me. I felt you turn my head. I wanted to speak to you, to say good-bye. But she was singing, don't you see? She was singing. And now she lets me sing along. When I sing with her, I can feel myself travel out, like a spider along a single thread, out into the place where she is. Into the darkness. It's lonely there, and black, and cold, but I know that at the end of the thread there she'll be, a friend for me forever."

"You're frightening me, Elaine."

"There aren't any trees on her starship, you know. That's how I stay here. I think of the trees and the hills and the birds and the grass and the wind, and how I'd lose all of that. She gets angry at me, and a little hurt. But it keeps me here. Except now I can hardly remember the trees at all. I try to remember, and it's like trying to remember the face of my mother. I can remember her dress and her hair, but her face is gone forever. Even when I look at a picture, it's a stranger. The trees are strangers to me now."

I stroked her forehead. At first she pulled her head away, then slid it back.

"I'm sorry," she said. "I usually don't like people to touch me there."

"I won't," I said.

"No, go ahead. I don't mind."

So I stroked her forehead again. It was cool and dry, and she lifted her head almost imperceptibly, to receive my touch. Involuntarily I thought of what the old woman had said the day before. *Woman troubles.* I was touching Elaine, and I thought of making love to her. I immediately put the thought out of my mind.

"Hold me here," she said. "Don't let me go. I want to go so badly. But I'm not meant for that. I'm just the right size, but not the right shape. Those aren't my arms. I know what my arms felt like."

"I'll hold you if I can. But you have to help."

"No drugs. The drugs pull my mind away from my body. If you give me drugs, I'll die."

"Then what can I do?"

"Just keep me here, any way you can."

Then we talked about nonsense, because we had been so serious, and it was as if she weren't having any problems at all. We got on to the subject of the church meetings.

"I didn't know you were religious," I said.

"I'm not. But what else is there to do on Sunday? They sing hymns, and I sing with them. Last Sunday there was a sermon that really got to me. The preacher talked about Christ in the sepulchre. About Him being there three days before the angel came to let Him go. I've been thinking about that, what it must have been like for Him, locked in a cave in the darkness, completely alone."

"Depressing."

"Not really. It must have been exhilarating for Him, in a way. If it was true, you know. To lie there on that stone bed, saying to Himself, 'They thought I was dead, but I'm here. I'm not dead.' "

"You make Him sound smug."

"Sure. Why not? I wonder if I'd feel like that, if I were with Anansa."

Anansa again.

"I can see what you're thinking. You're thinking, 'Anansa again.' "

"Yeah," I said. "I wish you'd erase her and go back to some more harmless friends."

Suddenly her face went angry and fierce.

"You can believe what you like. Just leave me alone."

I tried to apologize, but she wouldn't have any of it. She insisted on believing in this star woman. Finally I left, redoubling my cautions against letting her sleep. The nurses looked worried, too. They could see the change as easily as I could.

That night, because I was in Millard on a weekend, I called up Belinda. She wasn't married or anything at the moment. She came to my motel. We had dinner, made love, and watched television. She watched television, that is. I lay on the bed, thinking. And so when the test pattern came on and Belinda at last got up, beery and passionate, my mind was still on Elaine. As Belinda kissed and tickled me and whispered stupidity in my ear, I imagined myself without arms and legs. I lay there, moving only my head.

"What's the matter, you don't want to?"

I shook off the mood. No need to disappoint Belinda—I was the one who had called *her*. I had a responsibility. Not much of one, though. That was what was nagging at me. I made love to Belinda slowly and carefully, but with my eyes closed. I kept superimposing Elaine's face on Belinda's. Woman troubles. Even though Belinda's fingers played up and down my back, I thought I was making love to Elaine. And the stumps of arms and legs didn't revolt me as much as I would have thought. Instead, I only felt sad. A deep sense of tragedy, of loss, as if Elaine were dead and I could have saved her, like the prince in all the fairy tales; a kiss, so symbolic, and the princess awakens and lives happily ever after. And I hadn't done it. I had failed her. When we were finished, I cried.

"Oh, you poor sweetheart," Belinda said, her voice rich with sympathy. "What's wrong—you don't have to tell me." She cradled me for a while, and at last I went to sleep with my head pressed against her breasts. She thought I needed her. I suppose that, briefly, I did.

I did not go back to Elaine on Sunday as I had planned. I spent the entire day almost going. Instead of walking out the door, I sat and watched the incredible array of terrible Sunday morning television. And when I finally did go out, fully intending to go to the rest home and see how she was doing, I ended up driving, luggage in the back of the car, to my trailer, where I went inside and again sat down and watched television.

Why couldn't I go to her?

Just keep me here, she had said. Any way you can, she had said.

And I thought I knew the way. That was the problem. In the back of my mind all this was much too real, and the fairy tales were wrong. The prince didn't wake her with a kiss. He wakened the princess with a promise:

In his arms she would be safe forever. She awoke for the happily ever after. If she hadn't known it to be true, the princess would have preferred to sleep forever.

What was Elaine asking of me?

Why was I afraid of it?

Not my job. Unprofessional to get emotionally involved with a patient.

But then, when had I ever been a professional? I finally went to bed, wishing I had Belinda with me again, for whatever comfort she could bring. Why weren't all women like Belinda, soft and loving and undemanding?

Yet as I drifted off to sleep, it was Elaine I remembered, Elaine's face and hideous, reproachful stump of a body that followed me through all my dreams.

And she followed me when I was awake, through my regular rounds on Monday and Tuesday, and at last it was Wednesday, and still I was afraid to go to the Millard County Rest Home. I didn't get there until afternoon. Late afternoon, and the rain was coming down as hard as ever, and there were lakes of standing water in the fields, torrents rushing through the unprepared gutters of the town.

"You're late," the administrator said.

"Rain," I answered, and he nodded. But he looked worried.

"We hoped you'd come yesterday, but we couldn't reach you anywhere. It's Elaine."

And I knew that my delay had served its damnable purpose, exactly as I expected.

"She hasn't woken up since Monday morning. She just lies there, singing. We've got her on an IV. She's asleep."

She was indeed asleep. I sent the others out of the room.

"Elaine," I said.

Nothing.

I called her name again, several times. I touched her, rocked her head back and forth. Her head stayed wherever I placed it. And the song went on, softly, high and then low, pure and then gravelly. I covered her mouth. She sang on, even with her mouth closed, as if nothing were the matter.

I pulled down her sheet and pushed a pin into her belly, then into the thin flesh at her collarbone. No response. I slapped her face. No response. She was gone. I saw her again, connected to a starship, only this time I understood better. It wasn't her body that was the right size; it was her mind. And it was her mind that had followed the slender spider's thread out to Anansa, who waited to give her a body.

A job.

Shock therapy? I imagined her already-deformed body leaping and arching as the electricity coursed through her. It would accomplish nothing, except to torture unthinking flesh. Drugs? I couldn't think of any that could bring her back from where she had gone. In a way, I think, I even believed in Anansa, for the moment. I called her name. "Anansa, let her go. Let her come back to me. Please. I need her."

Why had I cried in Belinda's arms? Oh, yes. Because I had seen the princess and let her lie there unawakened, because the happily ever after was so damnably much work.

I did not do it in the fever of the first realization that I had lost her. It was no act of passion or sudden fear or grief. I sat beside her bed for hours, looking at her weak and helpless body, now so empty. I wished for her eyes to open on their own, for her to wake up and say, "Hey, would you believe the dream *I* had!" For her to say, "Fooled you, didn't I? It was really hard when you poked me with pins, but I fooled you."

But she hadn't fooled me.

And so, finally, not with passion but in despair, I stood up and leaned over her, leaned my hands on either side of her and pressed my cheek against hers and whispered in her ear. I promised her everything I could think of. I promised her no more rain forever. I promised her trees and flowers and hills and birds and the wind for as long as she liked. I promised to take her away from the rest home, to take her to see things she could only have dreamed of before.

And then at last, with my voice harsh from pleading with her, with her hair wet with my tears, I promised her the only thing that might bring her back. I promised her me. I promised her love forever, stronger than any songs Anansa could sing.

And it was then that the monstrous song fell silent. She did not awaken, but the song ended, and she moved on her own; her head rocked to the side, and she seemed to sleep normally, not catatonically. I waited by her bedside all night. I fell asleep in the chair, and one of the nurses covered me. I was still there when I was awakened in the morning by Elaine's voice.

"What a liar you are! It's still raining."

It was a feeling of power, to know that I had called someone back from places far darker than death. Her life was painful, and yet my promise of devotion was enough, apparently, to compensate. This was how I understood it, at least. This was what made me feel exhilarated, what kept me blind and deaf to what had really happened.

I was not the only one rejoicing. The nurses made a great fuss over her, and the administrator promised to write up a glowing report. "Publish," he said.

"It's too personal," I said. But in the back of my mind I was already trying to figure out a way to get the case into print, to gain something for my career. I was ashamed of myself for twisting what had been an honest, heartfelt commitment into personal advancement. But I couldn't ignore the sudden respect I was receiving from people to whom, only hours before, I had been merely ordinary.

"It's too personal," I repeated firmly. "I have no intention of publishing."

And to my disgust I found myself relishing the administrator's respect for that decision. There was no escape from my swelling self-satisfaction. Not as long as I stayed around those determined to give me cheap payoffs. Ever the wise psychologist, I returned to the only person who would give me gratitude instead of admiration. *The gratitude I had earned*, I thought. I went back to Elaine.

"Hi," she said. "I wondered where you had gone."

"Not far," I said. "Just visiting with the Nobel Prize committee."

"They want to reward you for bringing me here?"

"Oh, no. They had been planning to give me the award for having contacted a genuine alien being from outer space. Instead, I blew it and brought you back. They're quite upset."

She looked flustered. It wasn't like her to look flustered —usually she came back with another quip. "But what will they do to you?"

"Probably boil me in oil. That's the usual thing. Though, maybe they've found a way to boil me in solar energy. It's cheaper." A feeble joke. But she didn't get it.

"This isn't the way she said it was—she said it was—"

She. I tried to ignore the dull fear that suddenly churned in my stomach. *Be analytical*, I thought. *She could be anyone.*

"She said? Who said?" I asked.

Elaine fell silent. I reached out and touched her forehead. She was perspiring.

"What's wrong?" I asked. "You're upset."

"I should have known."

"Known what?"

She shook her head and turned away from me.

I knew what it was, I thought. I knew what it was, but we could surely cope. "Elaine," I said, "you aren't completely cured, are you? You haven't got rid of Anansa, have you? You don't have to hide it from me. Sure, I would have loved to think you'd been completely cured, but that would have been too much of a miracle. Do I look like a miracle worker? We've just made progress, that's all. Brought you back from catalepsy. We'll free you of Anansa eventually."

Still she was silent, staring at the rain-gray window.

"You don't have to be embarrassed about pretending to be completely cured. It was very kind of you. It made me feel very good for a little while. But I'm a grown-up. I can cope with a little disappointment. Besides, you're awake, you're back, and that's all that matters." Grown-up, hell! I was terribly disappointed, and ashamed that I wasn't more sincere in what I was saying. No cure after all. No hero. No magic. No great achievement. Just a psychologist who was, after all, not extraordinary.

But I refused to pay too much attention to those feelings. Be a professional, I told myself. She needs your help.

"So don't go feeling guilty about it."

She turned back to face me, her eyes full. "Guilty?" She almost smiled. "Guilty." Her eyes did not leave my face, though I doubted she could see me well through the tears brimming her lashes.

"You tried to do the right thing," I said.

"Did I? Did I really?" She smiled bitterly. It was a

strange smile for her, and for a terrible moment she no longer looked like my Elaine, my bright young patient. "I meant to stay with her," she said. "I wanted her with me, she was so alive, and when she finally joined herself to the ship, she sang and danced and swung her arms, and I said, 'This is what I've needed; this is what I've craved all my centuries lost in the songs.' But then I heard *you*."

"Anansa," I said, realizing at that moment who was with me.

"I heard *you*, crying out to her. Do you think I made up my mind quickly? She heard you, but she wouldn't come. She wouldn't trade her new arms and legs for anything. They were so new. But I'd had them for long enough. What I'd never had was—you."

"Where is she?" I asked.

"Out there," she said. "She sings better than I ever did." She looked wistful for a moment, then smiled ruefully. "And I'm here. Only I made a bad bargain, didn't I? Because I didn't fool you. You won't want me, now. It's Elaine you want, and she's gone. I left her alone out there. She won't mind, not for a long time. But then—then she will. Then she'll know I cheated her."

The voice was Elaine's voice, the tragic little body her body. But now I knew I had not succeeded at all. Elaine was gone, in the infinite outer space where the mind hides to escape from itself. And in her place— Anansa. A stranger.

"You cheated her?" I said. "How did you cheat her?"

"It never changes. In a while you learn all the songs, and they never change. Nothing moves. You go on forever until all the stars fail, and yet nothing ever moves."

I moved my hand and put it to my hair. I was startled at my own trembling touch on my head.

"Oh, God," I said. They were just words, not a supplication.

"You hate me," she said.

Hate her? Hate my little, mad Elaine? Oh, no. I had another object for my hate. I hated the rain that had cut her off from all that kept her sane. I hated her parents for not leaving her home the day they let their car drive them on to death. But most of all I remembered my days of hiding from Elaine, my days of resisting her need, of pretending that I didn't remember her or think of her or need her, too. She must have wondered why I was so long in coming. Wondered and finally given up hope, finally realized that there was no one who would hold her. And so she left, and when I finally came, the only person waiting inside her body was Anansa, the imaginary friend who had come, terrifyingly, to life. I knew whom to hate. I thought I would cry. I even buried my face in the sheet where her leg would have been. But I did not cry. I just sat there, the sheet harsh against my face, hating myself.

Her voice was like a gentle hand, a pleading hand touching me. "I'd undo it if I could," she said. "But I can't. She's gone, and I'm here. I came because of you. I came to see the trees and the grass and the birds and your smile. The happily ever after. That was what she had lived for, you know, all she lived for. Please smile at me."

I felt warmth on my hair. I lifted my head. There was no rain in the window. Sunlight rose and fell on the wrinkles of the sheet.

"Let's go outside," I said.

"It stopped raining," she said.

"A bit late, isn't it?" I answered. But I smiled at her.

"You can call me Elaine," she said. "You won't tell, will you?"

I shook my head. No, I wouldn't tell. She was safe

enough. I wouldn't tell because then they would take her away to a place where psychiatrists reigned but did not know enough to rule. I imagined her confined among others who had also made their escape from reality and I knew that I couldn't tell anyone. I also knew I couldn't confess failure, not now.

Besides, I hadn't really completely failed. There was still hope. Elaine wasn't really gone. She was still there, hidden in her own mind, looking out through this imaginary person she had created to take her place. Someday I would find her and bring her home. After all, even Grunty the ice pig had melted.

I noticed that she was shaking her head. "You won't find her," she said. "You won't bring her home. I won't melt and disappear. She *is* gone and you couldn't have prevented it."

I smiled. "Elaine," I said.

And then I realized that she had answered thoughts I hadn't put into words.

"That's right," she said, "let's be honest with each other. You might as well. You can't lie to me."

I shook my head. For a moment, in my confusion and despair, I had believed it all, believed that Anansa was real. But that was nonsense. Of course Elaine knew what I was thinking. She knew me better than I knew myself. "Let's go outside," I said. A failure and a cripple, out to enjoy the sunlight, which fell equally on the just and the unjustifiable.

"I don't mind," she said. "Whatever you want to believe: Elaine or Anansa. Maybe it's better if you still look for Elaine. Maybe it's better if you let me fool you after all."

The worst thing about the fantasies of the mentally ill is that they're so damned consistent. They never let up. They never give you any rest.

"I'm Elaine," she said, smiling. "I'm Elaine, pretending to be Anansa. You love me. That's what I came for. You promised to bring me home, and you did. Take me outside. You made it stop raining for me. You did everything you promised, and I'm home again, and I promise I'll never leave you."

She hasn't left me. I come to see her every Wednesday as part of my work, and every Saturday and Sunday as the best part of my life. I take her driving with me sometimes, and we talk constantly, and I read to her and bring her books for the nurses to read to her. None of them know that she is still unwell—to them she's Elaine, happier than ever, pathetically delighted at every sight and sound and smell and taste and every texture that they touch against her cheek. Only *I* know that she believes she is not Elaine. Only *I* know that I have made no progress at all since then, that in moments of terrible honesty I call her Anansa, and she sadly answers me.

But in a way I'm content. Very little has changed between us, really. And after a few weeks I realized, with certainty, that she was happier now than she had ever been before. After all, she had the best of all possible worlds, for her. She could tell herself that the real Elaine was off in space somewhere, dancing and singing and hearing songs, with arms and legs at last, while the poor girl who was confined to the limbless body at the Millard County Rest Home was really an alien who was very, very happy to have even that limited body.

And as for me, I kept my commitment to her, and I'm happier for it. I'm still human—I still take another woman into my bed from time to time. But Anansa doesn't mind. She even suggested it, only a few days after she woke up. "Go back to Belinda sometimes," she said. "Belinda loves you, too, you know. I won't mind at all." I still can't remember when I spoke to her of Belinda, but at least she didn't mind, and so there aren't really any discontentments in my life. Except.

Except that I'm not God. I would like to be God. I would make some changes.

When I go to the Millard County Rest Home, I never enter the building first. She is never in the building. I walk around the outside and look across the lawn by the trees. The wheelchair is always there; I can tell it from the others by the pillows, which glare white in the sunlight. I never call out. In a few moments she always sees me, and the nurses wheel her around and push the chair across the lawn.

She comes as she has come hundreds of times before. She plunges toward me, and I concentrate on watching her, so that my mind will not see my Elaine surrounded by blackness, plunging through space, gathering dust, gathering songs, leaping and dancing with her new arms and legs that she loves better than me. Instead I watch the wheelchair, watch the smile on her face. She is happy to see me, so delighted with the world outside that her body cannot contain her. And when my imagination will not be restrained, I am God for a moment. I see her running toward me, her arms waving. I give her a left hand, a right hand, delicate and strong; I put a long and girlish left leg on her, and one just as sturdy on the right.

And then, one by one, I take them all away.

PRIOR RESTRAINT

I MET Doc Murphy in a writing class taught by a mad Frenchman at the University of Utah in Salt Lake City. I had just quit my job as a coat-and-tie editor at a conservative family magazine, and I was having a little trouble getting used to being a slob student again. Of a shaggy lot, Doc was the shaggiest and I was prepared to be annoyed by him and ignore his opinions. But his opinions were not to be ignored. At first because of what he did to me. And then, at last, because of what had been done to him. It has shaped me; his past looms over me whenever I sit down to write.

Armand the teacher, who had not improved on his French accent by replacing it with Bostonian, looked puzzled as he held up my story before the class. "This is commercially viable," he said. "It is also crap. What else can I say?"

It was Doc who said it. Nail in one hand, hammer in the other, he crucified me and the story. Considering that I had already decided not to pay attention to him, and considering how arrogant I was in the lofty position of being the one student who had actually sold a novel, it is surprising to me that I listened to him. But underneath the almost angry attack on my work was something else: A basic respect, I think, for what a good writer should be. And for that small hint in my work that a good writer might be hiding somewhere in me.

So I listened. And I learned. And gradually, as the Frenchman got crazier and crazier, I turned to Doc to learn how to write. Shaggy though he was, he had a far crisper mind than anyone I had ever known in a business suit.

We began to meet outside class. My wife had left me two years before, so I had plenty of free time and a pretty large rented house to sprawl in; we drank or read or talked, in front of a fire or over Doc's convincing veal parmesan or out chopping down an insidious vine that wanted to take over the world starting in my backyard. For the first time since Denae had gone I felt at home in my house—Doc seemed to know by instinct what parts of the house held the wrong memories, and he soon balanced them by making me feel comfortable in them again.

Or uncomfortable. Doc didn't always say nice things.

"I can see why your wife left you," he said once.

"You don't think I'm good in bed, either?" (This was a joke—neither Doc nor I had any unusual sexual predilections.)

"You have a neanderthal way of dealing with people, that's all. If they aren't going where you want them to go, club 'em a good one and drag 'em away."

It was irritating. I didn't like thinking about my wife. We had only been married three years, and not good years either, but in my own way I had loved her and I missed her a great deal and I hadn't wanted her to go when she left. I didn't like having my nose rubbed in it. "I don't recall clubbing *you*."

He just smiled. And, of course, I immediately thought back over the conversation and realized that he was right. I hated his goddam smile.

"OK," I said, "you're the one with long hair in the land of the last surviving crew cuts. Tell me why you like 'Swap' Morris."

"I don't like Morris. I think Morris is a whore selling someone else's freedom to win votes."

And I *was* confused, then. I had been excoriating good old "Swap" Morris, Davis County Commissioner, for having fired the head librarian in the county because she had dared to stock a "pornographic" book despite his objections. Morris showed every sign of being illiterate, fascist, and extremely popular, and I would gladly have hit the horse at his lynching.

"So you don't like Morris either—what did I say wrong?"

"Censorship is never excusable for any reason, says you."

"You *like* censorship?"

And then the half-serious banter turned completely serious. Suddenly he wouldn't look at me. Suddenly he only had eyes for the fire, and I saw the flames dancing in tears resting on his lower eyelids, and I realized again that with Doc I was out of my depth completely.

"No," he said. "No, I don't *like* it."

And then a lot of silence until he finally drank two full glasses of wine, just like that, and went out to drive home; he lived up Emigration Canyon at the end of a winding, narrow road, and I was afraid he was too drunk, but he only said to me at the door, "I'm not drunk. It takes half a gallon of wine just to get up to normal after an hour with you, you're so damn sober."

One weekend he even took me to work with him.

Doc made his living in Nevada. We left Salt Lake City on Friday afternoon and drove to Wendover, the first town over the border. I expected him to be an employee of the casino we stopped at. But he didn't punch in, just left his name with a guy; and then he sat in a corner with me and waited.

"Don't you have to work?" I asked.

"I'm working," he said.

"I used to work just the same way, but I got fired."

"I've got to wait my turn for a table. I told you I made my living with poker."

And it finally dawned on me that he was a freelance professional—a player—a cardshark.

There were four guys named Doc there that night. Doc Murphy was the third one called to a table. He played quietly, and lost steadily but lightly for two hours. Then, suddenly, in four hands he made back everything he had lost and added nearly fifteen hundred dollars to it. Then he made his apologies after a decent number of losing hands and we drove back to Salt Lake.

"Usually I have to play again on Saturday night," he told me. Then he grinned. "Tonight I was lucky. There was an idiot who thought he knew poker."

I remembered the old saw: Never eat at a place called Mom's, never play poker with a man named Doc, and never sleep with a woman who's got more troubles than you. Pure truth. Doc memorized the deck, knew all the odds by heart, and it was a rare poker face that Doc couldn't eventually see through.

At the end of the quarter, though, it finally dawned on me that in all the time we were in class together, I had never seen one of his own stories. He hadn't written a damn thing. And there was his grade on the bulletin board—A.

I talked to Armand.

"Oh, Doc writes," he assured me. "Better than you

do, and you got an A. God knows how, you don't have the talent for it."

"Why doesn't he turn it in for the rest of the class to read?"

Armand shrugged. "Why should he? Pearls before swine."

Still it irritated me. After watching Doc disembowel more than one writer, I didn't think it was fair that his own work was never put on the chopping block.

The next quarter he turned up in a graduate seminar with me, and I asked him. He laughed and told me to forget it. I laughed back and told him I wouldn't. I wanted to read his stuff. So the next week he gave me a three-page manuscript. It was an unfinished fragment of a story about a man who honestly thought his wife had left him even though he went home to find her there every night. It was some of the best writing I've ever read in my life. No matter how you measure it. The stuff was clear enough and exciting enough that any moron who likes Harold Robbins could have enjoyed it. But the style was rich enough and the matter of it deep enough even in a few pages that it made most other "great" writers look like chicken farmers. I reread the fragment five times just to make sure I got it all. The first time I had thought it was metaphorically about me. The third time I knew it was about God. The fifth time I knew it was about everything that mattered, and I wanted to read more.

"Where's the rest?" I asked.

He shrugged. "That's it," he said.

"It doesn't feel finished."

"It isn't."

"Well, finish it! Doc, you could sell this anywhere, even the *New Yorker*. For them you probably don't even *have* to finish it."

"Even the *New Yorker*. Golly."

"I can't believe you think you're too good for *anybody*, Doc. Finish it. I want to know how it ends."

He shook his head. "That's all there is. That's all there ever will be."

And that was the end of the discussion.

But from time to time he'd show me another fragment. Always better than the one before. And in the meantime we became closer, not because he was such a good writer—I'm not so self-effacing I like hanging around with people who can write me under the table—but because he was Doc Murphy. We found every decent place to get a beer in Salt Lake City—not a particularly time-consuming activity. We saw three good movies and another dozen that were so bad they were fun to watch. He taught me to play poker well enough that I broke even every weekend. He put up with my succession of girlfriends and prophesied that I would probably end up married again. "You're just weak willed enough to try to make a go of it," he cheerfully told me.

At last, when I had long since given up asking, he told me why he never finished anything.

I was two and a half beers down, and he was drinking a hideous mix of Tab and tomato juice that he drank whenever he wanted to punish himself for his sins, on the theory that it was even worse than the Hindu practice of drinking your own piss. I had just got a story back from a magazine I had been sure would buy it. I was thinking of giving it up. He laughed at me.

"I'm serious," I said.

"Nobody who's any good at all needs to give up writing."

"Look who's talking. The king of the determined writers." He looked angry. "You're a paraplegic making fun of a one-legged man," he said.

"I'm sick of it."

"Quit then. Makes no difference. Leave the field to the hacks. You're probably a hack, too."

Doc hadn't been drinking anything to make him surly, not drunk-surly, anyway. "Hey, Doc, I'm asking for encouragement."

"If you need encouragement, you don't deserve it. There's only one way a good writer can be stopped."

"Don't tell me you have a selective writer's block. Against endings."

"Writer's block? Jesus, I've never been blocked in my life. Blocks are what happen when you're not good enough to write the thing you know you have to write."

I was getting angry. "And *you*, of course, are always good enough."

He leaned forward, looked at me in the eyes. "I'm the best writer in the English language."

"I'll give you this much. You're the best who never finished anything."

"I finish everything," he said. "I finish everything, beloved friend, and then I burn all but the first three pages. I finish a story a week, sometimes. I've written three complete novels, four plays. I even did a screenplay. It would've made millions of dollars and been a classic."

"Says who?"

"Says—never mind who says. It was bought, it was cast, it was ready for filming. It had a budget of thirty million. The studio believed in it. Only intelligent thing I've ever heard of them doing."

I couldn't believe it. "You're joking."

"If I'm joking, who's laughing? It's true."

I'd never seen him look so poisoned, so pained. It was true, if I knew Doc Murphy, and I think I did. Do. "Why?" I asked.

"The Censorship Board."

"What? There's no such thing in America."

He laughed. "Not full-time anyway."

"Who the hell is the Censorship Board?"

He told me:

When I was twenty-two I lived on a rural road in Oregon, he said, outside of Portland. Mailboxes out on the road. I was writing, I was a playwright, I thought there'd be a career in that; I was just starting to try fiction. I went out one morning after the mailman had gone by. It was drizzling slightly. But I didn't much care. There was an envelope there from my Hollywood agent. It was a contract. Not an option—a sale. A hundred thousand dollars. It had just occurred to me that I was getting wet and I ought to go in when two men came out of the bushes—yeah, I know, I guess they go for dramatic entrances. They were in business suits. God, I hate men who wear business suits. The one guy just held out his hand. He said, "Give it to me now and save yourself a lot of trouble." Give it to him? I told him what I thought of his suggestion. They looked like the mafia, or like a comic parody of the mafia, actually.

They were about the same height, and they seemed almost to be the same person, right down to a duplicate glint of fierceness in the eyes; but then I realized that my first impression had been deceptive. One was blond, one dark-haired; the blond had a slightly receding chin that gave his face a meek look from the nose down; the dark one had once had a bad skin problem and his neck was treeish, giving him an air of stupidity, as if a face had been pasted on the front of the neck with no room for a head at all. Not mafia at all. Ordinary people.

Except the eyes. That glint in the eyes was not false, and that was what had made me see them wrong at first. Those eyes had seen people weep, and had cared, and had hurt them again anyway. It's a look that human eyes should never have.

"It's just the *contract*, for Christ's sake," I told them,

but the dark one with acne scars only told me again to hand it over.

By now, though, my first fear had passed; they weren't armed, and so I might be able to get rid of them without violence. I started back to the house. They followed me.

"What do you want my contract for?" I asked.

"That film will never be made," says Meek, the blond one with the missing chin. "We won't allow it to be made."

I'm thinking who writes their dialogue for them, do they crib it from Fenimore Cooper? "Their hundred thousand dollars says they want to try. I want them to."

"You'll never get the money, Murphy. And this contract and that screenplay will pass out of existence within the next four days. I promise you that."

I ask him, "What are you, a critic?"

"Close enough."

By now I was inside the door and they were on the other side of the threshold. I should have closed the door, probably, but I'm a gambler. I had to stay in this time because I had to know what kind of hand they had. "Plan to take it by force?" I asked.

"By inevitability," Tree says. And then he says, "You see, Mr. Murphy, you're a dangerous man; with your IBM Self-Correcting Selectric II typewriter that has a sluggish return so that you sometimes get letters printed a few spaces in from the end. With your father who once said to you, 'Billy, to tell you the honest-to-God truth, I don't know if I'm your father or not. I wasn't the only guy your Mom had been seeing when I married her, so I really don't give a damn if you live or die.' "

He had it right down. *Word for word*, what my father

told me when I was four years old. I'd never told anybody. And he had it word for word.

CIA, Jesus. That's pathetic.

No, they weren't CIA. They just wanted to make sure that I didn't write. Or rather, that I didn't publish.

I told them I wasn't interested in their suggestions. And I was right—they weren't muscle types. I closed the door and they just went away.

And then the next day as I was driving my old Galaxy along the road, under the speed limit, a boy on a bicycle came right out in front of me. I didn't even have a chance to brake. One second he wasn't there, and the next second he was. I hit him. The bicycle went under the car, but he mostly came up the top. His foot stuck in the bumper, jammed in by the bike. The rest of him slid up over the hood, pulling his hip apart and separating his spine in three places. The hood ornament disemboweled him and the blood flowed up the windshield like a heavy rainstorm, so that I couldn't see anything except his face, which was pressed up against the glass with the eyes open. He died on the spot, of course. And I wanted to.

He had been playing Martians or something with his brother. The brother was standing there near the road with a plastic ray gun in his hand and a stupid look on his face. His mother came out of the house screaming. I was screaming, too. There were two neighbors who saw the whole thing. One of them called the cops and ambulance. The other one tried to control the mother and keep her from killing me. I don't remember where I was going. All I remember is that the car had taken an unusually long time starting that morning. Another minute and a half, I think—a long time, to start a car. If it had started up just like usual, I wouldn't have hit the kid. I kept thinking that—it was all just a coincidence that I happened to be coming by just at that moment. A half-second sooner and he would have seen me and swerved. A half-second later and I would have seen him. Just coincidence. The only reason the boy's father didn't kill me when he came home ten minutes later was because I was crying so damn hard. It never went to court because the neighbors testified that I hadn't a chance to stop, and the police investigator determined that I hadn't been speeding. Not even negligence. Just terrible, terrible chance.

I read the article in the paper. The boy was only nine, but he was taking special classes at school and was very bright, a good kid, ran a paper route and always took care of his brothers and sisters. A real tear-jerker for the consumption of the subscribers. I thought of killing myself. And then the men in the business suits came back. They had four copies of my script, my screenplay. Four copies is all I had ever made—the original was in my file.

"You see, Mr. Murphy, we have every copy of the screenplay. You will give us the original."

I wasn't in the mood for this. I started closing the door.

"You have so much taste," I said. I didn't care how they got the script, not then. I just wanted to find a way to sleep until when I woke up the boy would still be alive.

They pushed the door open and came in. "You see, Mr. Murphy, until we altered your car yesterday, your path and the boy's never did intersect. We had to try four times to get the timing right, but we finally made it. It's the nice thing about time travel. If you blow it, you can always go back and get it right the next time."

I couldn't believe anyone would want to take credit for the boy's death. "What for?" I asked.

And they told me. Seems the boy was even more

talented than anyone thought. He was going to grow up and be a writer. A journalist and critic. And he was going to cause a lot of problems for a particular government some forty years down the line. He was especially going to write three books that would change the whole way of thinking of a large number of people. The wrong way.

"We're all writers ourselves," Meek says to me. "It shouldn't surprise you that we take our writing very seriously. More seriously than *you* do. Writers, the good writers, can change people. And some of the changes aren't very good. By killing that boy yesterday, you see, you stopped a bloody civil war some sixty years from now. We've already checked and there are some unpleasant side effects, but nothing that can't be coped with. Saved seven million lives. You shouldn't feel bad about it."

I remembered the things they had known about me. Things that nobody could have known. I felt stupid because I began to believe they might be for real. I felt afraid because they were calm when they talked of the boy's death. I asked, "Where do I come in? Why me?"

"Oh, it's simple. You're a very good writer. Destined to be the best of your age. Fiction. And this screenplay. In three hundred years they're going to compare you to Shakespeare and the poor old bard will lose. The trouble is, Murphy, you're a godawful hedonist and a pessimist to boot, and if we can just keep you from publishing anything, the whole artistic mood of two centuries will be brightened considerably. Not to mention the prevention of a famine in seventy years. History makes strange connections, Murphy, and you're at the heart of a lot of suffering. If you never publish, the world will be a much better place for everyone."

You weren't there, you didn't hear them. You didn't see them, sitting on my couch, legs crossed, nodding, gesturing like they were saying the most natural thing in the world. From them I learned how to write genuine insanity. Not somebody frothing at the mouth; just somebody sitting there like a good friend, saying impossible things, cruel things, and smiling and getting excited and—Jesus, you don't know. Because I believed them. They knew, you see. And they were *too* insane, even a madman could have come up with a better hoax than that. And I'm making it sound as if I believed them logically, but I didn't, I don't think I can persuade you, either, but trust me—if I know when a man is bluffing or telling the truth, and I do, these two were not bluffing. A child had died, and they knew how many times I had turned the key in the ignition. And there was truth in those terrible eyes when Meek said, "If you willingly refrain from publishing, you will be allowed to live. If you refuse, then you will die within three days. Another writer will kill you—accidently, of course. We only have authority to work through authors."

I asked them why. The answer made me laugh. It seems they were from the Authors' Guild. "It's a matter of responsibility. If you refuse to take responsibility for the future consequences of your acts, we'll have to give the responsibility to somebody else."

And so I asked them why they didn't just kill me in the first place instead of wasting time talking to me.

It was Tree who answered, and the bastard was crying, and he says to me, "Because we love you. We love everything you write. We've learned everything we know about writing from you. And we'll lose it if you die."

They tried to console me by telling me what good company I was in. Thomas Hardy—they made him give up novels and stick to poetry which nobody read and so it was safe. Meek tells me, "Hemingway decided to kill himself instead of waiting for us to do it. And there are some others who only had to refrain from writing a particular book. It hurt them, but Fitzgerald was still able to have a decent career with the other books he could write, and Perelman gave it to us in laughs, since he couldn't be allowed to write his real work. We only bother with great writers. Bad writers aren't a threat to anybody."

We struck a sort of bargain. I could go on writing. But after I had finished everything, I had to burn it. All but the first three pages. "If you finish it at all," says Meek, "we'll have a copy of it here. There's a library here that—uh, I guess the easiest way to say it is that it exists outside time. You'll be published, in a way. Just not in your own time. Not for about eight hundred years. But at least you can write. There are others who have to keep their pens completely still. It breaks our hearts, you know."

I knew all about broken hearts, yes sir, I knew all about it. I burned all but the first three pages.

There's only one reason for a writer to quit writing, and that's when the Censorship Board gets to him. Anybody else who quits is just a gold-plated jackass. "Swap" Morris doesn't even know what real censorship is. It doesn't happen in libraries. It happens on the hoods of cars. So go on, become a real estate broker, sell insurance, follow Santa Claus and clean up the reindeer poo, I don't give a damn. But if you give up something that I will never have, I'm through with you. There's nothing in you for me.

So I write. And Doc reads it and tears it to pieces; everything except this. This he'll never see. This he'd probably kill me for, but what the hell? It'll never get published. No no I'm too vain. You're reading it, aren't you? See how I put my ego on the line? If I'm really a good enough writer, if my work is important enough to change the world, then a couple of guys in business suits will come make me a proposition I can't refuse, and you won't read this at all, but you are reading it, aren't you? Why am I doing this to myself? Maybe I'm hoping they'll come and give me an excuse to quit writing now, before I find out that I've already written as well as I'm ever going to. But here I thumb my nose at those goddam future critics and they ignore me, they tell exactly what my work is worth.

Or maybe not. Maybe I really *am* good, but my work just happens to have a positive effect, happens not to make any unpleasant waves in the future. Maybe I'm one of the lucky ones who can accomplish something powerful that doesn't need to be censored to protect the future.

Maybe pigs have wings.

THE CHANGED MAN AND THE
KING OF WORDS

O NCE THERE WAS a man who loved his son more
than life. Once there was a boy who loved his
father more than death.

They are not the same story, not really. But I can't
tell you one without telling you the other.

The man was Dr. Alvin Bevis, and the boy was his
son, Joseph, and the only woman that either of them
loved was Connie, who in 1977 married Alvin, with
hope and joy, and in 1978 gave birth to Joe on the brink
of death and adored them both accordingly. It was an
affectionate family. This made it almost certain that
they would come to grief.

Connie could have no more children after Joe. She
shouldn't even have had *him*. Her doctor called her a
damn fool for refusing to abort him in the fourth month
when the problems began. "He'll be born retarded.
You'll die in labor." To which she answered, "I'll have
one child, or I won't believe that I ever lived." In her

seventh month they took Joe out of her, womb and all. He was scrawny and little, and the doctor told her to expect him to be mentally deficient and physically uncoordinated. Connie nodded and ignored him. She was lucky. She had Joe, alive, and silently she said to any who pitied her, *I am more a woman than any of you barren ones who still have to worry about the phases of the moon.*

Neither Alvin nor Connie ever believed Joe would be retarded. And soon enough it was clear that he wasn't. He walked at eight months. He talked at twelve months. He had his alphabet at eighteen months. He could read at a second-grade level by the time he was three. He was inquisitive, demanding, independent, disobedient, and exquisitely beautiful, with a shock of copper-colored hair and a face as smooth and deep as a coldwater pool.

His parents watched him devour learning and were sometimes hard pressed to feed him with what he needed. *He will be a great man,* they both whispered to each other in the secret conversations of night. It made them proud; it made them afraid to know that his learning and his safety had, by chance or the grand design of things, been entrusted to them.

Out of all the variety the Bevises offered their son in the first few years of his life, Joe became obsessed with stories. He would bring books and insist that Connie or Alvin read to him, but if it was not a storybook, he quickly ran and got another, until at last they were reading a story. Then he sat imprisoned by the chain of events as the tale unfolded, saying nothing until the story was over. Again and again "Once upon a time," or "There once was a," or "One day the king sent out a proclamation," until Alvin and Connie had every storybook in the house practically memorized. Fairy tales were Joe's favorites, but as time passed, he graduated to movies and contemporary stories and even history.

The problem was not the thirst for tales, however. The conflict began because Joe had to live out his stories. He would get up in the morning and announce that Mommy was Mama Bear, Daddy was Papa Bear, and he was Baby Bear. When he was angry, he would be Goldilocks and run away. Other mornings Daddy would be Rumpelstiltskin, Mommy would be the Farmer's Daughter, and Joe would be the King. Joe was Hansel, Mommy was Gretel, and Alvin was the Wicked Witch.

"Why can't I be Hansel's and Gretel's father?" Alvin asked. He resented being the Wicked Witch. Not that he thought it *meant* anything. He told himself it merely annoyed him to have his son constantly assigning him dialogue and action for the day's activities. Alvin never knew from one hour to the next who he was going to be in his own home.

After a time, mild annoyance gave way to open irritation; if it was a phase Joe was going through, it ought surely to have ended by now. Alvin finally suggested that the boy be taken to a child psychologist. The doctor said it was a phase.

"Which means that sooner or later he'll get over it?" Alvin asked. "Or that you just can't figure out what's going on?"

"Both," said the psychologist cheerfully. "You'll just have to live with it."

But Alvin did not like living with it. He wanted his son to call him Daddy. He *was* the father, after all. Why should he have to put up with his child, no matter how bright the boy was, assigning him silly roles to play whenever he came home? Alvin put his foot down. He refused to answer to any name but Father. And after a little anger and a lot of repeated attempts, Joe finally stopped trying to get his father to play a part. Indeed, as far as Alvin knew, Joe entirely stopped acting out stories.

It was not so, of course. Joe simply acted them out with Connie after Alvin had gone for the day to cut up DNA and put it back together creatively. That was how Joe learned to hide things from his father. He wasn't *lying*; he was just biding his time. Joe was sure that if only he found good enough stories, Daddy would play again.

So when Daddy was home, Joe did not act out stories. Instead he and his father played number and word games, studied elementary Spanish as an introduction to Latin, plinked out simple programs on the Atari, and laughed and romped until Mommy came in and told her boys to calm down before the roof fell in on them. *This is being a father*, Alvin told himself. *I am a good father*. And it was true. It was true, even though every now and then Joe would ask his mother hopefully, "Do you think that Daddy will want to be in *this* story?"

"Daddy just doesn't like to pretend. He likes your stories, but not acting them out."

In 1983 Joe turned five and entered school; that same year Dr. Bevis created a bacterium that lived on acid precipitation and neutralized it. In 1987 Joe left school, because he knew more than any of his teachers; at precisely that time Dr. Bevis began earning royalties on commercial breeding of his bacterium for spot cleanup in acidized bodies of water. The university suddenly became terrified that he might retire and live on his income and take his name away from the school. So he was given a laboratory and twenty assistants and secretaries and an administrative assistant, and from then on Dr. Bevis could pretty well do what he liked with his time.

What he liked was to make sure the research was still going on as carefully and methodically as was proper and in directions that he approved of. Then he went home and became the faculty of one for his son's very private academy.

It was an idyllic time for Alvin.

It was hell for Joe.

Joe loved his father, mind you. Joe played at learning, and they had a wonderful time reading *The Praise of Folly* in the original Latin, duplicating great experiments and then devising experiments of their own—too many things to list. Enough to say that Alvin had never had a graduate student so quick to grasp new ideas, so eager to devise newer ones of his own. How could Alvin have known that Joe was starving to death before his eyes?

For with Father home, Joe and Mother could not play.

Before Alvin had taken him out of school Joe used to read books with his mother. All day at home she would read *Jane Eyre* and Joe would read it in school, hiding it behind copies of *Friends and Neighbors*. Homer. Chaucer. Shakespeare. Twain. Mitchell. Galsworthy. Elswyth Thane. And then in those precious hours after school let out and before Alvin came home from work they would be Ashley and Scarlett, Tibby and Julian, Huck and Jim, Walter and Griselde, Odysseus and Circe. Joe no longer assigned the parts the way he did when he was little. They both knew what book they were reading and they would live within the milieu of that book. Each had to guess from the other's behavior what role had been chosen that particular day; it was a triumphant moment when at last Connie would dare to venture Joe's name for the day, or Joe call Mother by hers. In all the years of playing the games never once did they choose to be the same person; never once did they fail to figure out what role the other played.

Now Alvin was home, and that game was over. No more stolen moments of reading during school. Father frowned on stories. History, yes; lies and poses, no. And so, while Alvin thought that joy had finally come, for Joe and Connie joy was dead.

Their life became one of allusion, dropping phrases to each other out of books, playing subtle characters without ever allowing themselves to utter the other's name. So perfectly did they perform that Alvin never knew what was happening. Just now and then he'd realize that something was going on that he didn't understand.

"What sort of weather is this for January?" Alvin said one day looking out the window at heavy rain.

"Fine," said Joe, and then, thinking of "The Merchant's Tale," he smiled at his mother. "In May we climb trees."

"What?" Alvin asked. "What does that have to do with anything?"

"I just like tree climbing."

"It all depends," said Connie, "on whether the sun dazzles your eyes."

When Connie left the room, Joe asked an innocuous question about teleology, and Alvin put the previous exchange completely out of his mind.

Or rather tried to put it out of his mind. He was no fool. Though Joe and Connie were very subtle, Alvin gradually realized he did not speak the native language of his own home. He was well enough read to catch a reference or two. Turning into swine. Sprinkling dust. "Frankly, I don't give a damn." Remarks that didn't quite fit into the conversation, phrases that seemed strangely resonant. And as he grew more aware of his wife's and his son's private language, the more isolated he felt. His lessons with Joe began to seem not exciting but hollow, as if they were both acting a role. Taking parts in a story. The story of the loving father-teacher and the dutiful, brilliant student-son. It had been the best time of Alvin's life, better than any life he had created in the lab, but that was when he had believed it. Now it was just a play. His son's real life was somewhere else.

I didn't like playing the parts he gave me, years ago, Alvin thought. *Does he like playing the part that I have given him?*

"You've gone as far as I can take you," Alvin said at breakfast one day, "in everything, except biology of course. So I'll guide your studies in biology, and for everything else I'm hiring advanced graduate students in various fields at the university. A different one each day."

Joe's eyes went deep and distant. "You won't be my teacher anymore?"

"Can't teach you what I don't know," Alvin said. And he went back to the lab. Went back and with delicate cruelty tore apart a dozen cells and made them into something other than themselves, whether they would or not.

Back at home, Joe and Connie looked at each other in puzzlement. Joe was thirteen. He was getting tall and felt shy and awkward before his mother. They had been three years without stories together. With Father there, they had played at being prisoners, passing messages under the guard's very nose. Now there was no guard, and without the need for secrecy there was no message anymore. Joe took to going outside and reading or playing obsessively at the computer; more doors were locked in the Bevis home than had ever been locked before.

Joe dreamed terrifying, gentle nightmares, dreamed of the same thing, over and over; the setting was different, but always the story was the same. He dreamed of being on a boat, and the gunwale began to crumble wherever he touched it, and he tried to warn his parents, but they wouldn't listen, they leaned, it broke away under their hands, and they fell into the sea, drowning. He dreamed that he was bound up in a web, tied like a spider's victim, but the spider never, never, never came to taste of him, left him there to desiccate in helpless bondage, though he cried out and struggled. How could he explain such dreams to his parents? He remembered Joseph in Genesis, who spoke too much of dreams; remembered Cassandra; remembered Iocaste, who thought to slay her child for fear of oracles. *I am caught up in a story,* Joe thought, *from which I cannot escape. Each change is a fall; each fall tears me from myself. If I cannot be the people of the tales, who am I then?*

Life was normal enough for all that. Breakfast lunch dinner, sleep wake sleep, work earn spend own, use break fix. All the cycles of ordinary life played out despite the shadow of inevitable ends. One day Alvin and his son were in a bookstore, the Gryphon, which had the complete Penguin Classics. Alvin was browsing through the titles to see what might be of some use when he noticed Joe was no longer following him.

His son, all the slender five feet nine inches of him, was standing half the store away bent in avid concentration over something on the counter. Alvin felt a terrible yearning for his son. He was so beautiful and yet somehow in these dozen and one years of Joe's life, Alvin had lost him. Now Joe was nearing manhood and very soon it would be too late. *When did he cease to be mine?* Alvin wondered. *When did he become so much his mother's son? Why must he be as beautiful as she and yet have the mind he has? He is Apollo,* Alvin said to himself.

And in that moment he knew what he had lost. By calling his son Apollo he had told himself what he had taken from his son. A connection between stories the child acted out and his knowledge of who he was. The connection was so real it was almost tangible and yet Alvin could not put it into words could not bear the knowledge and so and so and so.

Just as he was sure he had the truth of things it slipped away. Without words his memory could not hold it, lost the understanding the moment it came. *I knew it all and I have already forgotten.* Angry at himself, Alvin strode to his son and realized that Joe was not doing anything intelligent at all. He had a deck of tarot cards spread before him. He was doing a reading.

"Cross my palm with silver," said Alvin. He thought he was making a joke but his anger spoke too loudly in his voice. Joe looked up with shame on his face. Alvin cringed inside himself. *Just by speaking to you I wound you.* Alvin wanted to apologize but he had no strategy for that so he tried to affirm that it had been a joke by making another. "Discovering the secrets of the universe?"

Joe half-smiled and quickly gathered up the cards and put them away.

"No," Alvin said, "No, you were interested: you don't have to put them away."

"It's just nonsense," Joe said.

You're lying, Alvin thought.

"All the meanings are so vague they could fit just about anything." Joe laughed mirthlessly.

"You looked pretty interested."

"I was just you know wondering how to program a computer for this wondering whether I could do a program that would make it make some sense. Not just the random fall of the cards you know. A way to make it respond to who a person really is. Cut through all the—"

"Yes?"

"Just wondering."

"Cut through all the ?"

"Stories we tell ourselves. All the lies that we believe about ourselves. About who we really are."

Something didn't ring true in the boy's words, Alvin knew. Something was wrong. And because in Alvin's world nothing could long exist unexplained he decided the boy seemed awkward because his father had made him ashamed of his own curiosity. *I am ashamed that I have made you ashamed*, Alvin thought. *So I will buy you the cards.*

"I'll buy the cards. And the book you were looking at."

"No Dad," said Joe.

"No it's all right. Why not? Play around with the computer. See if you can turn this nonsense into something. What the hell, you might come up with some good graphics and sell the program for a bundle." Alvin laughed. So did Joe. Even Joe's *laugh* was a lie.

What Alvin didn't know was this: Joe was not ashamed. Joe was merely afraid. For he had laid out the cards as the book instructed, but he had not needed the explanations, had not needed the names of the faces. He had known their names at once, had known their faces. It was Creon who held the sword and the scales. Ophelia, naked wreathed in green, with man and falcon, bull and lion around. Ophelia who danced in her madness. And I was once the boy with the starflower in the sixth cup, giving to my child-mother, when gifts were possible between us. The cards were not dice, they were names, and he laid them out in stories drawing them in order from the deck in a pattern that he knew was largely the story of his life. All the names that he had borne were in these cards, and all the shapes of past and future dwelt here, waiting to be dealt. It was this that frightened him. He had been deprived of stories for so long, his own story of father, mother, son was so fragile now that he was madly grasping at anything; Father mocked, but Joe looked at the story of the cards, and he believed. *I do not want to take these home. It puts myself wrapped in a silk in my own hands.* "Please don't," he said to his father.

But Alvin, who knew better, bought them anyway, hoping to please his son.

Joe stayed away from the cards for a whole day. He had only touched them the once; surely he need not toy with this fear again. It was irrational, mere wish fulfillment, Joe told himself. *The cards mean nothing. They are not to be feared. I can touch them and learn no truth from them.* And yet all his rationalism, all his certainty that the cards were meaningless, were, he knew, merely lies he was telling to persuade himself to try the cards again, and this time seriously.

"What did you bring *those* home for?" Mother asked in the other room.

Father said nothing. Joe knew from the silence that Father did not want to make any explanation that might be overheard.

"They're silly," said Mother. "I thought you were a scientist and a skeptic. I thought you didn't believe in things like this."

"It was just a lark," Father lied. "I bought them for Joe to plink around with. He's thinking of doing a computer program to make the cards respond somehow to people's personalities. The boy has a right to play now and then."

And in the family room, where the toy computer sat mute on the shelf, Joe tried not to think of Odysseus walking away from the eight cups, treading the lip of the ocean's basin, his back turned to the wine. *Forty-*

eight kilobytes and two little disks. This isn't computer enough for what I mean to do, Joe thought. *I will not do it, of course. But with Father's computer from his office upstairs, with the hard disk and the right type of interface, perhaps there is space and time enough for all the operations. Of course I will not do it. I do not care to do it. I do not dare to do it.*

At two in the morning he got up from his bed, where he could not sleep, went downstairs, and began to program the graphics of the tarot deck upon the screen. But in each picture he made changes, for he knew that the artist, gifted as he was, had made mistakes. Had not understood that the Page of Cups was a buffoon with a giant phallus, from which flowed the sea. Had not known that the Queen of Swords was a statue and it was her throne that was alive, an angel groaning in agony at the stone burden she had to bear. The child at the Gate of Ten Stars was being eaten by the old man's dogs. The man hanging upside down with crossed legs and peace upon his face, he wore no halo; his hair was afire. And the Queen of Pentacles had just given birth to a bloody star, whose father was not the King of Pentacles, that poor cuckold.

And as the pictures and their stories came to him, he began to hear the echoes of all the other stories he had read. Cassandra, Queen of Swords, flung her bladed words, and people batted them out of the air like flies, when if they had only caught them and used them, they would not have met the future unarmed. For a moment Odysseus bound to the mast was the Hanged Man; in the right circumstances. Macbeth could show up in the ever-trusting Page of Cups, or crush himself under the ambitious Queen of Pentacles, Queen of Coins if she crossed him. The cards held tales of power, tales of pain, in the invisible threads that bound them to one another. Invisible threads, but Joe knew they were there, and he had to make the pictures right, make the program right, so that he could find true stories when he read the cards.

Through the night he labored until each picture was right: the job was only begun when he fell asleep at last. His parents were worried on finding him there in the morning, but they hadn't the heart to waken him. When he awoke, he was alone in the house, and he began again immediately, drawing the cards on the TV screen, storing them in the computer's memory; as for his own memory, he needed no help to recall them all, for he knew their names and their stories and was beginning to understand how their names changed every time they came together.

By evening it was done, along with a brief randomizer program that dealt the cards. The pictures were right. The names were right. But this time when the computer spread the cards before him—This is you, this covers you, this crosses you—it was meaningless. The computer could not do what hands could do. It could not understand and unconsciously deal the cards. It was not a randomizer program that was needed at all, for the shuffling of the tarot was not done by chance.

"May I tinker a little with your computer?" Joe asked.

"The hard disk?" Father looked doubtful. "I don't want you to open it, Joe. I don't want to try to come up with another ten thousand dollars this week if something goes wrong." Behind his words was a worry: *This business with the tarot cards has gone far enough, and I'm sorry I bought them for you, and I don't want you to use the computer, especially if it would make this obsession any stronger.*

"Just an interface, Father. You don't use the parallel port anyway, and I can put it back afterward."

"The Atari and the hard disk aren't even compatible."

"I know," said Joe.

But in the end there really couldn't be much argument. Joe knew computers better than Alvin did, and they both knew that what Joe took apart, Joe could put together. It took days of tinkering with hardware and plinking at the program. During that time Joe did nothing else. In the beginning he tried to distract himself. At lunch he told Mother about books they ought to read; at dinner he spoke to Father about Newton and Einstein until Alvin had to remind him that he was a biologist, not a mathematician. No one was fooled by these attempts at breaking the obsession. The tarot program drew Joe back after every meal, after every interruption, until at last he began to refuse meals and ignore the interruptions entirely.

"You have to eat. You can't die for this silly game," said Mother.

Joe said nothing. She set a sandwich by him, and he ate some of it.

"Joe, this had gone far enough. Get yourself under control," said Father.

Joe didn't look up. "I'm under control," he said, and he went on working.

After six days Alvin came and stood between Joe and the television set. "This nonsense will end now," Alvin said. "You are behaving like a boy with serious problems. The most obvious cure is to disconnect the computer, which I will do if you do not stop working on this absurd program at once. We try to give you freedom, Joe, but when you do this to us and to yourself, then—"

"That's all right," said Joe. "I've mostly finished it anyway." He got up and went to bed and slept for fourteen hours.

Alvin was relieved. "I thought he was losing his mind."

Connie was more worried than ever. "What do you think he'll do if it doesn't work?"

"Work? How could it work? Work at what? Cross my palm with silver and I'll tell your future."

"Haven't you been *listening* to him?"

"He hasn't said a word in days."

"He believes in what he's doing. He thinks his program will tell the truth."

Alvin laughed. "Maybe your doctor, what's-his-name, maybe he was right. Maybe there was brain damage after all."

Connie looked at him in horror. "God, Alvin."

"A joke, for Christ's sake."

"It wasn't funny."

They didn't talk about it, but in the middle of the night, at different times, each of them got up and went into Joe's room to look at him in his sleep.

Who are you? Connie asked silently. *What are you going to do if this project of yours is a failure? What are you going to do if it succeeds?*

Alvin, however, just nodded. He refused to be worried. Phases and stages of life. Children go through times of madness as they grow.

Be a lunatic thirteen-year-old, Joe, if you must. You'll return to reality soon enough. You're my son, and I know that you'll prefer reality in the long run.

The next evening Joe insisted that his father help him test the program. "It won't work on me," Alvin said. "I don't believe in it. It's like faith healing and taking vitamin C for colds. It never works on skeptics."

Connie stood small near the refrigerator. Alvin noticed the way she seemed to retreat from the conversation.

"Did you try it?" Alvin asked her.

She nodded.

"Mom did it four times for me," Joe said gravely.

"Couldn't get it right the first time?" Father asked. It was a joke.

"Got it right every time," Joe said.

Alvin looked at Connie. She met his gaze at first, but then looked away in—what? Fear? Shame? Embarrassment? Alvin couldn't tell. But he sensed that something painful had happened while he was at work. "Should I do it?" Alvin asked her.

"No," Connie whispered.

"Please," Joe said. "How can I test it if you won't help? I can't tell if it's right or wrong unless I know the people doing it."

"What kind of fortuneteller are you?" Alvin asked. "You're supposed to be able to tell the future of strangers."

"I don't tell the future," Joe said. "The program just tells the truth."

"Ah, truth!" said Alvin. "Truth about what?"

"Who you really are."

"Am I in disguise?"

"It tells your names. It tells your story. Ask Mother if it doesn't."

"Joe," Alvin said, "I'll play this little game with you. But don't expect me to regard it as *true*. I'll do almost anything for you, Joe, but I won't lie for you."

"I know."

"Just so you understand."

"I understand."

Alvin sat down at the keyboard. From the kitchen came a sound like the whine a cringing hound makes, back in its throat. It was Connie, and she was terrified. Her fear, whatever caused it, was contagious. Alvin shuddered and then ridiculed himself for letting this

upset him. He was in control, and it was absurd to be
afraid. He wouldn't be snowed by his own son.

"What do I do?"

"Just type things in."

"What things?"

"Whatever comes to mind."

"Words? Numbers? How do I know what to write if
you don't tell me?"

"It doesn't matter what you write. Just so you write
whatever you feel like writing."

I don't feel like writing anything, Alvin thought. *I
don't feel like humoring this nonsense another moment.* But he could not say so, not to Joe; he had to be
the patient father, giving this absurdity a fair chance.
He began to come up with numbers, with words. But
after a few moments there was no randomness, no free
association in his choice. It was not in Alvin's nature
to let chance guide his choices. Instead he began recit-
ing on the keyboard the long strings of genetic-code
information on his most recent bacterial subjects, fragments of names, fragments of numeric data, progressing
in order through the DNA. He knew as he did it that
he was cheating his son, that Joe wanted something of
himself. But he told himself, *What could be more a
part of me than something I made?*

"Enough?" he asked Joe.

Joe shrugged. "Do you think it is?"

"I could have done five words and you would have
been satisfied?"

"If you think you're through, you're through," Joe
said quietly.

"Oh, you're very good at this," Alvin said. "Even the
hocus-pocus."

"You're through then?"

"Yes."

Joe started the program running. He leaned back and waited. He could sense his father's impatience, and he found himself relishing the wait. The whirring and clicking of the disk drive. And then the cards began appearing on the screen. This is you. This covers you. This crosses you. This is above you, below you, before you, behind you. Your foundation and your house, your death and your name. Joe waited for what had come before, what had come so predictably, the stories that had flooded in upon him when he read for his mother and for himself a dozen times before. But the stories did not come. Because the cards were the same. Over and over again, the King of Swords.

Joe looked at it and understood at once. Father had lied. Father had consciously controlled his input, had ordered it in some way that told the cards that they were being forced. The program had not failed. Father simply would not be read. The King of Swords, by himself, was power, as all the Kings were power. The King of Pentacles was the power of money, the power of the bribe. The King of Wands was the power of life, the power to make new. The King of Cups was the power of negation and obliteration, the power of murder and sleep. And the King of Swords was the power of words that others would believe. Swords could say, "I will kill you," and be believed, and so be obeyed. Swords could say, "I love you," and be believed, and so be adored. Swords could lie. And all his father had given him was lies. What Alvin didn't know was that even the choice of lies told the truth.

"Edmund," said Joe. Edmund was the lying bastard in *King Lear*.

"What?" asked Father.

"We are only what nature makes us. And nothing more."

"You're getting this from the cards?"

Joe looked at his father, expressing nothing.

"It's all the same card," said Alvin.

"I know," said Joe.

"What's this supposed to be?"

"A waste of time," said Joe. Then he got up and walked out of the room.

Alvin sat there, looking at the little tarot cards laid out on the screen. As he watched, the display changed, each card in turn being surrounded by a thin line and then blown up large, nearly filling the screen. The King of Swords every time. With the point of his sword coming out of his mouth, and his hands clutching at his groin. *Surely*, Alvin thought, *that was not what was drawn on the Waite deck.*

Connie stood near the kitchen doorway, leaning on the refrigerator. "And that's all?" she asked.

"Should there be more?" Alvin asked.

"God," she said.

"What happened with you?"

"Nothing," she said, walking calmly out of the room. Alvin heard her rush up the stairs. And he wondered how things got out of control like this.

Alvin could not make up his mind how to feel about his son's project. It was silly, and Alvin wanted nothing to do with it, wished he'd never bought the cards for him. For days on end Alvin would stay at the laboratory until late at night and rush back again in the morning without so much as eating breakfast with his family. Then, exhausted from lack of sleep, he would get up late, come downstairs, and pretend for the whole day that nothing unusual was going on. On such days he discussed Joe's readings with him, or his own genetic experiments; sometimes, when the artificial cheer had been maintained long enough to be believed, Alvin would even discuss Joe's tarot program. It was at such times that Alvin offered to provide Joe with introductions, to get him better computers to work with, to advise him on the strategy of development and publication. Afterward Alvin always regretted having helped Joe, because what Joe was doing was a shameful waste of a brilliant mind. It also did not make Joe love him any more.

Yet as time passed, Alvin realized that other people were taking Joe seriously. A group of psychologists administered batteries of tests to hundreds of subjects—who had also put random data into Joe's program. When Joe interpreted the tarot readouts for these people, the correlation was statistically significant. Joe himself rejected those results, because the psychological tests were probably invalid measurements themselves. More important to him was the months of work in clinics, doing readings with people the doctors knew intimately. Even the most skeptical of the participating psychologists had to admit that Joe knew things about people that he could not possibly know. And most of the psychologists said openly that Joe not only confirmed much that they already knew but also provided brilliant new insights. "It's like stepping into my patient's mind," one of them told Alvin.

"My son is brilliant, Dr. Fryer, and I want him to succeed, but surely this mumbo jumbo can't be more than luck."

Dr. Fryer only smiled and took a sip of wine. "Joe tells me that you have never submitted to the test yourself."

Alvin almost argued, but it was true. He never had *submitted*, even though he went through the motions. "I've seen it in action," Alvin said.

"Have you? Have you seen his results with someone you know well?"

Alvin shook his head, then smiled. "I figured that

since I didn't believe in it, it wouldn't work around me."

"It isn't magic."

"It isn't science, either," said Alvin.

"No, you're right. Not science at all. But just because it isn't science doesn't mean it isn't true."

"Either it's science or it isn't."

"What a clear world you live in," said Dr. Fryer. "All the lines neatly drawn. We've run double-blind tests on his program, Dr. Bevis. Without knowing it, he has analyzed data taken from the same patient on different days, under different circumstances: the patient has even been given different instructions in some of the samples so that it wasn't random. And you know what happened?"

Alvin knew but did not say so.

"Not only did his program read substantially the same for all the different random inputs for the same patient, but the program also spotted the ringers. Easily. And then it turned out that the ringers were a consistent result for the woman who wrote the test we happened to use for the non-random input. Even when it shouldn't have worked, it worked."

"Very impressive," said Alvin, sounding as unimpressed as he could.

"It *is* impressive."

"I don't know about that," said Alvin. "So the cards are consistent. How do we know that they *mean* anything, or that what they mean is *true*?"

"Hasn't it occurred to you that your *son* is why it's true?"

Alvin tapped his spoon on the tablecloth, providing a muffled rhythm.

"Your son's computer program objectifies random input. But only your son can read it. To me that says that it's his *mind* that makes his method work, not his program. If we could figure out what's going on inside your son's head, Dr. Bevis, then his method would be science. Until then it's an art. But whether it is art or science, he tells the truth."

"Forgive me for what might seem a slight to your profession," said Alvin, "but how in God's name do *you* know whether what he says is true?"

Dr. Fryer smiled and cocked his head. "Because I can't conceive of it being wrong. We can't test his interpretations the way we tested his program. I've tried to find objective tests. For instance, whether his findings agree with my notes. But my notes mean nothing, because until your son reads my patients, I really don't understand them. And after he reads them, I can't conceive of any other view of them. Before you dismiss me as hopelessly subjective, remember please, Dr. Bevis, that I have every reason to fear and fight against your son's work. It undoes everything that I have believed in. It undermines my own life's work. And Joe is just like you. He doesn't think psychology is a science, either. Forgive *me* for what might seem a slight to your son, but he is troubled and cold and difficult to work with. I don't like him much. So why do I believe him?"

"That's your problem, isn't it?"

"On the contrary, Dr. Bevis. Everyone who's seen what Joe does, believes it. Except for you. I think that most definitely makes it *your* problem."

Dr. Fryer was wrong. Not everyone believed Joe.

"No," said Connie.

"No what?" asked Alvin. It was breakfast. Joe hadn't come downstairs yet. Alvin and Connie hadn't said a word since "Here's the eggs" and "Thanks."

Connie was drawing paths with her fork through the

yolk stains on her plate. "Don't do another reading with Joe."

"I wasn't planning on it."

"Dr. Fryer told you to believe it, didn't he?" She put her fork down.

"But I didn't believe Dr. Fryer."

Connie got up from the table and began washing the dishes. Alvin watched her as she rattled the plates to make as much noise as possible. Nothing was normal anymore. Connie was angry as she washed the dishes. There was a dishwasher, but she was scrubbing everything by hand. Nothing was as it should be. Alvin tried to figure out why he felt such dread.

"You will do a reading with Joe," said Connie, "*because* you don't believe Dr. Fryer. You always insist on verifying everything for yourself. If you believe, you must question your belief. If you doubt, you doubt your own disbelief. Am I not right?"

"No." *Yes.*

"And I'm telling you this once to have faith in your doubt. There is no truth whatever in his God-*damned* tarot."

In all these years of marriage, Alvin could not remember Connie using such coarse language. But then she hadn't said god-damn; she had said God-*damned*, with all the theological overtones.

"I mean," she went on, filling the silence. "I mean how can anyone take this seriously? The card he calls Strength—a woman closing a lion's mouth, yes, fine, but then he makes up a God-*damned* story about it, how the lion wanted her baby and she *fed it to him*." She looked at Alvin with fear. "It's sick, isn't it?"

"He said that?"

"And the Devil, forcing the lovers to stay together. He's supposed to be the firstborn child, chaining Adam

and Eve together. That's why Iocaste and Laios tried to
kill Oedipus. Because they hated each other, and the
baby would force them to stay together. But then they
stayed together anyway because of shame at what they
had done to an innocent child. And then they told everyone that asinine lie about the oracle and her proph-
ecy."

"He's read too many books."

Connie trembled. "If he does a reading of you, I'm
afraid of what will happen."

"If he feeds me crap like that, Connie, I'll just bite
my lip. No fights, I promise."

She touched his chest. Not his shirt, his chest. It felt
as if her finger burned right through the cloth. "I'm not
worried that you'll fight," she said. "I'm afraid that
you'll believe him."

"Why would I believe him?"

"We don't live in the Tower, Alvin!"

"Of course we don't."

"I'm not Iocaste, Alvin!"

"Of course you aren't."

"Don't believe him. Don't believe anything he says."

"Connie, don't get so upset." Again: "Why would I
believe him?"

She shook her head and walked out of the room. The
water was still running in the sink. She hadn't said a
word. But her answer rang in the room as if she had
spoken: "Because it's true."

Alvin tried to sort it out for hours. Oedipus and Iocaste.
Adam, Eve, and the Devil. The mother feeding her baby
to the lion. As Dr. Fryer had said, it isn't the cards, it
isn't the program, it's Joe. Joe and the stories in his
head. Is there a story in the world that Joe hasn't read?
All the tales that man has told himself, all the visions
of the world, and Joe knew them. Knew and believed

them. Joe the repository of all the world's lies, and now he was telling the lies back, and they believed him, every one of them believed him.

No matter how hard Alvin tried to treat this nonsense with the contempt it deserved, one thing kept coming back to him. Joe's program had known that Alvin was lying, that Alvin was playing games, not telling the truth. Joe's program was valid at least that far. *If his method can pass that negative test, how can I call myself a scientist if I disbelieve it before I've given it the* positive test *as well?*

That night while Joe was watching M*A*S*H reruns, Alvin came into the family room to talk to him. It always startled Alvin to see his son watching normal television shows, especially old ones from Alvin's own youth. The same boy who had read *Ulysses* and made sense of it without reading a single commentary, and he was laughing out loud at the television.

It was only after he had sat beside his son and watched for a while that Alvin realized that Joe was not laughing at the places where the laugh track did. He was not laughing at the jokes. He was laughing at Hawkeye himself.

"What was so funny?" asked Alvin.

"Hawkeye," said Joe.

"He was being serious."

"I know," said Joe. "But he's so sure he's *right*, and everybody believes him. Don't you think that's funny?"

As a matter of fact, no, I don't. "I want to give it another try, Joe," said Alvin.

Even though it was an abrupt change of subject, Joe understood at once, as if he had long been waiting for his father to speak. They got into the car, and Alvin drove them to the university. The computer people immediately made one of the full-color terminals available. This time Alvin allowed himself to be truly random, not thinking at all about what he was choosing, avoiding any meaning as he typed. When he was sick of typing, he looked at Joe for permission to be through. Joe shrugged. Alvin entered one more set of letters and then said, "Done."

Joe entered a single command that told the computer to start analyzing the input, and father and son sat together to watch the story unfold.

After a seemingly eternal wait, in which neither of them said a word, a picture of a card appeared on the screen.

"This is you," said Joe. It was the King of Swords.

"What does it mean?" asked Alvin.

"Very little by itself."

"Why is the sword coming out of his mouth?"

"Because he kills by the words of his mouth."

Father nodded. "And why is he holding his crotch?"

"I don't know."

"I thought you knew," said Father.

"I don't know until I see the other cards." Joe pressed the return key, and a new card almost completely covered the old one. A thin blue line appeared around it, and then it was blown up to fill the screen. It was Judgment, an angel blowing a trumpet, awakening the dead, who were gray with corruption, standing in their graves. "This covers you," said Joe.

"What does it mean?"

"It's how you spend your life. Judging the dead."

"Like God? You're saying I think I'm God?"

"It's what you do, Father," said Joe. "You judge everything. You're a scientist. I can't help what the cards say."

"I study life."

"You break life down into its pieces. Then you make your judgment. Only when it's all in fragments like the flesh of the dead."

Alvin tried to hear anger or bitterness in Joe's voice, but Joe was calm, matter-of-fact, for all the world like a doctor with a good bedside manner. Or like a historian telling the simple truth.

Joe pressed the key, and on the small display another card appeared, again on top of the first two, but horizontally. "This crosses you," said Joe. And the card was outlined in blue, and zoomed close. It was the Devil.

"What does it mean, crossing me?"

"Your enemy, your obstacle. The son of Laios and Iocaste."

Alvin remembered that Connie had mentioned Iocaste. "How similar is this to what you told Connie?" he asked.

Joe looked at him impassively. "How can I know after only three cards?"

Alvin waved him to go on.

A card above. "This crowns you." The Two of Wands, a man holding the world in his hands, staring off into the distance, with two small saplings growing out of the stone parapet beside him. "The crown is what you think you are, the story you tell yourself about yourself. Lifegiver, the God of Genesis, the Prince whose kiss awakens Sleeping Beauty and Snow White."

A card below. "This is beneath you, what you most fear to become." A man lying on the ground, ten swords piercing him in a row. He did not bleed.

"I've never lain awake at night afraid that someone would stab me to death."

Joe looked at him placidly. "But, Father, I told you, swords are words as often as not. What you fear is death at the hands of storytellers. According to the cards, you're the sort of man who would have killed the messenger who brought bad news."

According to the cards, or according to you? But Alvin held his anger and said nothing.

A card to the right. "This is behind you, the story of your past." A man in a sword-studded boat, poling the craft upstream, a woman and child sitting bowed in front of him. "Hansel and Gretel sent into the sea in a leaky boat."

"It doesn't look like a brother and sister," said Alvin. "It looks like a mother and child."

"Ah," said Joe. A card to the left. "This is before you, where you know your course will lead." A sarcophagus with a knight sculpted in stone upon it, a bird resting on his head.

Death, thought Alvin. Always a safe prediction. And yet not safe at all. The cards themselves seemed malevolent. They all depicted situations that cried out with agony or fear. That was the gimmick, Alvin decided. Potent enough pictures will seem to be important whether they really mean anything or not. Heavy with meaning like a pregnant woman, they can be made to bear anything.

"It isn't death," said Joe.

Alvin was startled to have his thoughts so appropriately interrupted.

"It's a monument after you're dead. With your words engraved on it and above it. Blind Homer. Jesus. Mahomet. To have your words read like scripture."

And for the first time Alvin was genuinely frightened by what his son had found. Not that this future frightened him. Hadn't he forbidden himself to hope for it, he wanted it so much? No, what he feared was the way he felt himself say, silently, *Yes, yes, this is True. I will not be flattered into belief*, he said to himself. But underneath every layer of doubt that he built between himself and the cards he believed. Whatever Joe told him, he would believe, and so he denied belief now, not because of disbelief but because he was afraid. Perhaps that was why he had doubted from the start.

Next the computer placed a card in the lower right-hand corner. "This is your house." It was the Tower, broken by lightning, a man and a woman falling from it, surrounded by tears of flame.

A card directly above it. "This answers you." A man under a tree, beside a stream, with a hand coming from a small cloud, giving him a cup. "Elijah by the brook, and the ravens feed him."

And above that a man walking away from a stack of eight cups, with a pole and traveling cloak. The pole is a wand, with leaves growing from it. The cups are arranged so that a space is left where a ninth cup had been. "This saves you."

And then, at the top of the vertical file of four cards, Death. "This ends it." A bishop, a woman, and a child kneeling before Death on a horse. The horse is trampling the corpse of a man who had been a king. Beside the man lie his crown and a golden sword. In the distance a ship is foundering in a swift river. The sun is rising between pillars in the east. And Death holds a leafy wand in his hand, with a sheaf of wheat bound to it at the top. A banner of life over the corpse of the king. "This ends it," said Joe definitively.

Alvin waited, looking at the cards, waiting for Joe to explain it. But Joe did not explain. He just gazed at the monitor and then suddenly got to his feet. "Thank you, Father," he said. "It's all clear now."

"To you it's clear," Alvin said.

"Yes," said Joe. "Thank you very much for not lying this time." Then Joe made as if to leave.

"Hey, wait," Alvin said. "Aren't you going to explain it to me?"

"No," said Joe.

"Why not?"

"You wouldn't believe me."

Alvin was not about to admit to anyone, least of all

himself, that he did believe. "I still want to know. I'm curious. Can't I be curious?"

Joe studied his father's face. "I told Mother, and she hasn't spoken a natural word to me since."

So it was not just Alvin's imagination. The tarot program had driven a wedge between Connie and Joe. He'd been right. "I'll speak a natural word or two every day, I promise," Alvin said.

"That's what I'm afraid of," Joe said.

"Son," Alvin said. "Dr. Fryer told me that the stories you tell, the way you put things together, is the closest thing to truth about people that he's ever heard. Even if I don't believe it, don't I have the right to hear the truth?"

"I don't know if it *is* the truth. Or if there is such a thing."

"There is. The way things *are*, that's truth."

"But how *are* things, with people? What causes me to feel the way I do or act the way I do? Hormones? Parents? Social patterns? All the causes or purposes of all our acts are just stories we tell ourselves, stories we believe or disbelieve, changing all the time. But still we live, still we act, and all those acts have *some* kind of cause. The patterns all fit together into a web that connects everyone who's ever lived with everyone else. And every new person changes the web, adds to it, changes the connections, makes it all different. That's what I find with this program, how you believe you fit into the web."

"Not how I *really* fit?"

Joe shrugged. "How can I know? How can I measure it? I discover the stories that you believe most secretly, the stories that control your acts. But the very telling of the story changes the way you believe. Moves some things into the open, changes who you *are*. I undo my work by doing it."

"Then undo your work with me, and tell me the truth."

"I don't want to."

"Why not?"

"Because I'm in your story."

Alvin spoke then more honestly than he ever meant to. "Then for God's sake tell me the story, because I don't know who the hell you are."

Joe walked back to his chair and sat down. "I am Goneril and Regan, because you made me act out the lie that you needed to hear. I am Oedipus, because you pinned my ankles together and left me exposed on the hillside to save your own future."

"I have loved you more than life."

"You were always afraid of me, Father. Like Lear, afraid that I wouldn't care for you when I was still vigorous and you were enfeebled by age. Like Laios, terrified that my power would overshadow you. So you took *control*; you put me out of my place."

"I gave years to educating you—"

"Educating me in order to make me forever your shadow, your student. When the only thing that I really loved was the one thing that would free me from you— all the stories."

"Damnable stupid fictions."

"No more stupid than the fiction *you* believe. Your story of little cells and DNA, your story that there is such a thing as reality that can be objectively perceived. God, what an idea, to see with inhuman eyes, without interpretation. That's exactly how stones see, without interpretation, because without interpretation there isn't any *sight*."

"I think I know that much at least," Alvin said, trying to feel as contemptuous as he sounded. "I never said I was objective."

"*Scientific* was the word. What could be verified was

scientific. That was all that you would ever let me study, what could be verified. The trouble is, Father, that nothing in the world that matters at all is verifiable. What makes us who we are is forever tenuous, fragile, the web of a spider eaten and remade every day. I can never see out of your eyes. Yet I can never see any other way than through the eyes of every storyteller who ever taught me how to see. That was what you did to me, Father. You forbade me to hear any storyteller but you. It was *your* reality I had to surrender to. *Your* fiction I had to believe."

Alvin felt his past slipping out from under him. "If I had known those games of make-believe were so important to you, I wouldn't have—"

"You knew they were that important to me," Joe said coldly. "Why else would you have bothered to forbid me? But my mother dipped me into the water, all but my heel, and I got all the power you tried to keep from me. You see, Mother was not Griselde. She wouldn't kill her children for her husband's sake. When you exiled me, you exiled her. We lived the stories together as long as we were free."

"What do you mean?"

"Until you came home to teach me. We were free until then. We acted out all the stories that we could. Without you."

It conjured for Alvin the ridiculous image of Connie playing Goldilocks and the Three Bears day after day for years. He laughed in spite of himself, laughed sharply, for only a moment.

Joe took the laugh all wrong. Or perhaps took it exactly right. He took his father by the wrist and gripped him so tightly that Alvin grew afraid. Joe was stronger than Alvin had thought. "Grendel feels the touch of Beowulf on his hand," Joe whispered, "and he thinks,

Perhaps I should have stayed at home tonight. Perhaps I am not hungry after all."

Alvin tried for a moment to pull his arm away but could not. *What have I done to you, Joe?* he shouted inside himself. Then he relaxed his arm and surrendered to the tale. "Tell me my story from the cards," he said. "Please."

Without letting go of his father's arm, Joe began. "You are Lear, and your kingdom is great. Your whole life is shaped so that you will live forever in stone, in memory. Your dream is to create life. You thought I would be such life, as malleable as the little worlds you make from DNA. But from the moment I was born you were afraid of me. I couldn't be taken apart and recombined like all your little animals. And you were afraid that I would steal the swords from your sepulchre. You were afraid that you would live on as Joseph Bevis's father, instead of me forever being Alvin Bevis's son."

"I was jealous of my child," said Alvin, trying to sound skeptical.

"Like the father rat that devours his babies because he knows that someday they will challenge his supremacy, yes. It's the oldest pattern in the world, a tale older than teeth."

"Go on, this is quite fascinating." *I refuse to care.*

"All the storytellers know how this tale ends. Every time a father tries to change the future by controlling his children, it ends the same. Either the children lie, like Goneril and Regan, and pretend to be what he made them, or the children tell the truth, like Cordelia, and the father casts them out. I tried to tell the truth, but then together Mother and I lied to you. It was so much easier, and it kept me alive. She was Grim the Fisher, and she saved me alive."

Iocaste and Laios and Oedipus. "I see where this is going," Alvin said. "I thought you were bright enough not to believe in that Freudian nonsense about the Oedipus complex."

"Freud thought he was telling the story of all mankind when he was only telling his own. Just because the story of Oedipus isn't true for everyone doesn't mean that it isn't true for me. But don't worry, Father. I don't have to kill you in the forest in order to take possession of your throne."

"I'm not worried." It was a lie. It was a truthful understatement.

"Laios died only because he would not let his son pass along the road."

"Pass along any road you please."

"And I am the Devil. You and Mother were in Eden until I came. Because of me you were cast out. And now you're in hell."

"How neatly it all fits."

"For you to achieve your dream, you had to kill me with your story. When I lay there with your blades in my back, only then could you be sure that your sepulchre was safe. When you exiled me in a boat I could not live in, only then could you be safe, you thought. But I am the Horn Child, and the boat bore me quickly across the sea to my true kingdom."

"This isn't anything coming from the computer," said Alvin. "This is just you being a normal resentful teenager. Just a phase that everyone goes through."

Joe's grip on Alvin's arm only tightened. "I didn't die, I didn't wither, I have my power now, and you're not safe. Your house is broken, and you and Mother are being thrown from it to your destruction, and you know it. Why did you come to me, except that you knew you were being destroyed?"

Again Alvin tried to find a way to fend off Joe's story

with ridicule. This time he could not. Joe had pierced through shield and armor and cloven him, neck to heart. "In the name of God, Joe, how do we end it all?" He barely kept from shouting.

Joe relaxed his grip on Alvin's arm at last. The blood began to flow again, painfully; Alvin fancied he could measure it passing through his calibrated arteries.

"Two ways," said Joe. "There is one way you can save yourself."

Alvin looked at the cards on the screen. "Exile."

"Just leave. Just go away for a while. Let us alone for a while. Let me pass you by, stop trying to rule, stop trying to force your story on me, and then after a while we can see what's changed."

"Oh, excellent. A son divorcing his father. Not too likely."

"Or death. As the deliverer. As the fulfillment of your dream. If you die now, you defeat me. As Laios destroyed Oedipus at last."

Alvin stood up to leave. "This is rank melodrama. Nobody's going to die because of this."

"Then why can't you stop trembling?" asked Joe.

"Because I'm angry, that's why," Alvin said. "I'm angry at the way you choose to look at me. I love you more than any other father I know loves his son, and this is the way you choose to view it. How sharper than a serpent's tooth—"

"How sharper than a serpent's tooth it is to have a thankless child. Away, away!"

"Lear, isn't it? You gave me the script, and now I'm saying the goddamn lines."

Joe smiled a strange, sphinxlike smile. "It's a good exit line, though, isn't it?"

"Joe, I'm not going to leave, and I'm not going to drop dead, either. You've told me a lot. Like you said, not the truth, not *reality*, but the way you see things. That helps, to know how you see things."

Joe shook his head in despair. "Father, you don't understand. It was *you* who put those cards up on the screen. Not I. My reading is completely different. Completely different, but no better."

"If I'm the King of Swords, who are you?"

"The Hanged Man," Joe said.

Alvin shook his head. "What an ugly world you choose to live in."

"Not neat and pretty like yours, not bound about by rules the way yours is. Laws and principles, theories and hypotheses, may they cover your eyes and keep you happy."

"Joe, I think you need help," said Alvin.

"Don't we all," said Joe.

"So do I. A family counselor maybe. I think we need outside help."

"I've told you what you can do."

"I'm not going to run away from this, Joe, no matter how much you want me to."

"You already have. You've been running away for months. These are *your* cards, Father, not mine."

"Joe, I want to help you out of this—unhappiness."

Joe frowned. "Father, don't you understand? The Hanged Man is smiling. The Hanged Man has won."

Alvin did not go home. He couldn't face Connie right now, did not want to try to explain what he felt about what Joe had told him. So he went to the laboratory and lost himself for a time in reading records of what was happening with the different subject organisms. Some good results. If it all held up, Alvin Bevis would have taken mankind a long way toward being able to read the DNA chain. There was a Nobel in it. More important still, there was real change. *I will have changed the world*, he thought. And then there came into his mind the picture of the man holding the world in his hands, looking off into the distance. The Two of Wands. His dream. Joe was right about that. Right about Alvin's longing for a monument to last forever.

And in a moment of unusual clarity Alvin saw that Joe was right about everything. Wasn't Alvin even now doing just what the cards called for him to do to save himself, going into hiding with the Eight of Cups? His house was breaking down, all was being undone, and he was setting out on a long journey that would lead him to solitude. Greatness, but solitude.

There was one card that Joe hadn't worked into his story, however. The Four of Cups. "This answers you," he had said. The hand of God coming from a cloud. Elijah by the brook. *If God were to whisper to me, what would He say?*

He would say, Alvin thought, that there is something profoundly wrong, something circular in all that Joe has done. He has synthesized things that no other mind in the world could have brought together meaningfully. He is, as Dr. Fryer said, touching on the borders of Truth. But, by God, there is something wrong, something he has overlooked. Not a *mistake*, exactly. Simply a place where Joe has not put two true things together in his own life: Stories make us who we are: the tarot program identifies the stories we believe: by hearing the tale of the tarot, we have changed who we are: therefore—

Therefore, no one knows how much of Joe's tarot story is believed because it is true, and how much becomes true because it is believed. Joe is not a scientist. Joe is a tale-teller. But the gifted, powerful teller of tales soon lives in the world he has created, for as more and more people believe him, his tales become true.

We do not have to be the family of Laios. I do not

have to play at being Lear. I can say no to this story, and make it false. Not that Joe could tell any other story, because this is the one that he believes. But I can change what he believes by changing what the cards say, and I can change what the cards say by being someone else.

King of Swords. Imposing my will on others, making them live in the world that my words created. And now my son, too, doing the same. But I can change, and so can he, and then perhaps his brilliance, his insights can shape a better world than the sick one he is making us live in.

And as he grew more excited, Alvin felt himself fill with light, as if the cup had poured into him from the cloud. He believed, in fact, that he had already changed. That he was already something other than what Joe said he was.

The telephone rang. Rang twice, three times, before Alvin reached out to answer it. It was Connie.

"Alvin?" she asked in a small voice.

"Connie," he said.

"Alvin, Joe called me." She sounded lost, distant.

"Did he? Don't worry, Connie, everything's going to be fine."

"Oh, I know," Connie said. "I finally figured it out. It's the thing that Helen never figured out. It's the thing that Iocaste never had the guts to do. Enid knew it, though, Enid could do it. I love you, Alvin." She hung up.

Alvin sat with his hand on the phone for thirty seconds. That's how long it took him to realize that Connie sounded *sleepy*. That Connie was trying to change the cards, too. By killing herself.

All the way home in the car, Alvin was afraid that he was going crazy. He kept warning himself to drive carefully, not to take chances. He wouldn't be able to save Connie if he had an accident on the way. And then there would come a voice that sounded like Joe's, whispering, That's the story you tell yourself, but the truth is you're driving slowly and carefully, hoping she will die so everything will be simple again. It's the best solution. Connie has solved it all, and you're being *slow* so she can succeed, but telling yourself you're being *careful* so you can live with yourself after she's dead.

No, said Alvin again and again, pushing on the accelerator, weaving through the traffic, then forcing himself to slow down, not to kill himself to save two seconds. Sleeping pills weren't *that* fast. And maybe he was wrong; maybe she hadn't taken pills. Or maybe he was thinking that in order to slow himself down so that Connie would die and everything would be simple again—

Shut up, he told himself. *Just get there*, he told himself.

He got there, fumbled with the key, and burst inside. "Connie!" he shouted.

Joe was standing in the archway between the kitchen and the family room.

"It's all right," Joe said. "I got here when she was on the phone to you. I forced her to vomit, and most of the pills hadn't even dissolved yet."

"She's awake?"

"More or less."

Joe stepped aside, and Alvin walked into the family room. Connie sat on a chair, looking catatonic. But as he came nearer, she turned away, which at once hurt him and relieved him. At least she was not hopelessly insane. So it was not too late for change.

"Joe," Alvin said, still looking at Connie. "I've been thinking. About the reading."

Joe stood behind him, saying nothing.

"I believe it. You told the truth. The whole thing, just as you said."

Still Joe did not answer. *Well, what can he say, anyway?* Alvin asked himself. *Nothing. At least he's listening.* "Joe, you told the truth. I really screwed up the family. I've had to have the whole thing my way, and it really screwed things up. Do you hear me, Connie? I'm telling both of you, I agree with Joe about the past. But not the future. There's nothing magical about those cards. They don't tell the future. They just tell the outcome of the pattern, the way things will end if the pattern isn't changed. But we can change it, don't you see? That's what Connie was trying to do with the pills, change the way things turn out. Well, *I'm* the one who can really change, by changing me. Can you see that? I'm changed already. As if I drank from the cup that came to me out of the cloud, Joe. I don't have to control things the way I did. It's all going to be better now. We can build up from, up from—"

The ashes, those were the next words. But they were the wrong words, Alvin could sense that. All his words were wrong. It had seemed true in the lab, when he thought of it; now it sounded dishonest. Desperate. Ashes in his mouth. He turned around to Joe. His son was not listening silently. Joe's face was contorted with rage, his hands trembling, tears streaming down his cheeks.

As soon as Alvin looked at him, Joe screamed at him. "You can't just let it be, can you! You have to do it again and again and again, don't you!"

Oh, I see, Alvin thought. *By wanting to change things, I was just making them more the same. Trying to control the world they live in. I didn't think it through well enough. God played a dirty trick on me, giving me that cup from the cloud.*

"I'm sorry," Alvin said.

"No!" Joe shouted. "There's nothing you can say!"

"You're right," Alvin said, trying to calm Joe. "I should just have—"

"Don't say *anything*!" Joe screamed, his face red.

"I won't, I won't," said Alvin. "I won't say another—"

"*Nothing! Nothing! Nothing!*"

"I'm just agreeing with you, that's—"

Joe lunged forward and screamed it in his father's face. "God damn you, don't talk at all!"

"I see," said Alvin, suddenly realizing. "I see—as long as I try to put it in words, I'm forcing my view of things on the rest of you, and if I—"

There were no words left for Joe to say. He had tried every word he knew that might silence his father, but none would. Where words fail, there remains the act. The only thing close at hand was a heavy glass dish on the side table. Joe did not mean to grab it, did not mean to strike his father across the head with it. He only meant his father to be still. But all his incantations had failed, and still his father spoke, still his father stood in the way, refusing to let him pass, and so he smashed him across the head with the glass dish.

But it was the dish that broke, not his father's head. And the fragment of glass in Joe's hand kept right on going after the blow, followed through with the stroke, and the sharp edge of the glass cut neatly through the fleshy, bloody, windy part of Alvin's throat. All the way through, severing the carotid artery, the veins, and above all the trachea, so that no more air flowed through Alvin's larynx. Alvin was wordless as he fell backward, spraying blood from his throat, clutching at the pieces of glass imbedded in the side of his face.

"Uh-oh," said Connie in a high and childish voice.

Alvin lay on his back on the floor, his head propped

up on the front edge of the couch. He felt a terrible throbbing in his throat and a strange silence in his ears where the blood no longer flowed. He had not known how noisy the blood in the head could be, until now, and now he could not tell anyone. He could only lie there, not moving, not turning his head, watching.

He watched as Connie stared at his throat and slowly tore at her hair; he watched as Joe carefully and methodically pushed the bloody piece of glass into his right eye and then into his left. *I see now,* said Alvin silently. *Sorry I didn't understand before. You found the answer to the riddle that devoured us, my Oedipus. I'm just not good at riddles, I'm afraid.*

is the old pole lamp that no longer went with the decor when the living room was redecorated. But picture me, not as you found me, still and lifeless, but rather as I am at this moment, with my left hand neatly holding the paper. My right hand moves smoothly across the page, reaching up now and then to dip the quill in the blood that has pooled in the ragged mass of muscle, veins, and stumpy bone between my shoulders.

Why do I, being dead, bother to write to you now? If I didn't choose to write before I killed myself, perhaps I should have abided by that decision after death; but it was not until I had actually carried out my plan that I finally had something to say to you. And having something to say, writing became my only choice, since ordinary diction is beyond one who lacks larynx, mouth, lips, tongue, and teeth. All my tools of articulation have been shredded and embedded in the plasterboard. I have achieved utter speechlessness.

Do you marvel that I continue to move my arms and hands after my head is gone? I'm not surprised: My brain has been disconnected from my body for many years. All my actions long since became habits. Stimuli would pass from nerves to spinal cord and rise no further. You would greet me in the morning or lob your comments at me for hours in the night and I would utter my customary responses without these exchanges provoking a single thought in my mind. I scarcely remember being alive for the last years—or, rather, I remember being alive, but can't distinguish one day from another, one Christmas from any other Christmas, one word you said from any other word you might have said. Your voice has become a drone, and as for my own voice, I haven't listened to a thing I said since the last time I humiliated myself before you, causing you to curl your lip in distaste and turn over the next three cards in your solitaire game. Nor can I remember which of the many lip-curlings and card-turnings in my memory was the particular one that coincided with my last self-debasement before you. Now my habitual body continues as it has for all these years, writing this memoir of my suicide as one last, complex, involuntary twitching of the muscles in my arm and hand and fingers.

I'm sure you have detected the inconsistency. You have always been able to evade my desperate attempts at conveying meaning. You simply wait until you can catch some seeming contradiction in my words, then use it as a pretext to refuse to listen to anything else I say because I am not being logical, and therefore am not rational, and you refuse to speak to someone who is not being rational. The inconsistency you have noticed is: If I am completely a creature of habit, how is it that I committed suicide in the first place, since that is a new and therefore non-customary behavior?

But you see, this is no inconsistency at all. You have schooled me in all the arts of self-destruction. Just as the left hand will sympathetically learn some measure of a skill practiced only with the right, so I have made such a strong habit of subsuming my own identity in yours that it was almost a reflex finally to perform the physical annihilation of myself.

Indeed, it is merely the culmination of long custom that when I made the most powerful statement of my life, my most dazzling performance, my finest hundredth of a second, in that very moment I lost my eyes and so will not be able to witness the response of my audience. I write to you, but you will not write or speak to me, or if you do, I shall not have eyes to read or ears to hear you. Will you scream? (Will someone else find me, and will *that* person scream? But it *must* be you.)

I imagine disgust, perhaps. Kneeling, retching on the old rug that was all we could afford to use in my basement corner.

And later, who will peel the ceiling plaster? Rip out the wallboard? And when the wall has been stripped down to the studs, what will be done with those large slabs of drywall that have been plowed with shot and sown with bits of my brain and skull? Will there be fragments of drywall buried with me in my grave? Will they even be displayed in the open coffin, neatly broken up and piled where my head used to be? It would be appropriate, I think, since a significant percentage of my corpse is there, not attached to the rest of my body. And if some fragment of your precious house were buried with me, perhaps you would come occasionally to shed some tears on my grave.

I find that in death I am not free of worries. Being speechless means I cannot correct misinterpretations. What if someone says, "It wasn't suicide: The gun fell and discharged accidentally"? Or what if *murder* is supposed? Will some passing vagrant be apprehended? Suppose he heard the shot and came running, and then was found, holding the shotgun and gibbering at his own blood-covered hands; or, worse, going through my clothes and stealing the hundred-dollar bill I always carry on my person. (You remember how I always joked that I kept it as busfare in case I ever decided to leave you, until you forbade me to say it one more time or you would not be responsible for what you did to me. I have kept my silence on that subject ever since—have you noticed?—for I want you always to be responsible for what you do.)

The poor vagrant could not have administered first aid to me—I'm quite sure that nowhere in the Boy Scout Handbook would he have read so much as a paragraph on caring for a person whose head has been torn away so thoroughly that there's not enough neck left to hold a tourniquet. And since the poor fellow couldn't help me, why shouldn't he help himself? I don't begrudge him the hundred dollars—I hereby bequeath him all the money and other valuables he can find on my person. You can't charge him with stealing what I freely give to him. I also hereby affirm that he did not kill me, and did not dip my drawing pen into the blood in the stump of my throat and then hold my hand, forming the letters that appear on the paper you are reading. You are also witness of this, for you recognize my handwriting. No one should be punished for my death who was not involved in causing it.

But my worst fear is not sympathetic dread for some unknown body-finding stranger, but rather that no one will discover me at all. Having fired the gun, I have now had sufficient time to write all these pages. Admittedly I have been writing with a large hand and much space between the lines, since in writing blindly I must be careful not to run words and lines together. But this does not change the fact that considerable time has elapsed since the unmissable sound of a shotgun firing. Surely some neighbor must have heard; surely the police have been summoned and even now are hurrying to investigate the anxious reports of a gunshot in our picturebook home. For all I know the sirens even now are sounding down the street, and curious neighbors have gathered on their lawns to see what sort of burden the police carry forth. But even when I wait for a few moments, my pen hovering over the page, I feel no vibration of heavy footfalls on the stairs. No hands reach under my armpits to pull me away from the page. Therefore I conclude that there has been no phone call. No one has come, no one will come, unless you come, *until* you come.

Wouldn't it be ironic if you chose this day to leave

me? Had I only waited until your customary homecoming hour, you would not have come, and instead of transplanting a cold rod of iron into my lap I could have walked through the house for the first time as if it were somewhat my own. As the night grew later and later, I would have become more certain you were not returning; how daring I would have been then! I might have kicked the shoes in their neat little rows on the closet floor. I might have jumbled up my drawers without dreading your lecture when you discovered it. I might have read the newspaper in the holy of holies, and when I needed to get up to answer a call of nature, I could have left the newspaper spread open on the coffee table instead of folding it neatly just as it came from the paperboy and when I came back there it would be, wide open, just as I left it, without a tapping foot and a scowl and a rosary of complaints about people who are unfit to live with civilized persons.

But you have not left me. I know it. You will return tonight. This will simply be one of the nights that you were detained at the office and if I were a productive human being I would know that there are times when one cannot simply drop one's work and come home because the clock has struck such an arbitrary hour as five. You will come in at seven or eight, after dark, and you will find the cat is not indoors, and you will begin to seethe with anger that I have left the cat outside long past its hour of exercise on the patio. But I couldn't very well kill myself with the cat in here, could I? How could I write you such a clear and eloquent missive as this, my sweet, with your beloved feline companion climbing all over my shoulders trying to lick at the blood that even now I use as ink? No, the cat had to remain outdoors, as you will see; I actually had a valid reason for having violated the rules of civilized living.

Cat or no cat, all the blood is gone and now I am

using my ballpoint pen. Of course, I can't actually see whether the pen is out of ink. I remember the pen running out of ink, but it is the memory of many pens running out of ink many times, and I can't recall how recent was the most recent case of running-out-of-ink, and whether the most recent case of pen-buying was before or after it.

In fact it is the issue of memory that most troubles me. How is it that, headless, I remember anything at all? I understand that my fingers might know how to form the alphabet by reflex, but how is it that I remember how to spell these words, how has so much language survived within me, how can I cling to these thoughts long enough to write them down? Why do I have the shadowy memory of all that I am doing now, as if I had done it all before in some distant past?

I removed my head as brutally as possible, yet memory persists. This is especially ironic for, if I remember correctly, memory is what I most hoped to kill. Memory is a parasite that dwells within me, a mutant creature that has climbed up my spine and now perches atop my ragged neck, taunting me as it spins a sticky thread out of its own belly like a spider, then weaves it into shapes that harden in the air and become bone. I am being cheated; human bodies are not supposed to be able to regrow body parts that are any more complex than fingernails or hair, and here I can feel with my fingers that the bone has changed. My vertebrae are once again complete, and now the base of my skull has begun to form again.

How quickly? Too fast! And inside the bone grow softer things, the terrible small creature that once inhabited my head and refuses even now to die. This little knob at the top of my spine is a new limbic node; I recognize it, for when I squeeze it lightly with my fingers I feel strange passions, half-forgotten passions.

Soon, though, such animality will be out of reach, for the tissues will swell outward to form a cerebellum, a folded gray cerebrum; and then the skull will close around it, sheathed in wrinkled flesh and scanty hair.

My undoing is undone, and far too quickly. What if my head is fully restored to my shoulders before you come home? Then you will find me in the basement with a bloody mess and no rational explanation for it. I can imagine you speaking of it to your friends. You can't leave me alone for a single hour, you poor thing, it's just a constant burden living with someone who is constantly making messes and then lying about them. Imagine, you'll say to them, a whole letter, so many pages, explaining how I killed myself—it would be funny if it weren't so sad.

You will expose me to the scorn of your friends; but that changes nothing. Truth is truth, even when it is ridiculed. Still, why should I provide entertainment for those wretched soulless creatures who live only to laugh at one whose shoe-latchets they are not fit to unlace? If you cannot find me headless, I refuse to let you know what I have done at all. You will not read this account until some later day, after I finally succeed in dying and am embalmed. You'll find these pages taped on the bottom side of a drawer in my desk, where you will have looked, not because you hoped for some last word from me, but because you are searching for the hundred-dollar bill, which I will tape inside it.

And as for the blood and brains and bone embedded in the plasterboard, even that will not trouble you. I will scrub; I will sand; I will paint. You will come home to find the basement full of fumes and you will wear your martyr's face and take the paint away and send me to my room as if I were a child caught writing on the walls. You will have no notion of the agony I suffered in your absence, of the blood I shed solely in the hope of getting free of you. You will think this was a day like any other day. But I will know that on this day, this one day like the marker between B.C. and A.D., I found the courage to carry out an abrupt and terrible plan that I did not first submit for your approval.

Or has this, too, happened before? Will I, in the maze of memory, be unable to recall which of many head-explodings was the particular one that led me to write this message to you? Will I find, when I open the drawer, that on its underside there is already a thick sheaf of papers tied there around a single hundred-dollar bill? There is nothing new under the sun, said old Solomon in Ecclesiastes. Vanity of vanities; all is vanity. Nothing like that nonsense from King Lemuel at the end of Proverbs: Many daughters have done virtuously, but thou excellest them all.

Let her own works praise her in the gates, ha! I say let her own head festoon the walls.

LOST BOYS

I'VE WORRIED FOR a long time about whether to tell this story as fiction or fact. Telling it with made-up names would make it easier for some people to take. Easier for me, too. But to hide my own lost boy behind some phony made-up name would be like erasing him. So I'll tell it the way it happened, and to hell with whether it's easy for either of us.

Kristine and the kids and I moved to Greensboro on the first of March, 1983. I was happy enough about my job—I just wasn't sure I wanted a job at all. But the recession had the publishers all panicky, and nobody was coming up with advances large enough for me to take a decent amount of time writing a novel. I suppose I could whip out 75,000 words of junk fiction every month and publish them under a half dozen pseud-onyms or something, but it seemed to Kristine and me that we'd do better in the long run if I got a job to ride out the recession. Besides, my Ph.D. was down the toilet. I'd been doing good work at Notre Dame, but when I had to take out a few weeks in the middle of a semester to finish *Hart's Hope*, the English Department was about as understanding as you'd expect from people who prefer their authors dead or domesticated. Can't feed your family? So sorry. You're a writer? Ah, but not one that anyone's written a scholarly essay about. So long, boy-oh!

So sure, I was excited about my job, but moving to Greensboro also meant that I had failed. I had no way of knowing that my career as a fiction writer wasn't over. Maybe I'd be editing and writing books about computers for the rest of my life. Maybe fiction was just a phase I had to go through before I got a *real* job.

Greensboro was a beautiful town, especially to a family from the western desert. So many trees that even in winter you could hardly tell there was a town at all. Kristine and I fell in love with it at once. There were local problems, of course—people bragged about Greensboro's crime rate and talked about racial tension and what-not—but we'd just come from a depressed northern industrial town with race riots in the high schools, so to us this was Eden. There were rumors that several child disappearances were linked to some serial kidnapper, but this was the era when they started putting pictures of missing children on milk cartons—those stories were in every town.

It was hard to find decent housing for a price we could afford. I had to borrow from the company against my future earnings just to make the move. We ended up in the ugliest house on Chinqua Drive. You know the house—the one with cheap wood siding in a neighborhood of brick, the one-level rambler surrounded by split-levels and two-stories. Old enough to be shabby, not old enough to be quaint. But it had a big fenced yard and enough bedrooms for all the kids and for my office, too—because we hadn't given up on my writing career, not yet, not completely.

The little kids—Geoffrey and Emily—thought the whole thing was really exciting, but Scotty, the oldest, he had a little trouble with it. He'd already had kindergarten and half of first grade at a really wonderful private school down the block from our house in South Bend. Now he was starting over in mid-year, losing all his friends. He had to ride a school bus with strangers. He resented the move from the start, and it didn't get better.

Of course, *I* wasn't the one who saw this. *I* was at work—and I very quickly learned that success at Compute! Books meant giving up a few little things like seeing your children. I had expected to edit books written by people who couldn't write. What astonished me was that I was editing books about computers written by people who couldn't *program*. Not all of them, of course, but enough that I spent far more time rewriting programs so they made sense—so they even *ran*—than I did fixing up people's language. I'd get to work at 8:30 or 9:00, then work straight through till 9:30 or 10:30 at night. My meals were Three Musketeers bars and potato chips from the machine in the employee lounge. My exercise was typing. I met deadlines, but I was putting on a pound a week and my muscles were all atrophying and I saw my kids only in the mornings as I left for work.

Except Scotty. Because he left on the school bus at 6:45 and I rarely dragged out of bed until 7:30, during the week I never saw Scotty at all.

The whole burden of the family had fallen on Kristine. During my years as a freelancer from 1978 till 1983, we'd got used to a certain pattern of life, based on the fact that Daddy was *home*. She could duck out and run some errands, leaving the kids, because I was home. If one of the kids was having discipline problems, I was there. Now if she had her hands full and needed something from the store; if the toilet clogged; if the Xerox jammed, then she had to take care of it herself, somehow. She learned the joys of shopping with a cart-ful of kids. Add to this the fact that she was pregnant and sick half the time, and you can understand why sometimes I couldn't tell whether she was ready for sainthood or the funny farm.

The finer points of child-rearing just weren't within our reach at that time. She knew that Scotty wasn't adapting well at school, but what could she do? What could I do?

Scotty had never been the talker Geoffrey was—he spent a lot of time just keeping to himself. Now, though, it was getting extreme. He would answer in monosyllables, or not at all. Sullen. As if he were angry, and yet if he was, he didn't know it or wouldn't admit it. He'd get home, scribble out his homework (did they give homework when *I* was in first grade?), and then just mope around.

If he had done more reading, or even watched TV, then we wouldn't have worried so much. His little brother Geoffrey was already a compulsive reader at age five, and Scotty used to be. But now Scotty'd pick up a book and set it down again without reading it. He didn't even follow his mom around the house or anything. She'd see him sitting in the family room, go in and change the sheets on the beds, put away a load of clean clothes, and then come back in and find him sitting in the same place, his eyes open, staring at *nothing*.

I tried talking to him. Just the conversation you'd expect:

"Scotty, we know you didn't want to move. We had no choice."

"Sure. That's OK."

"You'll make new friends in due time."

"I know."

"Aren't you ever happy here?"

"I'm OK."

Yeah, right.

But we didn't have *time* to fix things up, don't you see? Maybe if we'd imagined this was the last year of Scotty's life, we'd have done more to right things, even if it meant losing the job. But you never know that sort of thing. You always find out when it's too late to change anything.

And when the school year ended, things *did* get better for a while.

For one thing, I saw Scotty in the mornings. For another thing, he didn't have to go to school with a bunch of kids who were either rotten to him or ignored him. And he didn't mope around the house all the time. Now he moped around outside.

At first Kristine thought he was playing with our other kids, the way he used to before school divided them. But gradually she began to realize that Geoffrey and Emily always played together, and Scotty almost never played with them. She'd see the younger kids with their squirtguns or running through the sprinklers or chasing the wild rabbit who lived in the neighborhood, but Scotty was never with them. Instead, he'd be poking a twig into the tent-fly webs on the trees, or digging around at the open skirting around the bottom of the house that kept animals out of the crawl space. Once or twice a week he'd come in so dirty that Kristine had to heave him into the tub, but it didn't reassure her that Scotty was acting normally.

On July 28th, Kristine went to the hospital and gave birth to our fourth child. Charlie Ben was born having a seizure, and stayed in intensive care for the first weeks of his life as the doctors probed and poked and finally figured out that they didn't know what was wrong. It was several months later that somebody uttered the words "cerebral palsy," but our lives had already been transformed by then. Our whole focus was on the child in the greatest need—that's what you *do*, or so we thought. But how do you measure a child's need? How do you compare those needs and decide who deserves the most?

When we finally came up for air, we discovered that Scotty had made some friends. Kristine would be nursing Charlie Ben, and Scotty'd come in from outside and talk about how he'd been playing army with Nicky or how he and the guys had played pirate. At first she thought they were neighborhood kids, but then one day when he talked about building a fort in the grass (I didn't get many chances to mow), she happened to remember that she'd seen him building that fort all by himself. Then she got suspicious and started asking questions. Nicky who? I don't know, Mom. Just Nicky. Where does he live? Around. I don't know. Under the house.

In other words, imaginary friends.

How long had he known them? Nicky was the first, but now there were eight names—Nicky, Van, Roddy, Peter, Steve, Howard, Rusty, and David. Kristine and I had never heard of anybody having more than one imaginary friend.

"The kid's going to be more successful as a writer than I am," I said. "Coming up with eight fantasies in the same series."

Kristine didn't think it was funny. "He's so *lonely*, Scott," she said. "I'm worried that he might go over the edge."

It *was* scary. But if he was going crazy, what then?

We even tried taking him to a clinic, though I had no
faith at all in psychologists. Their fictional explanations of human behavior seemed pretty lame, and their
cure rate was a joke—a plumber or barber who performed at the same level as a psychotherapist would be
out of business in a month. I took time off work to
drive Scotty to the clinic every week during August,
but Scotty didn't like it and the therapist told us nothing more than what we already knew—that Scotty was
lonely and morose and a little bit resentful and a little
bit afraid. The only difference was that she had fancier
names for it. We were getting a vocabulary lesson when
we needed help. The only thing that seemed to be helping was the therapy we came up with ourselves that
summer. So we didn't make another appointment.

Our homegrown therapy consisted of keeping him
from going outside. It happened that our landlord's father, who had lived in our house right before us, was
painting the house that week, so that gave us an excuse.
And I brought home a bunch of video games, ostensibly
to review them for *Compute!*, but primarily to try to
get Scotty involved in something that would turn his
imagination away from these imaginary friends.

It worked. Sort of. He didn't complain about not going outside (but then, he never complained about anything), and he played the video games for hours a day.
Kristine wasn't sure she loved *that*, but it was an im-
provement—or so we thought.

Once again, we were distracted and didn't pay much
attention to Scotty for a while. We were having insect
problems. One night Kristine's screaming woke me up.
Now, you've got to realize that when Kristine screams,
that means everything's pretty much OK. When something really terrible is going on, she gets cool and quiet
and *handles* it. But when it's a little spider or a huge
moth or a stain on a blouse, then she screams. I ex-

pected her to come back into the bedroom and tell me about this monstrous insect she had to hammer to death in the bathroom.

Only this time, she didn't stop screaming. So I got up to see what was going on. She heard me coming—I was up to 230 pounds by now, so I sounded like Custer's whole cavalry—and she called out, "Put your shoes on first!"

I turned on the light in the hall. It was hopping with crickets. I went back into my room and put on my shoes.

After enough crickets have bounced off your naked legs and squirmed around in your hands you stop wanting to puke—you just scoop them up and stuff them into a garbage bag. Later you can scrub yourself for six hours before you feel clean and have nightmares about little legs tickling you. But at the time your mind goes numb and you just do the job.

The infestation was coming out of the closet in the boys' room, where Scotty had the top bunk and Geoffrey slept on the bottom. There were a couple of crickets in Geoff's bed, but he didn't wake up even as we changed his top sheet and shook out his blanket. Nobody but us even saw the crickets. We found the crack in the back of the closet, sprayed Black Flag into it, and then stuffed it with an old sheet we were using for rags.

Then we showered, making jokes about how we could have used some seagulls to eat up our invasion of crickets, like the Mormon pioneers got in Salt Lake. Then we went back to sleep.

It wasn't just crickets, though. That morning in the kitchen Kristine called me again: There were dead June bugs about three inches deep in the window over the sink, all down at the bottom of the space between the regular glass and the storm window. I opened the window to vacuum them out, and the bug corpses spilled all over the kitchen counter. Each bug made a nasty little rattling sound as it went down the tube toward the vacuum filter.

The next day the window was three inches deep again, and the day after. Then it tapered off. Hot fun in the summertime.

We called the landlord to ask whether he'd help us pay for an exterminator. His answer was to send his father over with bug spray, which he pumped into the crawl space under the house with such gusto that we had to flee the house and drive around all that Saturday until a late afternoon thunderstorm blew away the stench or drowned it enough that we could stand to come back.

Anyway, what with that and Charlie's continuing problems, Kristine didn't notice what was happening with the video games at all. It was on a Sunday afternoon that I happened to be in the kitchen, drinking a Diet Coke, and heard Scotty laughing out loud in the family room.

That was such a rare sound in our house that I went and stood in the door to the family room, watching him play. It was a great little video game with terrific animation: Children in a sailing ship, battling pirates who kept trying to board, and shooting down giant birds that tried to nibble away the sail. It didn't look as mechanical as the usual video game, and one feature I really liked was the fact that the player wasn't alone—there were other computer-controlled children helping the player's figure to defeat the enemy.

"Come on, Sandy!" Scotty said. "Come on!" Whereupon one of the children on the screen stabbed the pirate leader through the heart, and the pirates fled.

I couldn't wait to see what scenario this game would move to then, but at that point Kristine called me to come and help her with Charlie. When I got back,

Scotty was gone, and Geoffrey and Emily had a different game in the Atari.

Maybe it was that day, maybe later, that I asked Scotty what was the name of the game about children on a pirate ship. "It was just a game, Dad," he said.

"It's got to have a name."

"I don't know."

"How do you find the disk to put it in the machine?"

"I don't know." And he sat there staring past me and I gave up.

Summer ended. Scotty went back to school. Geoffrey started kindergarten, so they rode the bus together. Most important, things settled down with the newborn, Charlie—there wasn't a cure for cerebral palsy, but at least we knew the bounds of his condition. He wouldn't get *worse*, for instance. He also wouldn't get well. Maybe he'd talk and walk someday, and maybe he wouldn't. Our job was just to stimulate him enough that if it turned out he wasn't retarded, his mind would develop even though his body was so drastically limited. It was do-able. The fear was gone, and we could breathe again.

Then, in mid-October, my agent called to tell me that she'd pitched my Alvin Maker series to Tom Doherty at TOR Books, and Tom was offering enough of an advance that we could live. That plus the new contract for *Ender's Game*, and I realized that for us, at least, the recession was over. For a couple of weeks I stayed on at Compute! Books, primarily because I had so many projects going that I couldn't just leave them in the lurch. But then I looked at what the job was doing to my family and to my body, and I realized the price was too high. I gave two weeks' notice, figuring to wrap up the projects that only I knew about. In true paranoid fashion, they refused to accept the two weeks—they had me clean my desk out that afternoon. It left a bitter taste, to have them act so churlishly, but what the heck. I was free. I was home.

You could almost feel the relief. Geoffrey and Emily went right back to normal; I actually got acquainted with Charlie Ben; Christmas was coming (I start playing Christmas music when the leaves turn) and all was right with the world. Except Scotty. Always except Scotty.

It was then that I discovered a few things that I simply hadn't known. Scotty never played any of the video games I'd brought home from *Compute!* I knew that because when I gave the games back, Geoff and Em complained bitterly—but Scotty didn't even know what the missing games *were*. Most important, that game about kids in a pirate ship wasn't there. Not in the games I took back, and not in the games that belonged to us. Yet Scotty was still playing it.

He was playing one night before he went to bed. I'd been working on *Ender's Game* all day, trying to finish it before Christmas. I came out of my office about the third time I heard Kristine say, "Scotty, go to bed *now*!"

For some reason, without yelling at the kids or beating them or anything, I've always been able to get them to obey when Kristine couldn't even get them to acknowledge her existence. Something about a fairly deep male voice—for instance, I could always sing insomniac Geoffrey to sleep as an infant when Kristine couldn't. So when I stood in the doorway and said, "Scotty, I think your mother asked you to go to bed," it was no surprise that he immediately reached up to turn off the computer.

"*I'll* turn it off," I said. "Go!"

He still reached for the switch.

"Go!" I said, using my deepest voice-of-God tones.

He got up and went, not looking at me.

I walked to the computer to turn it off, and saw the

animated children, just like the ones I'd seen before. Only they weren't on a pirate ship, they were on an old steam locomotive that was speeding along a track. What a game, I thought. The single-sided Atari disks don't even hold a 100K, and here they've got two complete scenarios and all this animation and—

And there wasn't a disk in the disk drive.

That meant it was a game that you upload and then remove the disk, which meant it was completely RAM resident, which meant all this quality animation fit into a mere 48K. I knew enough about game programming to regard that as something of a miracle.

I looked around for the disk. There wasn't one. So Scotty had put it away, thought I. Only I looked and looked and couldn't find any disk that I didn't already know.

I sat down to play the game—but now the children were gone. It was just a train. Just speeding along. And the elaborate background was gone. It was the plain blue screen behind the train. No tracks, either. And then no train. It just went blank, back to the ordinary blue. I touched the keyboard. The letters I typed appeared on the screen. It took a few carriage returns to realize what was happening—the Atari was in memopad mode. At first I thought it was a pretty terrific copy-protection scheme, to end the game by putting you into a mode where you couldn't access memory, couldn't do anything without turning off the machine, thus erasing the program code from RAM. But then I realized that a company that could produce a game so good, with such tight code, would surely have some kind of sign-off when the game ended. And why did it end? Scotty hadn't touched the computer after I told him to stop. I didn't touch it, either. Why did the children leave the screen? Why did the train disappear? There was no way the computer could "know" that Scotty was through playing, especially since the game *had* gone on for a while after he walked away.

Still, I didn't mention it to Kristine, not till after everything was over. She didn't know anything about computers then except how to boot up and get Word-Star on the Altos. It never occurred to her that there was anything weird about Scotty's game.

It was two weeks before Christmas when the insects came again. And they shouldn't have—it was too cold outside for them to be alive. The only thing we could figure was that the crawl space under our house stayed warmer or something. Anyway, we had another exciting night of cricket-bagging. The old sheet was still wadded up in the crack in the closet—they were coming from under the bathroom cabinet this time. And the next day it was daddy longlegs spiders in the bathtub instead of June bugs in the kitchen window.

"Just don't tell the landlord," I told Kristine. "I couldn't stand another day of that pesticide."

"It's probably the landlord's father *causing* it," Kristine told me. "Remember he was here painting when it happened the first time? And today he came and put up the Christmas lights."

We just lay there in bed chuckling over the absurdity of that notion. We had thought it was silly but kind of sweet to have the landlord's father insist on putting up Christmas lights for us in the first place. Scotty went out and watched him the whole time. It was the first time he'd ever seen lights put up along the edge of the roof—I have enough of a case of acrophobia that you couldn't get me on a ladder high enough to do the job, so our house always went undecorated except the tree lights you could see through the window. Still, Kristine and I are both suckers for Christmas kitsch. Heck, we even play the Carpenters' Christmas album. So we thought it was great that the landlord's father wanted to do that for us. "It was my house for so many years," he said. "My wife and I always had them. I don't think this house'd look *right* without lights."

He was such a nice old coot anyway. Slow, but still strong, a good steady worker. The lights were up in a couple of hours.

Christmas shopping. Doing Christmas cards. All that stuff. We were busy.

Then one morning, only about a week before Christmas, I guess, Kristine was reading the morning paper and she suddenly got all icy and calm—the way she does when something *really* bad is happening. "Scott, read this," she said.

"Just *tell* me," I said.

"This is an article about missing children in Greensboro."

I glanced at the headline: CHILDREN WHO WON'T BE HOME FOR CHRISTMAS. "I don't want to hear about it," I said. I can't read stories about child abuse or kidnappings. They make me crazy. I can't sleep afterward. It's always been that way.

"You've got to," she said. "Here are the names of the little boys who've been reported missing in the last three years. Russell DeVerge, Nicholas Tyler—"

"What are you getting at?"

"Nicky. Rusty. David. Roddy. Peter. Are these names ringing a bell with you?"

I usually don't remember names very well. "No."

"Steve, Howard, Van. The only one that doesn't fit is the last one, Alexander Booth. He disappeared this summer."

For some reason the way Kristine was telling me this was making me very upset. *She* was so agitated about it, and she wouldn't get to the point. "So *what*?" I demanded.

"Scotty's imaginary friends," she said.

"Come on," I said. But she went over them with me—she had written down all the names of his imaginary friends in our journal, back when the therapist asked us to keep a record of his behavior. The names matched up, or seemed to.

"Scotty must have read an earlier article," I said. "It must have made an impression on him. He's always been an empathetic kid. Maybe he started identifying with them because he felt—I don't know, like maybe he'd been abducted from South Bend and carried off to Greensboro." It sounded really plausible for a moment there—the same moment of plausibility that psychologists live on.

Kristine wasn't impressed. "This article says that it's the first time anybody's put all the names together in one place."

"Hype. Yellow journalism."

"Scott, he got *all* the names right."

"Except one."

"I'm so relieved."

But I wasn't. Because right then I remembered how I'd heard him talking during the pirate video game. Come on Sandy. I told Kristine. Alexander, Sandy. It was as good a fit as Russell and Rusty. He hadn't matched a mere eight out of nine. He'd matched them all.

You can't put a name to all the fears a parent feels, but I can tell you that I've never felt any terror for myself that compares to the feeling you have when you watch your two-year-old run toward the street, or see your baby go into a seizure, or realize that somehow there's a connection between kidnappings and your child. I've never been on a plane seized by terrorists or had a gun pointed to my head or fallen off a cliff, so maybe there are worse fears. But then, I've been in a spin on a snowy freeway, and I've clung to the handles of my airplane seat while the plane bounced up and down in mid-air, and still those weren't like what I felt then, reading the whole article. Kids who just disappeared. Nobody saw anybody pick up the kids. Nobody saw anybody lurking around their houses. The kids just didn't come home from school, or played outside and never came in when they were called. Gone. And Scotty knew all their names. Scotty had played with them in his imagination. How did he know who they were? Why did he fixate on these lost boys?

We watched him, that last week before Christmas. We saw how distant he was. How he shied away, never let us touch him, never stayed with a conversation. He was aware of Christmas, but he never asked for anything, didn't seem excited, didn't want to go shopping. He didn't even seem to sleep. I'd come in when I was heading for bed—at one or two in the morning, long after he'd climbed up into his bunk—and he'd be lying there, all his covers off, his eyes wide open. His insomnia was even worse than Geoffrey's. And during the day, all Scotty wanted to do was play with the computer or hang around outside in the cold. Kristine and I didn't know what to do. Had we already lost him somehow?

We tried to involve him with the family. He wouldn't go Christmas shopping with us. We'd tell him to stay inside while we were gone, and then we'd find him outside anyway. I even unplugged the computer and hid all the disks and cartridges, but it was only Geoffrey and Emily who suffered—I still came into the room and found Scotty playing his impossible game.

He didn't ask for anything until Christmas Eve.

Kristine came into my office, where I was writing the scene where Ender finds his way out of the Giant's Drink problem. Maybe I was so fascinated with computer games for children in that book because of what

Scotty was going through—maybe I was just trying to pretend that computer games made sense. Anyway, I still know the very sentence that was interrupted when she spoke to me from the door. So very calm. So very frightened.

"Scotty wants us to invite some of his friends in for Christmas Eve," she said.

"Do we have to set extra places for imaginary friends?" I asked.

"They aren't imaginary," she said. "They're in the backyard, waiting."

"You're kidding," I said. "It's *cold* out there. What kind of parents would let their kids go outside on Christmas Eve?"

She didn't say anything. I got up and we went to the back door together. I opened the door.

There were nine of them. Ranging in age, it looked like, from six to maybe ten. All boys. Some in shirt sleeves, some in coats, one in a swimsuit. I've got no memory for faces, but Kristine does. "They're the ones," she said softly, calmly, behind me. "That one's Van. I remembered him."

"Van?" I said.

He looked up at me. He took a timid step toward me.

I heard Scotty's voice behind me. "Can they come in, Dad? I told them you'd let them have Christmas Eve with us. That's what they miss the most."

I turned to him. "Scotty, these boys are all reported missing. Where have they been?"

"Under the house," he said.

I thought of the crawl space. I thought of how many times Scotty had come in covered with dirt last summer.

"How did they get there?" I asked.

"The old guy put them there," he said. "They said I shouldn't tell anybody or the old guy would get mad and they never wanted him to be mad at them again. Only I said it was OK, I could tell *you*."

"That's right," I said.

"The landlord's father," whispered Kristine.

I nodded.

"Only how could he keep them under there all this time? When does he feed them? When—"

She already knew that the old guy didn't feed them. I don't want you to think Kristine didn't guess that immediately. But it's the sort of thing you deny as long as you can, and even longer.

"They can come in," I told Scotty. I looked at Kristine. She nodded. I knew she would. You don't turn away lost children on Christmas Eve. Not even when they're dead.

Scotty smiled. What that meant to us—Scotty smiling. It had been so long. I don't think I really saw a smile like that since we moved to Greensboro. Then he called out to the boys. "It's OK! You can come in!"

Kristine held the door open, and I backed out of the way. They filed in, some of them smiling, some of them too shy to smile. "Go on into the living room," I said. Scotty led the way. Ushering them in, for all the world like a proud host in a magnificent new mansion. They sat around on the floor. There weren't many presents, just the ones from the kids; we don't put out the presents from the parents till the kids are asleep. But the tree was there, lighted, with all our homemade decorations on it—even the old needlepoint decorations that Kristine made while lying in bed with desperate morning sickness when she was pregnant with Scotty, even the little puff-ball animals we glued together for that first Christmas tree in Scotty's life. Decorations older than he was. And not just the tree—the whole room was decorated with red and green tassels and little wooden villages and a stuffed Santa hippo beside a wicker sleigh and a large chimney-sweep nutcracker and anything else we hadn't been able to resist buying or making over the years.

We called in Geoffrey and Emily, and Kristine brought in Charlie Ben and held him on her lap while I told the stories of the birth of Christ—the shepherds and the wise men, and the one from the Book of Mormon about a day and a night and a day without darkness. And then I went on and told what Jesus lived for. About forgiveness for all the bad things we do.

"Everything?" asked one of the boys.

It was Scotty who answered. "No!" he said. "Not killing."

Kristine started to cry.

"That's right," I said. "In our church we believe that God doesn't forgive people who kill on purpose. And in the New Testament Jesus said that if anybody ever hurt a child, it would be better for him to tie a huge rock around his neck and jump into the sea and drown."

"Well, it *did* hurt, Daddy," said Scotty. "They never told me about that."

"It was a secret," said one of the boys. Nicky, Kristine says, because she remembers names and faces.

"You should have told me," said Scotty. "I wouldn't have let him touch me."

That was when we knew, really knew, that it was too late to save him, that Scotty, too, was already dead.

"I'm sorry, Mommy," said Scotty. "You told me not to play with them anymore, but they were my friends, and I wanted to be with them." He looked down at his lap. "I can't even cry anymore. I used it all up."

It was more than he'd said to us since we moved to Greensboro in March. Amid all the turmoil of emotions I was feeling, there was this bitterness: All this year, all our worries, all our efforts to reach him, and yet nothing brought him to speak to us except death.

But I realized now it wasn't death. It was the fact that when he knocked, we opened the door; that when he asked, we let him and his friends come into our house that night. He had trusted us, despite all the distance between us during that year, and we didn't disappoint him. It was trust that brought us one last Christmas Eve with our boy.

But we didn't try to make sense of things that night. They were children, and needed what children long for on a night like that. Kristine and I told them Christmas stories and we told about Christmas traditions we'd heard of in other countries and other times, and gradually they warmed up until every one of the boys told all about his own family's Christmases. They were good memories. They laughed, they jabbered, they joked. Even though it was the most terrible of Christmases, it was also the best Christmas of our lives, the one in which every scrap of memory is still precious to us, the perfect Christmas in which being together was the only gift that mattered. Even though Kristine and I don't talk about it directly now, we both remember it. And Geoffrey and Emily remember it, too. They call it "the Christmas when Scotty brought his friends." I don't think they ever really understood, and I'll be content if they never do.

Finally, though, Geoffrey and Emily were both asleep. I carried each of them to bed as Kristine talked to the boys, asking them to help us. To wait in our living room until the police came, so they could help us stop the old guy who stole them away from their families and their futures. They did. Long enough for the investigating officers to get there and see them, long enough for them to hear the story Scotty told.

Long enough for them to notify the parents. They came at once, frightened because the police had dared not tell them more over the phone than this: that they were needed in a matter concerning their lost boy. They came: with eager, frightened eyes they stood on our doorstep, while a policeman tried to help them understand. Investigators were bringing ruined bodies out from under our house—there was no hope. And yet if they came inside, they would see that cruel Providence was also kind, and *this* time there would be what so many other parents had longed for but never had: a chance to say good-bye. I will tell you nothing of the scenes of joy and heartbreak inside our home that night—those belong to other families, not to us.

Once their families came, once the words were spoken and the tears were shed, once the muddy bodies were laid on canvas on our lawn and properly identified from the scraps of clothing, then they brought the old man in handcuffs. He had our landlord and a sleepy lawyer with him, but when he saw the bodies on the lawn he brokenly confessed, and they recorded his confession. None of the parents actually had to look at him; none of the boys had to face him again.

But they knew. They knew that it was over, that no more families would be torn apart as theirs—as ours—had been. And so the boys, one by one, disappeared. They were there, and then they weren't there. With that the other parents left us, quiet with grief and awe that such a thing was possible, that out of horror had come one last night of mercy and of justice, both at once.

Scotty was the last to go. We sat alone with him in our living room, though by the lights and talking we were aware of the police still doing their work outside. Kristine and I remember clearly all that was said, but what mattered most to us was at the very end.

"I'm sorry I was so mad all the time last summer," Scotty said. "I knew it wasn't really your fault about moving and it was bad for me to be so angry but I just was."

For him to ask *our* forgiveness was more than we could bear. We were full of far deeper and more terrible regrets, we thought, as we poured out our remorse for all that we did or failed to do that might have saved his life. When we were spent and silent at last, he put it all in proportion for us. "That's OK. I'm just glad that you're not mad at me." And then he was gone.

We moved out that morning before daylight; good friends took us in, and Geoffrey and Emily got to open the presents they had been looking forward to for so long. Kristine's and my parents all flew out from Utah and the people in our church joined us for the funeral. We gave no interviews to the press; neither did any of the other families. The police told only of the finding of the bodies and the confession. We didn't agree to it; it's as if everybody who knew the whole story also knew that it would be wrong to have it in headlines in the supermarket.

Things quieted down very quickly. Life went on. Most people don't even know we had a child before Geoffrey. It wasn't a secret. It was just too hard to tell. Yet, after all these years, I thought it *should* be told, if it could be done with dignity, and to people who might understand. Others should know how it's possible to find light shining even in the darkest place. How even as we learned of the most terrible grief of our lives, Kristine and I were able to rejoice in our last night with our firstborn son, and how together we gave a good Christmas to those lost boys, and they gave as much to us.

AFTERWORD

In August 1988 I brought this story to the Sycamore Hill Writers Workshop. That draft of the story included a disclaimer at the end, a statement that the story was fiction, that Geoffrey is my oldest child and that no landlord of mine has ever done us harm. The reaction of the other writers at the workshop ranged from annoyance to fury.

Karen Fowler put it most succinctly when she said, as best I can remember her words, "By telling this story in first person with so much detail from your own life, you've appropriated something that doesn't belong to you. You've pretended to feel the grief of a parent who has lost a child, and you don't have a right to feel that grief."

When she said that, I agreed with her. While this story had been rattling around in my imagination for years, I had only put it so firmly in first person the autumn before, at a Halloween party with the students of Watauga College at Appalachian State. Everybody was trading ghost stories that night, and so on a whim I tried out this one; on a whim I made it highly personal, partly because by telling true details from my own life I spared myself the effort of inventing a character, partly because ghost stories are most powerful when the audience half-believes they might be true. It worked better than any tale I'd ever told out loud, and so when it came time to write it down, I wrote it the same way.

Now, though, Karen Fowler's words made me see it in a different moral light, and I resolved to change it forthwith. Yet the moment I thought of revising the story, of stripping away the details of my own life and replacing them with those of a made-up character, I felt a sick dread inside. Some part of my mind was rebelling against what Karen said. No, it was saying, she's wrong, you *do* have a right to tell this story, to claim this grief.

I knew at that moment what this story was *really* about, why it had been so important to me. It wasn't a simple ghost story at all; I hadn't written it just for fun. I should have known—I never write anything just for fun. This story wasn't about a fictional eldest child named "Scotty." It was about my real-life youngest child, Charlie Ben.

Charlie, who in the five and a half years of his life has never been able to speak a word to us. Charlie, who could not smile at us until he was a year old, who could not hug us until he was four, who still spends his days and nights in stillness, staying wherever we put him, able to wriggle but not to run, able to call out but not to speak, able to understand that he cannot do what his brother and sister do, but not to ask us why. In short, a child who is not dead and yet can barely taste life despite all our love and all our yearning.

Yet in all the years of Charlie's life, until that day at Sycamore Hill, I had never shed a single tear for him, never allowed myself to grieve. I had worn a mask of calm and acceptance so convincing that I had believed it myself. But the lies we live will always be confessed in the stories that we tell, and I am no exception. A story that I had fancied was a mere lark, a dalliance in the quaint old ghost-story tradition, was the most personal, painful story of my career—and, unconsciously, I had confessed as much by making it by far the most autobiographical of all my works.

Months later, I sat in a car in the snow at a cemetery in Utah, watching a man I dearly love as he stood, then knelt, then stood again at the grave of his eighteen-year-old daughter. I couldn't help but think of what Karen had said; truly I had no right to pretend that I was entitled to the awe and sympathy we give to those who have lost a child. And yet I knew that I couldn't leave this story untold, for that would also be a kind of lie. That was when I decided on this compromise: I would publish the story as I knew it had to be written, but then I would write this essay as an afterword, so that you would know exactly what was true and what was not true in it. Judge it as you will; this is the best that I know how to do.

AFTERWORD

————

AUTHORS HAVE NO more story ideas than anyone else. We all live through or hear about thousands of story ideas a day. Authors are simply more practiced at recognizing them as having the potential to become stories.

The real challenge is to move from the idea through the process of inventing the characters and their surroundings, structuring the tale, and discovering the narrative voice and the point of view, and finally writing it all down in a way that will be clear and effective for the reader. That's the part that separates people who wish they were writers or intend someday to write a book, and those of us who actually put the words down on paper and send them out in hope of finding an audience.

To the best of my memory, here are the origins of each of the stories in this book:

"EUMENIDES IN THE FOURTH
FLOOR LAVATORY"

I was working at *The Ensign* magazine as an assistant editor and sometime staff writer. Jay A. Parry was copy editor there, as he had been at Brigham Young University Press, where my editorial career began. In fact, Jay was the one who alerted me to the possibility of applying for a position at *The Ensign* and helped shepherd me through the process.

He and I and another editor, Lane Johnson, all had dreams of being writers. I had already had something of a career as a playwright, but when it came to prose fiction we were all new. We started taking lunch together down in the cafeteria of the LDS Church Office Building in Salt Lake City, riding the elevators down from the twenty-third floor, grabbing a quick salad, and then hunching over a table talking stories.

Naturally, when we actually wrote the stories down, we showed them to each other. In many ways we were the blind leading the blind—none of us had sold anything when we began. Yet we were all professional editors; we all worked in a daily mill of taking badly written articles, restructuring them, and then rewriting them smoothly and clearly. We might not have known how to sell fiction, but we certainly knew how to *write*. And we also knew how to see other people's work clearly and search for the soul of their story, in order to preserve that soul through any number of incarnations as text.

(Indeed, that may be the reason I have always been so skeptical of the whole contemporary critical scene, in which the text is regarded as some immutable miracle, to be worshiped or dissected as if it were the story itself. What anyone trained as an editor and rewriter knows that the text is *not* the story—the text is merely one attempt to place the story inside the memory of the audience. The text can be replaced by an infinite number of other attempts. Some will be better than others, but no text will be "right" for all audiences, nor will any one text be "perfect." The story exists only in the memory of the reader, as an altered version of the story intended (consciously or not) by the author. It is possible for the audience to create for themselves a better story than the author could ever have created in the text. Thus audiences have taken to their hearts miserably-written stories like *Tarzan of the Apes* by Edgar Rice Burroughs, because what they received transcended the text; while any number of beautifully written texts have been swallowed up without a trace, because the text, however lovely, did a miserable job of kindling a living story within the readers' memories.)

How other stories in this collection grew out of that friendship, those lunchtime meetings, will be recounted in their place. This story came rather late in that time. I had already left *The Ensign* magazine and was beginning my freelance career. I still had much contact with the *Ensign* staff because I was supposed to be finishing a project that I had not yet completed when I resigned my position as of 1 January 1978. In one conversation I had with Jay Parry, he mentioned a terrible dream he had had. "You can use it for a story if you want," he said. "I think there's a story in it, but it would be too terrible for me to write."

Jay lacks my vicious streak, you see; or perhaps it's just that he was already a father and I wasn't. I'm not altogether sure I could write this story after Kristine and I started having kids. At the time, though, Jay's nightmare image of a child with flipper arms drowning in a toilet seemed fascinating, even poignant.

I had recently read whatever story collection of Harlan Ellison's was current at the time, and I had discerned a pattern in his toughest, meanest tales—a sin-and-punishment motif in which terrible things only seemed to happen to the most appropriate people. It seemed obvious to me that the way to develop this deformed baby into a story was to have it come into the life of someone who deserved to be confronted with a twisted child.

After my first draft, however, I submitted the story to Francois Camoin, by then my teacher in writing classes at the University of Utah. I had taken writing classes before, and except for occasional helpful comments had found that their primary value was that they provided me with deadlines so I *had* to produce stories. Francois was different—he actually understood, not only how to write, but also how to *teach* writing, a skill that is almost completely missing among teachers of creative writing in America today. He didn't know everything—no one does—but compared to what I knew at the time he might as well have known everything! Even though I was selling my science fiction quite regularly, I still didn't understand, except in the vaguest way, why some of my stories worked and others didn't. Francois helped open up my own work to me, both its strengths and weaknesses.

As a playwright I had learned that I have a tendency to write in epigrams; as one critical friend put it, all my characters said words that were meant to be carved in stone over the entrance of a public building. That tendency toward clever didacticism was still showing up in my fiction (and probably still does). It was Francois who helped me understand that while the events of the story should be clear—what happened and why— the *meaning* of the story should be subtle, arcane; it should be left lying about for readers to discover, but never forced upon them. "This story is *about* guilt," said Francois. "In fact, the child, the tiny Fury, *is* guilt. When you have a word embodied in a story, the word itself should never appear. So don't ever say the word 'guilt' in this story."

I knew at once that he was right. It wasn't just a matter of removing the word, of course. It meant removing most sentences that had the word in it, and occasionally even whole paragraphs had to come out. It was a pleasurable process, though not without some pain—rather like peeling away dead skin after a bad sunburn. What was left was much stronger.

It appeared in a rather obscure place—Roy Torgeson's *Chrysalis* anthology series from Zebra books. But Terry Carr picked it up for his best-of-the-year fantasy anthology, so it got a little better exposure. My name is on it, but much of this story is owed to others: Jay, for the seminal image; Harlan, for the basic structure; and Francois, for the things that *aren't* in the text here printed.

"QUIETUS"

Like "Eumenides," this story began with someone else's nightmare. My wife woke up one morning upset by a strange lingering dream. We lived at the time in a rented Victorian house on J Street in the Avenues district of Salt Lake City. We were only a bit more than a block from the Emigration Ward LDS meetinghouse, where we attended church. In Kristine's dream, the bishop of our ward had called us up and told us that they were holding a funeral for a stranger the next day, but that tonight there was no place to keep the coffin. Would we be willing to let them bring it by and leave it in our living room until morning?

Kristine isn't in the habit of saying no to requests for help, even in her dreams, and so she agreed. She woke up from her dream just as she was opening the coffin lid.

That was all—a stranger's coffin in the living room. But I knew at once that there was a story in it, and what the story had to be. A coffin in your own living room can only have one body in it: your own. And so I sat down to write a story of a man who was haunting his own house without realizing it, until he finally opened the coffin and climbed in, accepting death.

What I *didn't* know when I started writing was *why* he was left outside his coffin for a while, and why he then reconciled himself to death. So I started writing as much of the story as I knew, hoping something would come to me. I told of the moment of his death in his office, though he didn't realize it was death; I wrote of his homecoming; but the ultimate meaning of the story came by accident. I can't remember now what my mistake was in the first draft. Something like this: During the office scene I had written that he had no children, but by the time I wrote his homecoming, I had forgotten his childlessness and had him hear children's voices or see their drawings on the refrigerator—or something to that effect. Only when I showed the first draft of the story's opening to Kristine did we (probably she) notice the contradiction.

It was one of those silly dumb authorial lapses that every writer commits. My first thought was simply to change one or the other reference so they were reconciled.

However, as I sat there, preparing to revise, I had an intuition that my "mistake" was no mistake at all, but rather my unconscious answer to the fundamental question in the story: Why couldn't he accept death at first? Instead of eliminating the contradiction, I enhanced it, switching back and forth. Now they have children, now they don't. He could not accept death until their childlessness was replaced with children.

If you want to get psychological about it, Kristine was pregnant with our first child at the time. My "mistake" may have been a traditional freudian slip, revealing my ambivalence about entering onto the irrevocable step of having and raising children. What matters more, however, is not the personal source of the feeling, but what I learned about the process of writing: Trust your mistakes. Over and over again since then, I have found that when I do something "wrong" in an early draft of the story, I should not eliminate it immediately. I should instead explore it and see if there's some way that the mistake can be justified, amplified, made part of the story. I have come to believe that a storyteller's best work comes, not from his conscious plans, but from his impulses and errors. That is where his unconscious mind wells up to the surface. That is how stories become filled, not with what the writer believes that he believes, or thinks he ought to care about, but rather with what he believes without question and cares about most deeply. That is how a story acquires its truth.

"DEEP BREATHING EXERCISES"

The idea for this story came simply enough. My son, Geoffrey, was a born insomniac. It took him hours to fall asleep every night, and we learned that the most effective way to get him to sleep was for me to hold him and sing to him. (For some reason he responded more to a baritone than a mezzo-soprano.) This would continue until he was four or five years old; by that time I was spending a couple of hours a night lying by his bed, reading in the dim light from the hall while humming the tune to "Away in a Manger." When he was a baby, though, I stood in his room, rocking back and forth, singing, nonsense songs that included tender lyrics like, "Go to sleep, you little creep, Daddy's about to die." Even when he finally seemed to have drifted off I learned that he was only faking, and if I laid him down too soon he'd immediately scream. I appreciate a call for an encore as much as the next guy, but enough is enough. Especially since Kristine was asleep in the other room. Most of the time I didn't begrudge her that—she would be up in the morning taking care of Geoffrey (always an early riser no matter how late he dropped off) while I slept in, so it all evened out. Still, there were many nights when I stood there, rocking back and forth, listening to both of them breathing during the breaks in my lullaby.

One night I realized that Geoffrey's breath on my shoulder was exactly in rhythm with my wife's breath as she slept in the other room. The two of them inhaling and exhaling in perfect unison. My mind immediately began to take the idea and wander with it. I thought: It doesn't matter how long Daddy stands here singing to the kid, the bond with his mother is always the strongest one, right down to the level of their breathing. Mother and child share the same breath so long together—it's no surprise that out of the womb the child still seeks to breathe with her, to cling to the rhythms of his first and best home. From there my thoughts wandered to the fact that the unborn child is so tied to the mother that if she dies, he dies with her.

Before Geoffrey fell asleep, the story was written in my mind: Breathing in unison is a sign, not that people were born together, but that they were now irrevocably doomed to die together.

"FAT FARM"

My life can be viewed as one long struggle with my own body. I wasn't hopelessly uncoordinated as a kid. If I tried, I could swing a bat or get a ball through a hoop. And I suppose that if I had worked at it, I could have held my own in childhood athletics. But some are born nerds, some choose nerdhood, and some have nerdiness thrust upon them. I chose. I just didn't *care* about sports or physical games of any kind. As a child, given the choice, I would always rather read a book. Soon enough, however, I learned that this was a mistake. By the time I got to junior high, I realized that young male Americans are valued only for their contribution to athletic contests—or so it seemed to me. The result was that to avoid abuse, I avoided athletic situations.

Then, when I was about fifteen, I passed some sort of metabolic threshold. I had always been an outrageously skinny kid—you could count my ribs through my shirt. All of a sudden, though, without any change that I was aware of in my eating habits, I began to gain weight. Not a lot—just enough that I softened in the belly. Began to get that faintly pudgy wormlike look that is always so attractive and fashionable, especially in teenage boys. As the years passed, I gained a little more weight and began to discover that the abuse heaped upon nerds in childhood is nothing like the open, naked bigotry displayed toward adults who are overweight. People who would never dream of mocking a cripple or making racial or ethnic slurs feel no qualms about poking or pinching a fat person's midriff and making obscenely personal remarks. My hatred of such people was limitless. Some of my acquaintances in those days had no notion how close they came to immediate death.

The only thing that keeps fat people from striking back is that, in our hearts, most of us fear that our tormentors are right, that we somehow deserve their contempt, their utter despite for us as human beings. Their loathing for us is only surpassed by our loathing for ourselves.

I had my ups and downs. I weighed 220 pounds when I went on my LDS mission to Brazil in 1971. Through much walking and exercise, and relatively little eating (though Brazilian ice cream is exquisite) I came home two years later weighing 176 pounds. I looked and felt great. And the weight stayed off, mostly, for several years. I became almost athletic. My first two summers home, I operated a summer repertory theatre at an outdoor amphitheatre, the Castle, on the hill behind the state mental hospital. We weren't allowed to drive right up to the Castle, so at the beginning of every rehearsal we would walk up a switchback road. Within a few weeks I was in good enough shape that I was running up the steepest part of the hill right among the younger kids, and reaching the stage of the Castle without being out of breath. We had a piano that we stored in a metal box at the base of the amphitheatre and carried—not rolled—up a stony walkway to the stage for rehearsals and performances of musicals (*Camelot*, *Man of La Mancha*, and my own *Father*, *Mother*, *Mother*, *and Mom*). Soon I was carrying one end of the piano alone. I reveled in the fact that my body could be slender and well-muscled, not wormlike at all.

But then I began my editorial career and my theatre company folded, leaving me with heavy debts. I spent every day then sedentary and tense, with a candy machine just around the corner. My only exercise was pushing quarters into the machine. By the time I got married in 1977 I was back up to 220 pounds. Freelance writing made things even worse. Whenever I needed a break, I'd get up, walk thirty feet into the kitchen, make some toast and pour some orange juice. All very healthy. And only about a billion calories a day. I was near 265 pounds when I wrote "Fat Farm." It was an exercise in self-loathing and desperate hope. I knew that I was capable of having a strong, healthy body, but lacked the discipline to create it for myself. I had actually gone through the experience of trading bodies—it just took me longer than it took the hero of the story. In a way, I suppose the story was a wish that someone would *make* me change.

Ironically, within a few months after writing "Fat Farm," our lives went through a transition. We were moving to a larger house. The first thing I did was take all my old thin clothes and give them away to charity. I knew that I would never be thin again. It was no longer an issue. I was going to be a fat person for the rest of my life. Orson Welles was my hero.

Then I began packing up our thousands of books and carrying and stacking the boxes. The exercise began to take up more and more of each day. I ate less and less, since I wasn't constantly looking for breaks from writing. By the time we got into our new place, I had dropped ten pounds. Just like that, without even trying.

So I kept it up. Eating little—I now followed a thousand-calorie balanced diet—and exercising more and more, within a year I was 185 pounds and was riding a bicycle many miles a day. And I stayed thin for several years. Not until I moved to North Carolina and got a sedentary job under extreme tension did I put the weight back on again. I sit here writing this with a current weight of 255 pounds. But that's down almost ten pounds from my holiday high, and I'm riding an exercise bike and enjoying the sensation of being hungry most of the time and—who knows?

In short, "Fat Farm" isn't fiction. It's my physical autobiography.

And it's no accident that the story ends with our hero set up to fulfill ugly violent assignments. The undercurrent of violence is real. I hereby warn all those who think it's all right to greet a friend by saying, "Put on a little weight, haven't you!" You would never dream of greeting a friend by saying, "Wow, that's quite an enormous pimple you've got on your nose there," or, "Can't you afford to buy clothes that look good or do you just have no taste?" If you did, you would expect to lose the friend. Well, be prepared. Some of us are about to run out of patience with your criminal boorishness. Someday one of you is going to glance down at our waistline, grin, and then—before you can utter one syllable of your offensive slur—we're going to break you into a pile of skinny little matchsticks. No jury of fat people would convict us.

"CLOSING THE TIMELID"

I think it was in a conversation with Jay and Lane that we began wondering what death might feel like. Maybe, after all our fear of it, the actual moment of death—not the injuries leading up to it, but the moment itself—was the most sublime pleasure imaginable. After a few months of letting this idea gel in the back of my mind, I hit on the device of using time travel as a way to let people experience death without dying.

Time travel is one of those all-purpose science fictional devices. You can do *anything* with it, depending on how you set up the rules. In this case, I made it so that the time-traveler's body *does* materialize in the past, and can be injured—but upon return the body is restored to its condition when it left, though still feeling whatever feelings it had just before the return. It's a fun exercise for science fiction writers, to think up new variations on the rules of time travel. Each variation opens up thousands of possible stories. That's why it's so discouraging to see how many time-travel stories use the same old tired clichés. These writers are like tourists with cameras. They don't actually come to experience a strange land. They just take snapshots of each other and move on. Snapshot science fiction might as well not be written. Why write a time-travel story if you don't think through the mechanics of your fantasy and find the implications of the particular rules of your time-travel device? As long as we're dealing in impossibilities, why not make them interesting and fresh?

But I digress. Being a preacher at heart, I found that with this story I had written a homily of hedonism as self-destruction. Absurd as these people may seem, their obsession with a perverse pleasure is no stranger than any other pleasure that seduces its seekers from the society of normal human beings. Drug users, homosexuals, corporate takeover artists, steroid-popping bodybuilders and athletes—all such groups have, at some time or another, constructed societies whose whole purpose is celebrating the single pleasure whose pursuit dominates their lives, while it separates them from the rest of the world, whose rules and norms they resent and despise. Furthermore, they pursue their pleasure at the constant risk of self-destruction. And then they wonder why so many other people look at them with something between horror and distaste.

"FREEWAY GAMES"

The origin of this idea is simple enough. I learned to drive a car only in my early twenties (the state of Utah required that you take driver's ed. before you could get a license, my high school didn't offer it, and I never had time to take it on my own), and so went through my aggressive teenage driving period when I was over twenty-one. Thus even as I went through my bouts of naked competitiveness and aggression on the highway, I was intellectually mature enough to recognize the madness of my behavior. And, rarely, that intellectual awareness curbed some of my stupidest impulses. For instance, long before freeway shootings in California, I realized that when you flash your brights at some bozo you're taking your life in your hands. No, the way to punish a freeway offender was to do it passively. Follow them. Just—follow. Not tailgating. Just—following. If they squirt ahead in traffic, don't leap out to follow. Just work your way up until a few minutes later, there you are again, following. If they really deserve a scare, take a little bit of time out of your life and take their exit with them. Follow them along residential streets. Watch them panic.

I never actually went to that extreme—never actually followed somebody off the freeway. But I did follow a couple of bozos long enough that it clearly made them nervous; yet I never did anything aggressive enough to make them mad. They could never *really* be sure that they were being followed. It was the cruelest thing I can remember doing.

I thought for a while of writing a humor piece about freeway games—ways to pass the time while on long commutes. But when I showed my first draft to Kristine, she said, "That isn't funny, that's *horrible*." So I set it aside.

Later, taking a writing course from Francois Camoin, I decided to write a story that had no science fiction or fantasy element in it. While trying to think of something to write about, I hit on that "freeway games" essay and realized that when Kristine said it was horrible, I should have realized that she really meant that the idea was *horror*. A horror story with no monster except the human being behind the wheel. Somebody who didn't know when to stop. Who kept pushing and pushing until somebody died. In short, me—only out of control. So I wrote a story about a normal nice person who suddenly discovers one day that he's a monster after all.

"A SEPULCHRE OF SONGS"

I remember reading a spate of stories about human beings who had been cyborgized—their brains put into machinery so that moving an arm actually moved a cargo bay door and walking actually fired up a rocket engine, that sort of thing. It seemed that almost all of these stories—and a lot of robot and android stories as well—ended up being rewrites of "Pinocchio." They always wish they could be a real boy.

In years since then, the fashion has changed and more sf writers celebrate rather than regret the body mechanical. Still, at the time the issue interested me. Couldn't there be someone for whom a mechanical body would be liberating? So I wrote a story that juxtaposed two characters, one a pinocchio of a spaceship, a cyborg that wished for the sensations of real life; the other a hopelessly crippled human being, trapped in a body that can never *act*, longing for the power that would come from a mechanical replacement. They trade places, and both are happy.

A simple enough tale, but I couldn't tell it quite that way. Perhaps because I wanted it to be truer than a fantasy, I told the story from the point of view of a human observer who could never know whether a *real* trade had taken place or whether the story was just a fantasy that made life livable for a young girl with no arms or legs. Thus it became a story about the stories we tell ourselves that make it possible to live with *anything*.

All this was many years before my third child, Charlie, was born. I never really believed that someday I would have a child who lies on his bed except when we put him in a chair, who stays indoors unless we take him out. In some ways his condition is better than that of the heroine of "Sepulchre of Songs"—he has learned to grasp things and can manipulate his environment a little, since his limbs are not utterly useless. In some ways his condition is worse—so far he cannot speak, and so he is far more lonely, far more helpless than one who can at least have conversation with others. And sometimes when I hold him or sit and look at him, I think back to this story and realize that the fundamental truth of it is something quite unrelated to the issue of whether a powerful mechanical body would be preferable to a crippled one of flesh and bone.

The truth is this: The girl in the story brought joy and love into the lives of others, and when she left her body (however you interpret her leaving), she lost the power to do that. I would give almost anything to see my Charlie run; I wake up some mornings full of immeasurable joy because in the dream that is just fading Charlie spoke to me and I heard the words of his mouth; yet despite these longings I recognize something else: You don't measure whether a life is worth living except by measuring whether that life is giving any good to other people and receiving any joy from them. Plenty of folks with healthy bodies are walking minuses, subtracting from the joy of the world wherever they go, never able to receive much satisfaction either. But Charlie gives and receives many delights, and our family would be far poorer if he weren't a part of us. It teaches us something of goodness when we are able to earn his smile, his laughter. And nothing delights him more than when he earns our smiles, our praise, and our joy in his company. If some cyborg starship passed by, imaginary or otherwise, offering to trade bodies with my little boy, I would understand it if he chose to go. But I hope that he would not, and I would miss him terribly if he ever left.

"PRIOR RESTRAINT"

This story is a bit of whimsy, based in part on some thoughts about censorship and in part on the experience of knowing Doc Murdock, a fellow writing student in Francois Camoin's class. Doc really did support himself at times by gambling, though the last I heard he was making money hand-over-fist as a tech writer. Couldn't happen to a nicer guy.

I almost never consciously base characters on real people or stories on real events. Part of the reason is that the person involved will almost always be offended, unless you treat him as a completely romantic figure, the way I did with Doc Murdock. But the most important reason is that you don't really *know* any of the people you know in real life—that is, you never, ever, *ever* know *why* they do what they do. Even if they tell you why, that's no help because they never understand themselves the complete cause of anything they do. So when you try to follow a real person that you actually know, you will constantly run into vast areas of ignorance and misunderstanding. I find that I tell much more truthful and powerful stories when I work with fully fictional characters, because *them* I can know right down to the core, and am never hampered by thinking, "Oh, he'd never do that," or, worse yet, "I'd better not show him doing *that* or so-and-so will kill me."

And, in a way, "Prior Restraint" is proof that for me, at least, modeling characters on real people is a bad idea. Because, while I think the story is fun, it's also one of my shallower works. Scratch the surface and there's nothing there. It was never much deeper than the conscious idea.

By the way, this story was a *long* time making it into print. I wrote the first version of it very early in my career; Ben Bova rejected it, in part on the grounds that it's not a good idea to write stories about people writing stories, if only because it reminds the reader that he's reading a story. His advice was mostly right, though sometimes you *want* to remind readers they're reading. Still, I liked this idea, flaws and all, and so I sent it off to Charlie Ryan at *Galileo*. He accepted it—but then *Galileo* folded. Charlie wrote to me and offered to send the story back. I knew, however, that I wouldn't be able to sell it to Ben Bova or, probably, anybody else. So when Charlie suggested that he'd like to hang onto it in case someday he was able to restart *Galileo* or some other magazine, I agreed.

It was almost a decade later that a letter came out of the blue, telling me that Charlie was going to edit *Aboriginal SF*, and could he please use "Prior Restraint"? By then I was well aware of the relative weakness of the story, particularly considering the things I'd learned about storytelling since then. It might be a bit embarrassing to have such a primitive work come out now, in the midst of much more mature stories. But Charlie had taken the story back in the days when most editors didn't return my phone calls and some sent me insulting rejections; why shouldn't he profit from it now that things had changed? As long as the story wasn't too embarrassing. So I asked him to send me a copy and let me see if I still liked it.

I did. It wasn't a subtle piece, but it was still a decent idea and, with a bit of revision to get rid of my stylistic excesses from those days, I felt that it could be published without embarrassing me. I don't know whether to be chagrined or relieved that nobody seemed to be able to tell the difference—that nobody said, " 'Prior Restraint' feels like *early* Card." Maybe I haven't learned as much in the intervening years as I thought!

"THE CHANGED MAN AND THE KING OF WORDS"

The genesis of this story is easy enough. I was living in South Bend, Indiana, where I was working on a doctorate at Notre Dame. One of my professors was Ed Vasta, one of the great teachers that come along only a few times in one's life. We both loved Chaucer, and he was receptive to my quirky ideas about literature; he also wrote science fiction, so that there was another bond between us. One night I was at a party at his house. After an hour of everybody grousing about the stupidity of Hesburgh's choosing a high school teacher named Gerry Faust as the football coach, we got on the subject of tarot. Ed was a semi-believer—that is, he didn't really believe in any occult phenomena, but he did think that the cards provided a focus, a framework for bringing intuitive understanding into the open.

Kristine and I are both very uncomfortable around any occult dealings, partly because we are very uncomfortable with the sort of people who believe in the occult. But this was Ed Vasta, a very rational man, and so I consented to a reading. I remember thinking that the process was fascinating, precisely because nothing happened that could not be explained by Vasta's own personal knowledge of me; and yet the cards did provide a way of relating that previous knowledge together in surprising and illuminating patterns.

The experience led me to write a story, combining tarot with my then-new obsession with computers. The story itself is a cliché, a deliberately oedipal story by an author who thinks Freud's notion of an Oedipus complex is an utter crock. It's one of the few times that I've ever mechanically followed a symbolic structure, and for that reason it remains unsatisfying to me. What I really cared about were the ideas—the computer and the tarot cards—and I have since explored the interrelationship between storytelling computers and human beings in such works as my novels *Ender's Game* and *Speaker for the Dead*.

"MEMORIES OF MY HEAD"

This story began very recently when Lee Zacharias, my writing teacher at the University of North Carolina at Greensboro, mentioned that suicide stories were common enough among young writers that she despaired of ever seeing a good one. I remembered that when I was teaching at Elon College the semester before I had gotten enough of those suicide endings to make the pronouncement to my students that I hereby *forbade* them to end a story with suicide. It was a cop-out, said

I—it was a confession that the writer had no idea how the story *really* ought to end.

Now, though, I was feeling a bit defiant. I had said that suicide stories were dumb, and now Lee was saying the same thing. Why not see if I could write one that was any good? And why not make it even more impossible by making it first person present tense, just because I detest present tense and have declared that first person is usually a bad choice?

The result is one of the strangest stories I've ever written. But I *like* it. I enjoyed using this epistolary form to tell the tale of a hideously malformed relationship between a couple who had lived together far longer than they had any reason to.

"LOST BOYS"

This story came with its own afterword. Let me only add that since its publication, it has been criticized somewhat for its supposed cheating—I promise at the beginning to tell the truth, and then I lie. I can only say that it is a long tradition in ghost stories to pretend to be telling the truth; part of the pleasure in the tale is to keep the reader wondering whether *this* time the story might not be real. The ghost stories *I've* enjoyed most and remember the best have been the ones told as if they were true and had really happened to the teller. I tip my hat to Jack McLaughlin, a wonderful grad student in the theatre department at BYU, who spooked a whole bunch of us undergrad acting students with a really hair-raising poltergeist story that Actually Happened To Him.

I also enjoy the fact that criticisms of my story for violating expectations have all come from the more literary, "experimental" wing of the science fiction community. It seems that they love experimentation and literary flamboyance—but only if it follows the correct line. If somebody dares to do something that is *surprisingly* shocking instead of *predictably* shocking, well, fie on them. Thus do the radicals reveal their orthodoxy.

The fact remains that "Lost Boys" is the most autobiographical, personal, and painful story I've ever written. I wrote it in the absolutely only way *I* could have written it. So even if the manner of its writing is a literary crime, as these critics say, I can only answer, "So shoot me." I'm in the business of telling true stories as well as I possibly can. I've never yet found any of their rules that helped me tell a story better; and if I had followed their rules on this story, I never could have told it at all.

SF AND FANTASY FROM
ORSON SCOTT CARD